Strangers in the Night

An Artisan Mystery

Patricia H. Rushford

License Notes

Dedication...

To my mom—My greatest fan.
1923 to 2011

Table of Contents

Prelude

May 26, 1961

"Strangers in the Night." Abbie Campbell, aka Annie Davis, loved that song—perhaps because she still harbored a schoolgirl crush on the blue-eyed singer. Frank Sinatra never failed to touch her heart with his love songs.

She closed her eyes as he sang about exchanging glances and falling in love. The record playing over the PA system wasn't nearly as good as hearing him in person, but Abbie enjoyed it just the same.

It would be wonderful to fall in love again, but she wouldn't. Couldn't. She couldn't allow herself that luxury.

Though the supper club was dimly lit, and romance seemed to float on the air, she had no business daydreaming about love. Still, longing filled her heart, and for a moment she imagined herself dancing with Frank Sinatra himself.

"Could I have this dance?" A mellow voice invaded her senses.

Abbie eased out of her daydream and looked up to find gorgeous blue eyes gazing down at her. A perfect smile. Wavy dark hair. He wasn't the real crooner, of course, but oh, so handsome. His gaze locked with hers, and she couldn't look away.

She took his hand and let him lead her to the dance floor. When his arms closed around her, Abbie's heart quickened.

Leave. Now. Get yourself out of here before you do something foolish.

She should have heeded the warning. Instead, she closed her eyes and rested her head against the stranger's shoulder.

Just this once.

His closeness stirred feelings she hadn't had since Nate's death almost two years before. She sighed, released her fears, and thought about how perfectly they fit together. He led, and she followed, wondering how this stranger could make her feel as though she'd known him all her life. He didn't speak, and she didn't dare to—afraid that words would somehow shatter the magic.

All too soon the song ended—fantasy faded, and Abbie, the real Abbie Campbell, came to her senses, reminding herself of how dangerous this simple dance could be for her and for Emma. How letting down her guard for just one moment could cause her to lose her daughter and the life—the facade—she'd worked so hard to maintain.

Chapter One

Abbie dropped onto a bistro chair in the courtyard near the Red River for a much-needed break. The Memorial Day Arts and Crafts Fair had been going strong for only two hours, yet she was already bushed. Being one of the volunteers had kept her hopping, but she'd never felt better. As an artist herself, Abbie loved every minute of it. She wished she could have done more—such as exhibiting her own work, but she couldn't take that chance. Better to stay in the background.

Lifting her face to the sun, she welcomed the delicate breeze. They couldn't have asked for better weather. Grand Forks could be brutally hot once winter decided to melt away and eventually the heat would be all consuming, but today was perfect. Quite a crowd had gathered, and the forty some vendors busily assisted customers.

From the nearby stage, a string quartet from the University of North Dakota provided fairgoers with strains of Bach and Beethoven. Later there would be a popular rock-and-roll group entertaining them with songs from the likes of Bobbie Darin and Buddy Holly, Elvis and the Beatles, and of course, Frank Sinatra, Dean Martin, and Sammy Davis, Jr.

Her favorite group would be performing that evening. The famed George Donaldson and his band, which had been playing at the Red River Supper Club, had agreed to provide dance music.

Abbie's mind tumbled back to her error in judgment at the supper club the night before, but she wouldn't let the memory get a foothold. It was only one mistake, and the man had been a complete stranger. What were the chances she'd ever see him again?

She couldn't imagine what had come over her and blamed her behavior on being overly tired.

Setting her iced tea on the small mosaic tabletop, Abbie slipped off her two-inch heels and pulled her thigh-length floral pastel dress toward her knees. She loved the mini-skirt look but hated the way the skirt rode up when she sat.

She would have propped her feet up on the empty chair beside her if it hadn't been pulled back by a man wearing sunglasses, dressed in a classy shirt and suit pants. He hung the suit jacket he'd been carrying onto the back of the chair and placed his briefcase on the grass beside him. She shaded her eyes and squinted up at him, thinking he seemed familiar. One of the vendors maybe?

"May I?" He had a kind voice and an inviting smile. Even so, wariness crept in.

"It's a free country." *And who is he? Why is he here?*

Her heart picked up its cadence as the now familiar paranoia set in. Was he a private detective? The police? Federal agents wore suits, didn't they? Black, like his, if she wasn't mistaken.

Had they found her?

She held her breath, waiting for the dreaded words telling her she was under arrest. When the words didn't come, she met his gaze again. Realization set in. This was the stranger from last night's dance.

She should have recognized him immediately, but the lighting and her mood had been different then and he hadn't been wearing sunglasses. He slipped off the glasses, and there was no mistaking those blue eyes.

"Abbie Campbell?"

Her throat went dry. She closed her eyes and waited for her heart to start beating again. How could he know her real name? Other than asking her to dance last night, he hadn't said a word. Probably because she'd stepped out of his arms at the end of the dance and left him standing in her wake.

Blue eyes or not, this man was dangerous. He shouldn't know her name. Had he been sizing her up at the dance? Closing in for the kill?

The jig is up. He's going to arrest you and drag you off to jail.

"Um, you are Abbie, aren't you?" His gentle voice penetrated her fear. His warm smile caught her off guard. And his eyes, those lovely blue eyes... Maybe he wasn't there to arrest her after all. Maybe she'd known him before all this craziness started. Perhaps she'd known him in another lifetime. High school? College? No. If she had met this man before, she would have remembered.

"Who wants to know?" she managed to ask. He stretched out a hand and smiled. "Jake Conners. I'm a real estate agent and developer...and a friend of your parents."

"A developer?" To her knowledge, her parents weren't into developing anything except maybe a new record album. Still, his western accent legitimized his claim to being from the northwest.

Abbie shook his hand, far too aware of its warmth and how she liked the way hers fit into it. Pulling her hand back, she motioned for him to sit. She needed to be on her guard and couldn't afford to be swayed by the man's charm. Still, if her parents really had sent him, she needed to hear him out.

"How do you know my parents?"

He hesitated. "They didn't tell you I was coming?"

She shook her head then tipped it to one side, considering. "Actually, they may have. I've been distracted for the last few days helping to put this art event together and haven't picked up my mail."

"Ah, that would explain it." He smiled again, and Abbie's wariness melted a little more.

Be careful, Abbie. If he knew to find you here, he might also know where you live.

"I'll bet." He glanced around, apparently impressed. "From the looks of the crowd, I'd say it's a huge success. I'm hoping to take it all in after we've had a chance to talk. Um, maybe you could show me around later?"

"Maybe. But first, you might want to tell me how you found me and what you want."

"Right." He shifted slightly. Nodding toward her glass, he said, "Do you mind if I get something to drink first? yours looks good."

"It's iced tea." She slipped her shoes back on. "I'll get one for you. The booth is over…"

He stood. "No need. I'll get it. Just promise me you won't go anywhere."

"I'll be right here." As if of their own accord, her lips curved into a smile as she watched him walk away. His dark hair and blue eyes still reminded her of Frank Sinatra.

Abbie had personally met the blue-eyed crooner twenty years ago. She'd been only eight at the time, but even back then his eyes and warm smile had captivated her. Perhaps that's why he'd become so famous. What woman could resist?

Her parents had performed with him at the Sands in Las Vegas and again at the famed Cotton Club in New York City. They had given her several of his signed albums. He'd even presented one of his records to her personally. Her collection of the famed singer's records, photos, and memorabilia were stored in a box in her parents' attic. Maybe someday she'd have a place to display them.

She was still a fan. Jake's eyes had that same dreamy quality. No wonder she'd been so pliable the night before. The thought brought her up short. She let her gaze drift back to him.

Yes, he's appealing, but there's no way you should be admiring anyone at this point, especially a man in a black suit at an art festival.

Abbie tipped her head back and massaged her neck and shoulders. She was exhausted, and if she had any sense, she'd disappear into the crowd and head over to Patsy's Café for a much-needed lunch break. Better yet, she should check on Emma, her four-year-old daughter.

The encounter with Jake Conners had sent up dozens of red flags. Abbie left her drink on the table, hurried to the nearby phone booth, and dialed her best friend, Margie. Since she'd come to Grand Forks, she and Margie had shared a home.

"Hi, Annie," Margie greeted. For safety's sake Margie always used Abbie's pseudonym. "How's the art fair? I was thinking of bringing the kids over this afternoon."

"Is everything okay there?" Abbie asked. "No strangers hanging around? No...problems?"

"Everything is fine. Emma is playing outside with Jimmy. She's safe."

"Good. I...I had a moment of panic. Anyway, the kids will love it here. There's an entire section for children. They can do artwork or have their faces painted. Just be careful."

"I always am. Why are you asking?"

"You can't be too careful, you know. I got worried."

"Well, no worries here. The kids are fine. We'll see you soon."

Abbie hung up without telling Margie about Jake. She hadn't mentioned him last night either, and wasn't sure why.

Margaret Lowe was the only person in Grand Forks who knew Abbie's real name and story—the only person she could really trust. They'd roomed together in college and had been best friends ever since. Margie had been the first one Abbie called when she'd been in trouble. They were both widowed, and Margie insisted Abbie and Emma live with her and Jimmy.

Originally, the arrangement had been temporary, but after a few months they'd settled into an equitable routine and become a family of sorts. Their arrangement suited Abbie, since buying a house would require her to dig into her bank funds and provide legal ID. The last thing she needed was to alert the authorities to her whereabouts.

Abbie made her way back to the table. Maybe Jake really did know her parents and maybe he was okay. But why hadn't they contacted her? Then again, as she'd told Jake, maybe they had tried. she'd have to go by the post office later.

* * * * *

To the delight of the little girl selling lemonade and iced tea, Jake paid a quarter for his ten-cent drink. He glanced back at Abbie and smiled. He couldn't believe his luck. It was as if God Himself had instigated their meeting. He had certainly felt that way last night.

Jake had driven into Grand Forks late yesterday afternoon. He'd checked into the Dakota Hotel, intent on resting for a few hours and having dinner. His plan had been to take the next two days to relax and familiarize himself with the town and begin his search for Abbie on Monday. But there he was last night, enjoying his meal and the music, when he spotted her.

Jake had no trouble recognizing Abbie. The college graduation picture her parents had given him was still taped to his dashboard. He'd talked to her all the way from the Oregon Coast to Grand Forks. She made his grueling trip seem—well, less grueling. Her smile had worked its magic in his heart. She'd changed her hair from blond to brown and the style had gone from long to short, but she still had the same gray-green eyes and classic features.

Last night had been a mistake. He shouldn't have approached her, but when he saw her across the room, a smile on her lips, her head tipped back as if she were about to kiss someone, he had to go. He had to know if it was really her.

He'd been as tongue-tied as a schoolboy with a crush. As much as he wanted to introduce himself then and there and tell her of his plans, he couldn't. Those moments with Abbie in his arms had been heaven. If things didn't work out, at least he'd have that magical memory.

And today. Jake's heart still hadn't slowed down since spotting her in that colorful short dress, not quite a mini, which was all the rage these days. Even so, the dress showed off her shapely legs. The minute she'd slipped off her shoes, he imagined himself on one knee, holding out a glass slipper for her shapely foot. He chuckled at the fantasy. What she'd needed at that moment was a foot massage, not a glass slipper.

He'd have done that too, if she'd allowed him the privilege.

Too soon for that kind of thinking. Business first.

He glanced over at the table again, still amazed at his luck.

Abbie was gone. A quick look around and the panic subsided. She stood in an open phone booth a few feet away. He watched her talking, and from the frown etched on her face, she was no doubt worried about him showing up out of the blue. He couldn't blame her. He was, after all, a stranger to her, and he would do well to remember that.

Jake, on the other hand, felt as though he'd known her forever. Her parents had shared countless details, yet not nearly enough.

When she made her way back to the table, he stepped away from the booth. His stomach grumbled in protest as the tantalizing scents from the food booths wafted around him. Maybe Abbie would join him for lunch.

* * * * *

Abbie admired the ease with which Jake set his iced tea on the table and lowered himself into the chair. She felt a level of comfort with him that under ordinary circumstances might be a good thing. Now, though, being a fugitive, she needed to be especially careful.

"Thanks for staying," he said.

She raised an eyebrow. "You said you knew my parents. I figured that was either a great pick-up line or it's the truth."

He laughed. "I can assure you it's true."

The rich baritone voice struck a chord deep within her. Abbie's cheeks grew warm. She picked up her tea, focusing on the ice cubes and the drink's amber color. "How are they?"

"Good. They miss you and Emma. It's been hard for them with you not being able to visit them."

He knew. Alarm swelled in her chest again as she wondered how much her parents had told him. She reminded herself that they'd trusted him enough to send him here. Maybe she could trust him as well.

The last two years had been hard for her as well. She loved her parents but visiting them had been out of the question. Now, here was a man who knew them. Abbie had so many questions.

"What about Skye and Tim?" She hadn't seen her younger siblings since she'd moved to Iowa with Nathan. Whenever she asked about them, her mother would tell her the same old story. "They're a bit rebellious, Abbie, but they'll grow out of it. They're doing fine, really."

Skye and Tim lived in Portland. They were not as easy to deal with, her mother would say, but times were changing.

Abbie knew better. On her last visit, right after Nate's death, Skye had opted not to come to the coast to see Abbie, insisting that she didn't want to have to listen to her goody-two-shoes sister lecture her about all the stuff she was doing wrong.

Abbie wasn't like that. Well, maybe she did at times try to steer them right, but she wasn't judgmental. The barb still stung. "Did my folks say anything about them?"

"Tim is fine. He graduated from the police academy and is looking into working for the Oregon State Police. Skye is another story."

Jake's dour expression indicated that he didn't want to talk about Skye, but Abbie pressed him. "What's wrong?"

He fingered the napkin under his drink. "Skye is staying with your folks for the time being. She recently left a rehab facility. Before that, she spent some time on the streets. There's no easy way to say this, Abbie. You can't sugarcoat it. She's sick. She's a drug addict and she's killing herself."

Abbie groaned. "I...I didn't know." She should have been home, helping her mother, taking care of her little sister. "Mom never told me."

"They said I was supposed to break it to you gently." He frowned. "I didn't do so well on that part of my mission, did I?"

"Bad news is always hard to deliver. Thank you for giving it to me straight." She wanted more details, but Jake seemed reluctant.

"I'll tell you more about Skye later," he said, "She's not the reason I'm here. Your parents sent me here to talk with you. I have a proposition."

"A proposition?" Abbie struggled to transition from Skye to Jake's odd comment.

He bent to pick up his briefcase and set it on the table. "It's complicated."

"Wait." She held a hand up to stop him. "Do you mind if we discuss it over lunch? Unless you've already eaten."

"I haven't and I'm starving." Jake stood and waited while she did the same. "Lead the way."

Abbie left the remainder of her tea on the table. Jake took a moment to drain his before setting his glass beside hers.

They'd walked a block toward Patsy's Bakery and Café before Abbie spoke. "I should have asked this sooner, but how do you know my parents?"

"As I said, I'm a real estate agent. I sold them their home in Oceanside. I also do some investing and property development."

That made sense. her parents had bought the house shortly before Nate's death. She vaguely remembered them talking about their realtor. Rather than downsize to a smaller home, they'd gone larger. Mom wanted a house big enough to accommodate the entire family, as well as their hobbies, and a soundproof room to practice their music. Had they mentioned Jake's name? She wasn't certain. A measure of relief came. Perhaps he was on the level. Abbie let herself relax a bit more.

"This looks like a great restaurant." Jake nodded toward the glassed-in displays of fresh-baked breads, pastries, and desserts.

"My favorite for breakfast and lunch. The owners have a farm just north of here and they use fresh produce. Everything is delicious."

They walked across the black-and-white checkered linoleum and slid into a shiny red vinyl booth by the window. The light-flashing jukebox on the back wall played Ricky Nelson's "Be Bop Baby."

"Hi, Annie."

Sherrie, the waitress, was the owner's teenage daughter. Grinning, she sashayed over in her tight blue capris and matching blouse and hat. She plopped menus down in front of them. Her gaze moved to Jake. "Who's your friend?"

"Jake Conners."

"Hi, Jake." Admiration oozed out of every pore. Sherrie hesitated a moment then lifted the carafe. "Coffee?"

"No thanks," Abbie said. "I'd like some water though."

"Sure." Jake moved his cup closer. Sherrie filled the cup and seemed as taken by his blue eyes as Abbie had been.

They looked over the menu, and when Sherrie returned, Abbie ordered the beef stew special. Jake opted for the soup and a roast beef sandwich on rye.

"Coming right up." Sherrie grinned.

Jake nodded toward the waitress. "She called you Annie."

"Annie Davis. I had to change it after…"

"It's a dangerous choice," Jake said. "It's too close to your real name."

"I suppose it is. But it's worked so far." Dangerous choice? How much had her parents told him?

For several minutes they sat in strained silence, listening to Theresa Brewer belt out "Sweet Old-fashioned Girl."

Around about the middle of "Hang Down Your Head, Tom Dooley," and comforted by familiar surroundings and wonderful smells, Abbie began to relax again. Sherrie brought their meals, and Abbie was surprised when Jake asked a blessing.

"This looks good. I'm glad you suggested coming here." He picked up a sandwich half and took a bite.

Abbie lifted her spoon and stirred her stew. "What are my parents up to and how, or should I ask why, did they persuade you to come all the way out here to talk to me?"

Jake swallowed and wiped his mouth on his napkin. "They want me to make you an offer you can't refuse."

"Ah, the proposition." She read the skepticism in his eyes and voice. "But you're not so sure."

"Personally, I think it's a great idea." He hesitated. "I won't lie to you, Abbie. There's a lot of money in this for me. The deal hinges on you being willing to make it happen. Your dad knew he wouldn't be able to persuade you on the phone or in a letter, so he sent me." He grinned and winked. "And I never was one to turn down an offer to meet a pretty girl."

Although heat rose in her cheeks, Abbie discarded the last statement and the wink that went with it. She ducked her head and pretended interest in the stew. She wanted to hear more, yet she didn't. She had a feeling that he was going to ask her to go back to Oregon. Something she couldn't do—at least not if she wanted to keep her daughter and stay out of prison.

Chapter Two

Jake went back to eating his sandwich while Abbie finished her stew. Once it was gone, she felt ready to move ahead. She could at least hear him out. "I'm assuming this offer involves buying property or opening a business of some sort."

Jake sipped his coffee. "A business, yes, but it's more than that. The property they want to buy is a town in the Coastal Mountain range, only about twenty minutes southeast of Oceanside. The depression cut hard into the economy there a few years back and the owner needs to sell."

"An entire town?"

"Look, Abbie." He moved his plate forward and placed his arms on the table, leaning toward her. "Your parents told me what you've been going through."

Abbie stiffened, aghast that they would break her confidence. And to a real estate agent. What were they thinking? Jake could easily have gone to the police. Maybe he had.

As if reading the alarm in her eyes, he said, "Relax. your secret is safe with me. I guess they figured I should know the whole story if I'm going to help you."

"Help me?" Abbie tossed her napkin on her plate and took a drink of water. *Oh, Mom and Pops, what have you done?* "They told you everything?"

"Enough." He glanced around. "Maybe this isn't the best place to talk. Can we go somewhere more private?"

"Of course." The lunch crowd had descended on the popular café, and Abbie felt claustrophobic. Besides that, someone apparently liked little Richard a lot more than she did, and the keep-a-knockin' screeches were giving her a headache.

When they rose, Jake tossed a ten-dollar bill on the table. More than enough to cover both meals. Sherrie would be thrilled.

She led Jake back to the art fair and to the riverfront park nearby where they could talk without being overheard. She crumpled onto a lone bench. For almost two years she'd been a fugitive. She had been so careful not to allow anyone access to her life. Now, her parents had apparently betrayed her. Not only had they told Jake Conners where she lived, but also that she'd kidnapped her daughter.

She clasped the front of the bench on either side of her and leaned forward, feeling as though she might lose the stew she'd just eaten.

"What exactly did they tell you?" She felt raw and exposed as old wounds began to rupture.

"Abbie." He reached for her hand.

She pulled away, but his touch, however brief, loosened flood-gates inside her. Tears escaped their confines and slid down her face. She pulled a tissue from her bag and wiped them away.

Jake stretched his arm out on the back of the bench, brushing his hand against her shoulder. "I can't imagine what you've been through. Losing your husband was bad enough, but losing your baby and then having Emma taken from you. No one could possibly blame you for what you did."

She blew her nose. "I broke the law when I ran away with Emma."

"And you've been looking over your shoulder ever since." The compassion she saw in his face wrapped itself around her.

She nodded. "I should have stayed and gone to court, but I was terrified of losing Emma permanently."

"The court isn't that quick to take children away from their parents." He said it with such conviction, she almost believed him.

"You don't know Leah."

"Your mother-in-law."

Abbie nodded, wondering how well her parents knew this man. They must trust him implicitly to reveal so much. Her parents were open and friendly, but they'd ferociously guarded her secret. Until now.

"From what your parents told me, she's quite a bulldozer."

Abbie frowned. "It isn't like that. Leah was only trying to do what she thought would be best for Emma. The truth is, I was not being a good mother. After Nate died, I fell apart. I let Leah take care of Emma and then when I lost the baby, I was too tired and depressed to do anything."

"You were grieving. That's not being a bad mother."

"True, but in Leah's eyes, I had failed. I shouldn't have been surprised. She never did like me much. I wasn't good enough for Nate and I made a lousy farmer's wife."

Abbie straightened, drawing herself together. "I made a lot of mistakes. I never imagined that Leah might see my actions or inactions as neglect. I thought she was being kind when she took care of Emma for me. I never expected her to accuse me of being an unfit mother. Leah gained custody by going to a judge who was also her friend."

Abbie hauled in a deep breath. "Anyway, I took Emma and ran away from it all. I have a friend here, and she's helped me piece together a new life. I still don't know how you managed to find me. Not even my parents have an address other than the post office."

"They gave me a picture." His lips curled in a half smile. "Truth is, I didn't know how I was going to find you. There are thirty-five thousand people here, but I was prepared to talk to every one of them if need be. The amazing thing is that I decided to eat at the supper club last night and there you were."

"So much for being anonymous." That Jake had found her so easily rattled her sense of security to the core. Yet, on another level, Abbie felt a strange sense of relief.

"Abbie. I'm not a threat." He caught her gaze and held it.

Taken aback by the intensity and sincerity of those blue eyes, Abbie looked away. "I hope not."

"I want to help you."

"How do you plan to do that?"

"First, we need to get you back to Oregon."

"That's not going to happen. I can't…"

"Hear me out." Jake leaned down to open his briefcase. "There's a place called Cold Creek for sale near the Oregon coast."

She shook her head. "You mentioned before it was a town, but I don't understand."

"Cold Creek is an old lumber town that fell on hard times. They were doing great until the stock market fell in '29 The owner died shortly after that and the widow has been selling off bits and pieces of property ever since to people who had previously rented and wanted to stay."

Abbie glanced down at the aerial photo Jake handed her. The circled area included a mountain, a lake, forests, a creek, and a small town with a main street and about twenty houses, along with a number of small cabins. She handed the photo back. "That's a lot of property."

"Isabelle Johansson has weathered the storms pretty well." He smiled. "She's considered the town's matriarch. She's decided to sell off the entire town except for her home and some acreage around it. Isabelle is luckier than a lot of folks. At least she owns the property free and clear and it's close enough to the coast to make it appealing.

Real estate prices are projected to climb—especially in resort areas. Bear Lake borders the town and is one of the most beautiful places around. Unfortunately, a lot of people have had to move to the cities in order to find jobs. That's left several buildings vacant, especially in the downtown area, so it's a bit run-down. It'll need a lot of work."

Abbie sighed. "I don't see what this has to do with me. Are you saying my parents want to buy this town?"

"Actually, they want to buy it with you." He rubbed the back of his neck. "It's complicated. your parents want to turn the place into an artist colony, and they want you to run it. They said, and I quote, 'Tell Abbie it's time to stop hiding and come home. This is what she's always wanted.'"

Excitement stirred in her chest. her parents knew her well. Ever since she'd visited the Artists' Way in Rhode Island during college, she'd dreamed of being a part of a place like that. "I can't." She sighed. "I'm wanted for kidnapping. I can't afford to go back, no matter how wonderful it sounds."

"I really don't think you need to worry about this so-called kidnapping. I have a good friend who's a lawyer."

"You talked to a lawyer about me?"

"He raised his hands. "Not about you. Not specifically. I asked him about custody cases in general. From what he told me, I have no doubt you can fight it and win." He lowered his hands and cast her an apologetic look. "Besides, your parents have already put earnest money on it."

She ran her hands through her hair. "Why do I feel like I'm being manipulated?"

"Because you are." He grinned, easing the insanity of it all. "They are really into this artists' retreat. They understand that they can't force you." He chuckled then and added, "Actually, your dad suggested that if you wouldn't accept the offer, I should kidnap you and Emma and bring you back."

"That's not funny," she quipped. "It's not possible. I can't take the chance."

"Can't or won't?" Jake leaned toward her. "I know it's scary, but can you really walk away? Do you want to be looking over your shoulder for the rest of your life?"

"I'll do it." The words slipped out before she could stop them.

Abbie couldn't believe what she'd said. Resurfacing meant facing charges of kidnapping and possibly losing Emma for good.

Still, on some level, Abbie knew she couldn't go on being a fugitive forever. Her parents were right. The offer was too good to refuse. It was time to go home, not so much for the artist colony, though that did appeal to her. She had to see Skye and reconnect with her family. For Emma's sake as well as her own, she needed to stop running.

Chapter Three

Jake never imagined she'd give in so easily. He expected a long and arduous argument. In a way, he wanted to back up and tell her to wait. She didn't even know him, for Pete's sake.

She'd asked him where he was staying and told him she'd be in touch. She'd be ready to leave in the morning if he was okay with that. Then off she went to check on some paintings. At least that's what she'd said. He'd been too shocked to do much more than nod.

Maybe she was thinking of running again. The thought slammed him alongside the head. He had no idea where she lived or how to find her. Not even her parents knew that. They wrote to a post office address. That was one of the places he had planned to go on Monday on his quest to find her.

Jake prayed that he hadn't spooked Abbie. He hated the thought of having to go back to Oregon empty-handed.

Not certain what else to do, he browsed around the art fair for a while then headed back to the hotel. He'd make a couple of phone calls and take a nap and maybe come back for the evening's entertainment. Maybe he'd be lucky, and Abbie would be there. Maybe he'd ask her to dance. And maybe, she'd say yes. At the hotel he made a call to Abbie's parents in Oceanside. Lyle Grant answered almost immediately.

"I found her."

The declaration brought resounding cheers from Lyle and his wife, Carlene who was talking in the background. "Abbie has agreed to come back to Oregon with me."

"That was quick." Lyle sounded pleased. "I'll have to add a bonus. I knew you were the right man for the job."

"I wouldn't celebrate quite yet. Abbie could change her mind."

"You told her about Skye?"

"I did."

Lyle breathed a heavy sigh. "She won't."

As they said their good-byes, Jake couldn't help but wonder why the Grants didn't just write to Abbie about her sister and about the property for that matter. Then it occurred to him that talking one-on-one with Abbie was a much more humane way of breaking the news and encouraging her to come home.

He was glad they'd sent him. Jake had been able to answer her questions and provide a measure of comfort and security. At least he hoped that was the case. On the other hand, he may have only been instrumental in chasing her even farther away.

Jake placed the telephone earpiece on the cradle, hoping his report to Lyle Grant was correct. He didn't want to disappoint his clients, but it was more than that. Maybe it was his imagination or maybe the fact that he'd stared at Abbie's picture most of the way to North Dakota, but his heart ached for the Grant family. He felt connected to them. Theirs had certainly become much more than a realtor/client relationship.

Jake shook his head to dispel his thoughts and switched modes. Picking up the receiver again, he dialed the number for his real estate office in Oceanside.

Prior to the trip east, he'd left his agent, Barbara Nichols, in charge, and had given her the phone number of the hotel in Grand Forks in case she needed to contact him.

Barbara hadn't called, nor did she answer now. According to the answering service gal, Barbara hadn't called in for messages since Friday afternoon. He wished people would be more dependable.

Barbara usually was, but then Jake didn't usually take trips lasting more than three days. "Give the messages to me now in case I need to call any of our clients." Opening his briefcase, Jake removed a pen and notepad and began writing. Ten messages in all and most were clients that Barbara should have dealt with.

"Thanks, Sarah," he said, trying to keep the annoyance out of his voice. "Tell Barb to call me the minute you hear from her. If I'm not here she needs to leave a message with the front desk."

"Will do."

He checked his watch and deducted two hours for the time-zone change. Barb might be out to lunch or with clients. He'd try again later.

Jake made the necessary phone calls to their clients—nothing that couldn't wait really, but he wanted to keep them happy.

Frustrated, Jake went back down to the front desk and snagged a copy of the *Grand Forks Herald*. For the next hour, he sat in the lobby of the hotel, watching people and reading articles about President Kennedy's arrival in France. Not surprisingly, politics took second to fashion as France fell in love with the first lady. He couldn't blame them. Jackie Kennedy commanded attention everywhere she went. She was the perfect first lady: elegant, soft-spoken, wealthy, and a mother.

Kennedy had made a good choice in a mate, or perhaps the choice had been made for him. After all, the Kennedy family was the closest thing the United States had to royalty.

Before heading out for his evening meal, Jake tried calling Barbara again; no answer at the office or at her home. Barbara normally would have called to check in, but in the real estate business, time was rarely one's own. He doubted there was a problem but couldn't help but worry.

Chapter Four

That evening, when Abbie told Margie about Jake and her parents' offer, her doubts returned with the driving force of a tornado. It didn't help that she had picked up her mail from the post office and found nothing from her parents.

"I wish I could have met him." Margie pulled her knitting bag from beside the sofa and lifted out the maroon sweater she was making. "I trust your judgment and everything, but you wouldn't be the first person to get sidetracked by a good-looking man."

"Did I say he was good-looking?" Abbie remembered no such thing.

"You didn't have to." Margie adjusted her needles and began working a purl stitch. "I can tell by the way you talk about him."

"Humph." Had she really given Margie that impression of Jake or was Margie just guessing? "Just because he has blue eyes like Sinatra and a dreamy smile doesn't mean I was swayed by his charms."

"When are you seeing him again? I want to be there." Margie said it as if she were the better judge of character. Maybe she was. Abbie had to admit that she herself was being led more by her heart than her brain.

"I'm supposed to hook up with him in the morning." Abbie pressed a throw pillow against her chest, hoping to ease the discomfort that had lingered all afternoon.

"I don't like it, Annie." Margie began to knit. "It's too soon, too fast. Are you sure you can trust him?"

"I don't know. I tried calling Mom and Dad from a payphone downtown to verify what he said, but they didn't answer." She regretted her hasty response to Jake, but for those few minutes, desire to see her parents and Skye and to go back home overrode common sense. That and those trusting blue eyes.

"Then wait until you can get hold of them." She paused to look at her instructions. "Besides, how can you expect to be ready so soon?"

"It's not like we have much to pack. But you're right. only…if he were with the police, he'd have arrested me, don't you think?"

"Probably." She peered at Abbie over her glasses. "It's not the police I'm worried about. It's Leah. What if she hired this Jake guy to find you? He wins your trust by making up some wild story about your parents and Skye and this property to lure you into a trap. He takes you along and ditches you somewhere then takes off with Emma."

"I can't imagine anyone going to such lengths." A lump the size of a boulder lodged in Abbie's throat. Could Leah have discovered where she'd gone? "Besides, he sold a house to my parents. Jake lives in Oceanside."

"So, he says. Do you know that for sure? Did he give you a business card? Did you ask for his identification?"

"No, I… he's staying at the Dakota Hotel."

"Tell me you didn't give him our address." Margie lowered her knitting.

"I didn't. I'm supposed to call him tomorrow morning."

"That's something." Margie sighed. "We should really check this guy out." She placed her knitting back in the basket and headed for the kitchen. Lifting the receiver, she began to dial.

"Who are you calling?" Abbie demanded.

"My friend Charlie at the police department." Into the phone she said, "Yes, hello, can I talk to Charlie Wells?"

Abbie's pulse ratcheted up. "Are you crazy?" She spoke in as loud a whisper as she dared. "Getting the police involved is paramount to a prison sentence for me."

Margie covered the mouthpiece. "Relax, will you? I won't even mention your name. Besides, Charlie doesn't know anything about your background."

Margie turned her attention back to the phone. "Hi, Charlie. Margie here. Good. No." She chuckled. "I haven't forgotten. Listen, I need a favor. There's a stranger in town who's looking to sell a friend of mine some property out west. I'm wondering if you could check him out for me. See if he's legit."

She listened a moment, and Abbie, her stomach churning, sank back against the sofa. On one level, she needed to know if Jake was who he claimed to be. On the other, she was afraid to find out. Afraid that his offer might be bogus. Margie was right to question her sanity. Saying yes to a man she didn't know—saying yes to an offer that was far too good to be true, and worse, agreeing to drive all the way back to Oregon with him—made no sense whatsoever. Still, she'd told him that she'd need to call her parents to verify his story and he'd agreed that she should. Didn't that mean he was being honest?

Margie gave Jake's name to Charlie. "He's a realtor from Oceanside, Oregon. That's about all the information I have." After a moment, she said, "Thanks a bunch, Charlie. I owe you one."

Her giggle suggested that Charlie might be growing into more of a friend than Margie let on. Charlie had been her husband's partner when they'd gotten into a clash with some local thieves. Her husband, Nick, had taken a bullet in the chest and later died. Margie hung up and came back to her knitting.

A cold dread shuddered through Abbie. She pulled the afghan that was draped over the back of the sofa around her. Drawing up her knees, she covered her legs as well.

"What did he say?"

"He'll call the police in Oceanside. We should know within an hour."

Chapter Five

On a warm Monday morning, three days after Jake's arrival in Grand Forks, Abbie, Emma, and Jake rolled out of Grand Forks in Jake's new white 1961 Cadillac convertible. He'd bought the car, he told her, just before making the trip. He'd wanted a nice car to bring her home in.

In a way, the car defined the man who drove it—a classy gentleman with good taste, but not always practical. Abbie leaned back for a moment, running her hands over the luxurious white leather bench with its fold-down armrest, drawing in the new car scent.

It had been a long time since she'd ridden in a car so elegant. In her youth, there'd often been limousines and specially designed coaches on railway cars—the opulence that often came with successful show-business people like her parents.

She'd given it all up when she married Nate. Young and so much in love, she'd looked forward to their new life on the farm he and his brother Daniel shared with his parents. That had been a lifetime and a hundred heartaches ago.

Panic sliced through her again as it had so often since meeting Jake. Had she made the right decision? She already missed Margie, and they'd only crossed the border into Montana. Once Charlie gave the all clear, Jake passed Margie's scrutiny with flying colors.

Abbie left with Margie's blessing, promising to call as soon as she arrived at her parents'.

"I'll be praying," Margie said as she waved their final goodbye. Abbie hoped her friend's prayers would be enough.

I'll be praying. Abbie couldn't help but think about how often she had prayed over the years. Even though she had taken Emma illegally, she felt God had been with her. Had God really helped her escape? If so, then why did she feel this urgency to go back?

Leah prayed too. Abbie had heard Leah use those same words nearly every day. Leah, so full of faith and good works, and so determined to do God's will.

Two years ago, Leah insisted it was God's will that she take custody of Emma. *"You're not fit to be a mother. You're a bad seed, just like your parents. It's terrible the way they carouse around in bars, smoking, drinking, dancing. And they raised you to be just like them."*

Remnants of anger and resentment rose in Abbie as bitter bile. If Leah was right about God being on her side, then what was Abbie to believe? Abbie had grown up knowing a loving God, full of grace and truth.

Leah had shown nothing but contempt for Abbie and her family. Yes, her parents had played in supper clubs all around the country. Yes, they danced and played beautiful music. Her father had smoked, but everyone in his circle did. Nearly everyone.

Abbie closed her eyes, trying to keep the tears at bay and the old wounds from splitting open. Glancing now at Jake's profile, she felt strangely reassured. He had given her sound advice. It was time to stop running. She was doing the right thing, and that alone brought a certain peace. Jake had promised that somehow everything would work out. She hoped so.

"Mommy?"

Abbie turned around. "What, sweetie?"

Emma leaned against the back of the front bench seat. In a stage whisper she asked, "Mommy, can I sit up there with you and Unca Jake? It's lonely back here all by myself."

"Lonely?" Jake chuckled and winked at Emma in the rearview mirror. "We can't have that, now can we?" He pushed in the armrest that separated him from Abbie and patted the seat beside him. "Come on."

Emma grinned and crawled into the front seat with Abbie guiding her feet. Her shoes had been removed early on to protect Jake's white seats.

"What do you say to Uncle Jake?"

"Thank you, Unca Jake." She leaned against him and five minutes later was asleep. Emma had taken a shine to Jake the moment she met him. Abbie might have too if not for the barriers she carried in her heart.

"Is he going to be my daddy?" Emma had whispered to Abbie during Jake's first visit to Margie's. Abbie had hurriedly told her he could be her uncle, but not her daddy.

Abbie hadn't slept much since Jake's appearance in Grand Forks last Friday. His presence and the idea of going home to face kidnapping charges triggered an explosion of events and memories she had tried to put behind her. Memories of nearly losing Emma, of Nate's death, and thoughts of what might have been if Nate had lived.

Abbie closed her eyes, willing sleep to come.

What came instead was a memory she couldn't escape. A heart-wrenching day she would never forget.

She and Leah had been canning peaches on a hot August day.

"Want something to drink?" Abbie kneaded her fists against her lower back, trying to ease the pain that came whenever she was on her feet too long. Her big belly and the extra weight of the baby weren't helping. Emma, now two, had been much easier. Or maybe time and circumstances had simply deemed it so.

Sweat dripped down her back, adding to the moisture already dampening her sleeveless cotton shirt. Pulling out the pitcher of the iced tea she'd made that morning, Abbie pressed it against one cheek then the other.

Iowa in August could be wretched. Maybe next year at this time she, Nate, Emma, and the baby would be settled into their home in the northwest, enjoying the cool Oregon Coast breeze.

"Humph," Leah grumbled. "We'll never get these peaches done if you keep taking breaks. But…"

"I'll take that as a yes." Abbie pulled down two tall glasses and filled them with ice. The blast of frigid air from the freezer made the beads of sweat on her face and chest tingle.

Nate should have let her buy the air conditioner as she'd wanted to do their first summer here. Murray and Leah didn't have the money, and she would have offered, but Nate refused to let her spend any of her trust fund on the farm, saying he wanted her to save it for something important. He'd even asked her not to mention "the money" to his family—as though having it was a deep dark sin. He was funny that way—intent on supporting his family without her financial help. Now she wondered if Nate felt the same way about her parents as Leah did. He wanted nothing to do with their money.

A brief flare of anger rose and fizzled. It was too hot, and she was too tired to get riled up. She sighed instead. Men could be so stubborn at times. In the past year, however, Nate seemed willing to talk about living somewhere other than the farm.

She filled the glasses with the cinnamon-colored brew that was made with a blend of black teas and peach juice. It smelled as sweet as the peaches they were canning. After pouring the tea, she put the pitcher back, once again reveling in the brief but welcome chill.

Abbie set Leah's tea on the counter and took a long drink of her own.

"Thank you." Leah rinsed her hands and reached for the iced tea. After taking a drink she said, "This is nice." Abbie had to smile. Despite Leah's stern temperament, the woman could be likeable at times. Abbie felt another pang of guilt.

Her in-laws worked hard, and Leah went out of her way to include Abbie as one of the family. She hadn't approved of the marriage from the beginning, and Abbie doubted they'd ever be close. They were simply too different, which was one of the reasons Abbie wanted her own home. There she could have a craft room with lots of light and no one to tell her that sketching and painting were a waste of time.

Abbie turned the overhead fan on high and went back to the sink and the peaches waiting to be packed into jars.

The phone rang and Leah grumbled. "Get that, would you, Abbie? It's probably Janet reminding me to bring cookies to church on Sunday."

"Sure." Abbie dutifully lifted the bell-shaped hearing device to her ear. But it wasn't Janet.

"Hello, darling. How are you?"

"Mom." Abbie sank into the chair next to the phone, happy to hear her mother's voice. "How are you? And Pops? He's okay, isn't he?" Lyle grant had recently suffered a bout with the flu. She worried about them though she needn't have. They weren't old—in fact her mother was a young fifty-five. Dad was sixty.

"Your father is fine. We both are." Her mother hesitated. "He says hi. We're doing a special outdoor concert in Oceanside tonight."

"Sounds like fun." Abbie smiled just thinking about them out on the stage, singing familiar favorites that their band had made popular. Her mother chuckled. "Should be a blast. Your dad's been practicing his sax all day."

"I wish I could be there."

"I wish you could be here too, sweetheart. It's been too long. Remember those road trips we used to take with you kids? You all would sing along with your father and me."

"Of course, I remember." Tears gathered, and Abbie used the back of her wrist to wipe them away. "I do, Mom." She glanced toward the kitchen where Leah kept looking over her shoulder and glaring at her. "I really don't have time to reminisce. Peaches are waiting to be canned."

Her mother sighed. "You work too hard. How is Emma?"

"She's terrific and so excited about the baby."

"I wish I could be there with you."

"I do too." Abbie swallowed around the lump in her throat. She wanted so much for her parents to come and stay, but there was no room at the house, and even if there had been, Leah had made it clear from the beginning that "those people" were not welcome in her home.

"Honey, the reason I called… did you get a chance to talk to Nate about moving out here?"

Abbie's breath caught. "Yes, last night. He said it sounded…promising."

Those hadn't been his exact words. Nate had told her she could look at property in Oregon and visit her parents if she wanted. She'd gotten the distinct impression that he didn't want her to go. He'd talked again about building them a house on the farm over by the pond—something he'd been promising for years. The time had never been right. Would it ever be? Funny how he only mentioned that when she talked about moving out West.

"That's wonderful," her mother said. "So, you're all coming then."

"No." Abbie cleared her throat. "Nate can't take the time off right now but said Emma and I could go without him. I have train reservations for September sixth."

"Oh, I was hoping you could come sooner," her mother said.

"I can't leave now. I need to help Leah with the canning. The sixth is only a few weeks away."

"That's getting close to your due date. Will you be okay to travel?"

"I think so. If not, I'll have to come later." She wasn't due until mid-October, so she'd have plenty of time.

"I can't wait." Her mother hesitated. "Tell Emma her Nana Carlene and Papa Lyle love her and give her a big hug and kiss from us. Skye says hello too. Are you showing Emma our pictures, so she knows us?"

"Of course."

"I'll line up some places for us to look at when you come. It'll save you some time."

"Sounds good, Mom, but I really have to go." Abbie pushed herself out of the chair. A knot formed in the pit of her stomach when she said good-bye.

She hung up and took several deep breaths before going back into the kitchen, vacillating between excitement and trepidation. *What if I find a home for us and Nate refuses to move?*

She didn't know how much longer she could stay on the farm and maintain her sanity. Every day seemed more of a struggle. Part of that was the pregnancy, but not all. She missed her family and her art, and the mountains and greenery of the Pacific northwest.

Your place is with your husband, Abbie reminded herself. According to Leah, the farm was the perfect place to raise children. *Am I being selfish? Is this where God wants me? If so, then why has He created such a strong desire in me to go home?* Abbie ran a hand through her blond hair and reluctantly joined Leah in the kitchen. "My mother," she explained.

"I know." Leah cast a sidelong glance at Abbie, disapproval narrowing her eyes. "I heard you say you've made train reservations. You're planning another trip out there?"

"They want me to look at some property near the coast."

"Property." Leah spit out the word as if it were an obscenity. "What on earth for? you're not planning on leaving us, are you?"

"Nate and I have talked about moving out west for a while now."

Leah chuckled. "You can forget that nonsense. Mark my words, Abbie, Nate has no intention of moving out west or anywhere else. He's a farm boy and always will be. You should know that by now."

He could farm in Oregon if he wanted to. Abbie didn't bother arguing. Nate had said they'd move one day soon. But would they? Did he tell her that to placate her?

Was Leah right? Abbie washed her hands then packed the sliced peaches into one of the dozen or so clean quart jars that still waited on the counter.

They worked in strained silence for several minutes before Abbie spotted their neighbor's pickup truck racing along the gravel road heading into town. "Mr. Olson sure seems in a hurry. Wonder what's going on." She dropped peaches into another jar.

Leah's round face crinkled in concern as she wiped her hands on her soiled apron. "Sure, hope neither of them is sick. Jim and Mary Beth aren't getting any younger. He needs more help than what those kids of theirs give them, that's for sure."

Always the critic. Not wanting to be critical herself, Abbie backed out of the thought. Her mind far from her task, she finished up the last of the peaches Leah had cleaned and blanched. She watched as Leah put the hot, sanitized quart jars into the water bath where they would stay for twenty-five minutes.

The women had put up over a hundred jars, and that was after Leah made her prize-winning peach freezer jam. When the jars cooled, she and Leah would carry them down to the root cellar with the rest of the fruits and vegetables they'd already put up for the winter.

Abbie pulled out one of the eight kitchen chairs sitting around the scarred table and was just about to sit when she heard a truck pull in and a door slam. Someone stomped up the stairs and strode across the back porch. The door flew open and Daniel stepped inside.

His frantic gaze ripped from Abbie to his mother and back again. For what seemed an eternity, he stood there, hunched over, tears streaking his face. His jeans, shirt, and hands were splattered in blood. "Nathan is dead." The words spewed out of his mouth and hung in the air like a deadly gas.

"No..." Abbie doubled over, not needing or wanting to hear the rest.

In the ensuing hours, Abbie learned that Nate had been trampled and gored by the neighbor's bull. He had stepped between old Mr. Olson and the charging animal, hoping to divert the bull's attention. Nate had run toward the fence, but the bull charged after him. Nate fell before he could make it. They called her husband a hero, but that didn't make the loss any easier.

Losing Nate had been more than Abbie could bear, or so she thought. While she mourned, barely able to get out of bed in the mornings, Leah took over the funeral arrangements.

Leah took over everything, including Emma. They buried Nate in the Campbell family plot behind St. Mark's Church, which stood alone in the country, ten miles from Manchester, Iowa.

Four days later, she lost the baby. Little Ashley Mae lay in the grave next to her daddy, a chunk of Abbie's heart buried with them.

Between grief and pain and losing so much blood in the miscarriage, Abbie felt incapable of doing anything and spent nearly a month in bed. She was thankful that Leah made certain hers and Emma's needs were met.

Abbie knew now that what she saw as Leah's compassion was simply a gathering of evidence to prove Abbie was incapable of caring for Emma.

On a rainy day in late September, Abbie and Emma boarded the train to Oregon to be with her parents. Abbie hadn't been ready to buy property but planned to stay with her parents until the time was right. When she returned to the farm to pack up their things, she learned that Leah had been given custody of Emma.

In Abbie's absence, Leah had sought help from a judge, an old friend, who awarded her custody. Abbie could move to Oregon if she wanted to, but she wouldn't be taking Emma with her.

She'd stayed at the farm for all of two weeks before the escape. Abbie should have fought the accusations and the court order then and there, but she'd had no fight left in her.

Severe depression from her losses had drained her, leaving her helpless and afraid. Somehow, Abbie's survival instincts kicked in, and she made plans to take Emma and run as far away from the farm as she could get.

The day finally arrived. Leah had her quilting bee at the church and Murray had gone to an auction. She, Daniel, and Emma were home alone. Abbie talked Daniel into taking them shopping in Des Moines. She needed clothes for Emma, she'd said. That much was true. The girl was growing like a wildflower.

The escape went off without a hitch. While Daniel waited in a nearby café, Abbie entered a large department store, where she picked up a suitcase set and several items of clothing along with grooming needs.

Leaving through a different door, she hired a taxi and went straight to the bus depot where she bought tickets to Grand Forks and let Margie know she was coming.

Poor Daniel. She hated using him like that, but what other choice did she have? Maybe when this was all over, she'd call him and apologize. She had at least left a note in the truck so he wouldn't worry that she and Emma had been abducted but knew it would do little to ease the hurt. Daniel had been a friend. He'd trusted her, and she had betrayed him.

Chapter Six

Abbie drew in a deep breath; the scent of new leather and spicy aftershave brought her out of the past.

Jake glanced at her. "A penny for your thoughts."

"They're not worth that much." A smile inched its way to her lips.

"Are you having second thoughts?" His gaze fell to her clenched hands, and she pulled them apart to smooth her skirt.

"I'm way beyond second thoughts. I can't get my brain wrapped around the idea that we're going back home."

"If it's any consolation, your folks have talked to their attorney, Leo Morrison. That's the friend I told you about."

It wasn't any consolation at all. Dread rose in the pit of her stomach. She clasped her hands in her lap again to keep them from shaking. "I'm not sure that's such a good idea. Doesn't that mean I'll have to turn myself in?"

"Not right away. Leo will get the entire story and gather all the facts in the case."

"They should have waited." She pulled in a long breath. "How much does he know?"

"I left that up to your parents. We want him to have as much information as possible before we get there. When we arrive, you can sit down with him and go over everything." Jake reached across the back of the seat to massage her shoulder. "It'll be all right, Abbie. Trust me."

She caught his gaze for just a moment before looking out at the green pastureland of Montana. Her heart quickened at the realization that she'd soon be home.

Trust me, he'd said. Easier said than done.

* * * * *

Jake would have given anything to erase the worry lines etched across Abbie's brow. He'd finally coaxed the full story out of her—about her husband's death and losing the baby. She didn't deserve the treatment she'd gotten from her in-laws. He still couldn't believe she'd agreed to travel with him. Fortunately, he'd found a friend in Charlie.

It had been about nine in the evening when he'd heard a knock on his hotel door. He'd opened it and found himself eye to eye with a cop. Jake suspected the shock must have registered on his face, because Charlie held up a hand and grinned—a sort of I-come-in-peace signal.

They'd talked for over an hour. Turned out that Charlie had attended the University of Oregon around the same time Jake had. They parted friends, and Charlie promised to call the next time he visited his parents in Oregon.

Jake almost wished he'd been able to confide in Charlie. But that wasn't going to happen. As kind as he appeared, Charlie was a cop. He would have to do his job even if it meant arresting Abbie for kidnapping her daughter.

With Charlie's blessing he had been cleared to bring Abbie home. Now it was just a matter of getting her safely back to Oceanside.

Thinking about his hometown brought on yet another concern. Barbara Nichols.

"You look worried." The gentle timbre of Abbie's voice brought Jake out of his reverie.

He glanced at her and smiled. "I guess I am."

"About me?" She frowned.

"Not entirely." He studied her a moment. "You know all those calls I've been making?" He'd tried phoning at lunch and again when they stopped for gas.

She nodded. "I've been wondering about that."

"I work with a woman named Barbara Nichols. I've been trying to get ahold of her since I got to Grand Forks, but she isn't answering her phone."

"That's been four days. I can see why you'd be concerned. Does she have family or friends you could call?"

"Her parents live in Portland, but I don't have the number. She may have had to make a trip there. It's odd, though, that she didn't call me at the hotel." He pinched the bridge of his nose and then reached up to adjust the visor. The afternoon sun was dipping toward the west.

"I suppose I shouldn't worry, but I left a dozen messages with my answering service and even called our secretary. Sandy took some vacation days to be with her daughter who just had a baby." He was babbling on without meaning to. Maybe he was more worried than he'd been willing to admit. "To make a long story short, Sandy went into the office, heard all my messages, but said there weren't any from Barbara. She wasn't home and her car was gone. Sandy is the one who suggested Barb might have gone into Portland. She'll keep trying to reach her."

"Maybe you should call the police?"

"I thought about it, but nothing's happened to indicate there might be trouble. I'll see what Sandy says the next time I talk to her."

Abbie smiled. "Maybe she needed to get away."

He nodded. "Could be. She's been pretty stressed out lately. Speaking of which, I should have Sandy call Barbara's boyfriend. "Travis might know something. I'll call again at our next stop."

And Jake did, every time they stopped for a meal or at a motel for the night. On Wednesday he urged Sandy to call the police.

"They'll look into it," Sandy told him when he called the office the next morning. "But since her car is gone, they're not apt to do much investigating. Honestly, Jake, I know money is tight for the police department, but you'd think they could do more. At least they're going to keep an eye out for her car."

By the time they reached Oceanside, his worry had breached safe levels.

* * * * *

Jake pulled into the Grants' driveway around noon on Thursday. While the Grants welcomed Abbie and Emma, he unloaded their bags and personal belongings and deposited them on the porch. He then headed back to the happy group. Jake felt elated that he could be a part of the homecoming. Skye hadn't joined them, and he wondered about that. Had she run off again?

Jake had only seen Skye once, and to him she looked as though she might die before he could get Abbie home.

"How can we ever thank you?" Carlene said to Jake when he told them he needed to go.

"You're not staying for lunch?" Lyle asked.

"I wish I could, but I need to get back to my office." Sick with worry over Barbara, he told Abbie and Emma good-bye. Emma cried and hugged him when he tried to leave. Her tears did funny things to his heart. He couldn't ever remember anyone crying for him to stay with them. Oh, maybe one or two high school girlfriends, but never a sweet little girl with a beautiful mother.

"Don't go, Unca Jake. You can stay here with us." Emma had a headlock on him, and Abbie had to pry her loose.

"Jake has to go to work, Emma. We'll see him again soon."

"I'll come back, Emma," he promised. His gaze slipped to Abbie. He was tempted to pull her into his arms and kiss her.

"Thanks for all your help." Abbie leaned forward and tentatively kissed his cheek.

47

Carlene hugged him. "Don't be a stranger."

Lyle shook his hand. "When you figure out all your expenses, let me know and I'll write you a check."

"You don't need to do that."

"Nonsense." Lyle clapped him on the back. "A deal is a deal."

Jake wanted to argue. Bringing Abbie back had been a blessing for him. True, the trip had started out as a business deal, but it had become so much more. How did one take money for helping a woman like Abbie and a precious childlike Emma—a mother and child he was beginning to care about far too much.

He'd talk to Lyle later. Right now, though, he had to find out what had happened to Barbara.

Chapter Seven

Abbie watched the white Cadillac pull out of the driveway. They all waved, and Jake waved back. In a way she felt a little jealous of Emma's innocence and how she had clung to Jake, not wanting to lose him even for a moment. Truth be told, Abbie hadn't wanted him to leave either. She used her thumb to wipe away residual tears and reassured Emma again. "It's okay, sweetheart. Uncle Jake has to go to his own house."

"He'll be back, dear." Her mother laid an arm across Abbie's shoulder and it dawned on her that her mother wasn't talking to Emma.

"What?" Abbie shook her head. "I wasn't..."

Her mother gave her a knowing smile and thankfully changed the subject. "Let's go inside. We have a surprise for you. Oh..." She squeezed Abbie's shoulder. "I see our surprise has ventured outside."

Abbie turned and spotted a pencil-thin, disheveled woman sitting on the porch swing, smoking a cigarette and staring at them. Shock slammed into Abbie's chest and tore every thought of Jake from her mind. "Oh my..." she stopped, unable to take another step. She let Emma slide down her hip and leg. "Is that..."

"Skye." Her mother's whispered response held as much or more pain than Abbie felt. Jake had mentioned Skye being sick, but Abbie never expected anything like this. "What happened to her?" Drugs, Abbie knew, but how could it have gotten this bad?

"It's a long story, but let's not worry about that right now. We'll have plenty of time to talk later."

Carlene nudged Abbie forward and took Emma's hand. In a cheerful voice she said, "Come on, sweetheart. let's go see your Auntie Skye."

Abbie swallowed the lump in her throat and followed her mother. She hadn't seen Skye since marrying Nate and moving to Iowa. The sad part was she wouldn't have recognized her sister if she'd met her on the street. Hollow eyes continued to stare at them, reminding Abbie of emaciated children from third-world countries.

Skye stopped rocking and rose from the swing then bent down to crush the cigarette in an ashtray. Tears filled Skye's eyes as she grasped the railing and hobbled down the steps toward them.

"Oh, Skye," Abbie gasped. "She threw her arms open wide, and her sister stepped into the embrace. Abbie's brain bubbled over with questions, but this wasn't the time. She held her baby sister as tightly as she dared.

"It's about time you got here." Skye pulled back and brushed at her cheeks with the back of her hand.

Abbie held her sister's hand and turned to bring Emma and her mother closer. "Emma, sweetie, this is my little sister. Remember the pictures I showed you?"

"Skye." Emma grinned and waved a hand in the air. "Like the sky."

"That's right." Skye tossed Abbie a questioning glance. "Your mommy told you about me?"

Emma nodded. "She shows me pictures and we say prayers every night. But you don't look very much like the picture. And you're not very little."

"Emma, shush." Sending her sister an apologetic look, she added, "We look at pictures of you, Nana and Papa, and Tim almost every night and we pray for all of you." Looking at Skye now, Abbie wondered if God had answered any of those prayers.

Pops slipped by them and climbed the steps to the porch, where he picked up two of the suitcases. "I should help him." Abbie released her sister and grabbed one of the bags.

Once the suitcases had been set in the rooms that Emma and Abbie would occupy, everyone gathered in the living room, a large, light-filled room that looked over the sand, rocks, and the ocean beyond. The tide was in, coming almost to the base of the hill upon which the house stood.

The décor was simple and beachy, with nearly all the pictures depicting the sea. One of them Abbie recognized as a painting she had done while in college. The walls were painted in light aquamarine and peach and seemed to bring the outdoors inside. There were a few too many decorations and knickknacks—lighthouses, salt and pepper shakers for Abbie's taste. She supposed her mother's tendency to collect came from living so many years without a real home.

Skye had settled herself in a hammock that hung from the ceiling. With blankets wrapped around her, she looked as though she'd slipped into a cocoon.

Emma sat cross-legged beside her, rocking a baby doll and cooing, "It's all right, baby. Mommy's got you. It's going to be okay."

Tears sprang into Abbie's eyes. But she caught them and whisked them away with a tissue she fished out of her pocket.

Her first instinct was to pick up her little girl and reassure her, knowing that when Emma loved on her doll, it was often because she herself felt frightened or insecure. But for now, Emma was dealing well with whatever fears she had. They would talk later.

Abbie had so often said those very words to Emma— especially after they left the farm in Iowa. A curtain of guilt shrouded her as she remembered how brokenhearted Emma had been. She loved her grandma and grandpa Campbell and her uncle Daniel. Abbie had taken back her child, but in the process, she'd stolen relationships that might have been.

Lord, I'm so sorry. I never meant to hurt Emma. I didn't want to hurt anyone.

Abbie pushed the guilt aside, knowing there'd be no going back and knowing she'd do the same thing again if she had to. She turned her mind toward the here and now.

"How's that coffee coming, love?" Pops sank into a huge leather recliner that went with nothing in the room, yet strangely went with everything. It sat directly in front of the television set, with other chairs of lesser import arranged in a horseshoe shape. From each chair, one had a view of the water as well as the television set.

Abbie moseyed into the kitchen, which was an extension of the living room, only at a slightly higher level so one could watch the sea while cooking. A long breakfast bar/counter separated the two areas.

"What can I do to help you, Mom?"

"I'm almost done." Carlene pulled forward a cookie jar, from which she selected about a dozen cookies. "Oatmeal chocolate chip. Your grandmother used to make them for us all the time, remember?"

Abbie nodded. Grandma Olsen lived in a retirement home nearby. "How is grandma?"

"Feisty as ever." Carlene arranged the cookies on the plate. "You'll see her soon. She comes to the house and bakes for me sometimes. Right now, she's on a senior cruise in the Caribbean. How do you want your coffee? Still taking a little coffee in your cream and sugar?"

Abbie chuckled at the old joke. "I'm down to two spoons of cream and one sugar cube."

Carlene lifted the cream from the tray and handed it, along with a cup, to Abbie. "I'll let you fix your own and then you can bring the tray. I'll take the cookies. My arm is acting up."

"Probably from carrying Emma. She's not a baby anymore."

"Don't remind me." Guilt struck at Abbie again. She'd stolen time with Emma away from her parents as well. Maybe coming back would repair the damage.

Unless Leah takes Emma and I go to jail.

Stop it. Abbie couldn't let herself think that way. Jake had promised her it would work out in her favor. She had to believe that. Abbie poured herself some coffee, added the cream and sugar. After a couple of stirs, she placed it on the tray and joined the others in the living room.

Abbie served her father first, then Skye, thinking it should be the other way around. Pops wouldn't have minded in the least, but that was how things were done. Emma scooted over to the coffee table where Abbie set her fruit drink and cookie.

Carlene picked up her own mug and settled into a cushioned rocking chair, which sat parallel to her husband's. Abbie imagined them sitting there in the evenings watching their favorite television shows. She picked up her cup and took a chair between her mother and Skye.

Once they had their goodies, the room fell silent until Pops asked about the trip and how things were in Grand Forks. Did she like it there? Had she and Jake enjoyed the trip?

Abbie answered each question in turn, wishing she could ask a few questions of her own. The family tiptoed around the issues that had brought them all together and they did it quite well. Years of practice, Abbie supposed. For now, it was a good thing. Emma didn't need to hear about their problems.

"I'm glad you're here, Abs." Skye managed a smile, though it seemed to hurt her mouth.

"I am too." Abbie patted her sister's bony hand then tore her gaze from Skye's gaunt face to the cream-diluted coffee.

How are you? Are you eating? Have you stopped taking drugs? Are you dying? all questions Abbie wanted to ask but didn't.

"So…" Mom eased out of the awkward silence. "How is Margie?"

"Good. She says to tell you hello. I think our being with her these last couple of years has been good for her. For both of us." Abbie smiled. "She has a friend, Charlie, and I think they're pretty close to being a couple."

Another silent patch.

"Did Jake take you to see the property on your way into town?" Pops asked as he lifted a hand-thrown pottery mug to his lips.

"No. He thought about it, but we both agreed it would be better to wait. I wanted to settle in here and he…" She frowned. "His partner seems to be missing."

Her mom perked up. "Barbara?"

Abbie nodded. "He's been trying to reach her for days. But she's not returning his calls. I don't suppose either of you have seen her?"

"As a matter of fact, we have." Pops grinned. "Jake had already left for Iowa and we wanted to see the property again. We're still pinching ourselves. Doesn't seem possible we could find such a beautiful place."

"Barbara was kind enough to take us out there." Her mother pursed her lips. "She seemed fine. Said she wanted to go anyway—something about having another look."

"The last time we saw her was when we'd finished exploring. She got in her car and followed us out to the highway."

Pops frowned. "Nice gal, sure hope she's okay."

"Do you remember what day that was? Jake says he hasn't heard from her since the twenty-sixth of May."

"It was before that," Mom said. "The twenty-fifth." Abbie made a mental note to let Jake know about Barbara's visit to Cold Creek. She couldn't help but wonder if that visit had something to do with the realtor's disappearance.

Emma fell asleep on the plush seafoam-green carpet, and Mom reached into an old wooden trunk near her chair and pulled out a crocheted afghan—probably one Grandma Olsen had made. She tucked it gently around Emma, pausing to lean forward to kiss her cheek.

"It's been a long day." Abbie stood as she gathered up Emma's glass and plate.

Skye untangled herself from the cocoon. "For me too. I need to take my meds and maybe get a nap before dinner." She smiled. "I didn't sleep much last night. All I could think about was where you might be and when you might come and..."

"She was like a little kid," Pops said. "Remember when you guys were little and you used to ask, 'are we there yet?' about drove me crazy."

"I remember," Abbie said. "Some of those trips were excruciatingly long."

"I know, but we had fun." His smile widened. "We used to sing songs to make the time go by faster."

Carlene nodded. "We also sang them as practice for our performances."

"They were good times." Abbie squeezed her mother's hand.

Pops shifted in his chair. "We were family."

"What are we now, Pops?" Skye challenged, her tone taking on a sharp edge.

"It was different. We didn't have kids on drugs...."

"Didn't we? You drank, Pops. Every night. And sometimes you took uppers so you could stay awake."

"So, you're blaming me for all this trouble you've gotten yourself into?"

"Shush." Carlene pushed out of her chair. "Come on, you two, let's not argue. Not today. Not in front of Abbie and Emma."

Abbie's gaze flickered over Skye and her father. "It sounds like we need to talk, but Mom's right. Not now."

"Not ever, if Pops has anything to say about it," Skye countered.

Their father said nothing as he left his chair and walked out the front door.

Skye rose and shuffled across the floor. Clinging to the banister, she slowly and painfully ascended the stairs.

"We offered to give her a room down here." Her mother lowered her head and pinched the bridge of her nose.

"She refused." Abbie nodded. "Always the stubborn one."

"Takes after her father." Carlene sighed. "He's taking this so hard. Blames himself for not being stricter with her in high school when all this started."

"And what about Skye's accusations?"

Mom shook her head. "He drank some, but he was never drunk or mean. She's wrong about dad taking drugs. All he ever took back then was pills to lower his blood pressure, and sometimes he took pills the doctor gave him to help him sleep. He was never an addict."

Abbie never remembered her father being a user, but Skye had gotten the notion from somewhere. A lot of performers used drugs and drank heavily. It was part of the culture. "Even if Pops never took street drugs, Skye had a lot of role models." Abbie wanted to know more, but she also wanted to change the subject. "How is Tim?"

"Good. He's hoping to get a job with the state police in this area, and if he does, he'll be moving back home for a while."

"That's what Jake was saying." Abbie helped her mother take the cups and tray back into the kitchen.

"How do you like our Jake?

Our Jake? "He's very nice."

"Oh, he's more than that." Mom gave that knowing smile.

Abbie would have commented, but Emma had awakened from her nap. "Looks like this might be a good time to unpack and get settled in." She picked up her daughter and headed for the stairs.

"I'll walk up with you," Mom said. "Make sure everything is to your liking."

Abbie and Emma would be staying in two of the four upstairs bedrooms, which connected via a large European-style bathroom. Emma's room looked as though it had been newly decorated in pinks and hints of other pastels. The bed, dressed in princess-style ruffles and eyelets, had a canopy with yet more ruffles.

The furnishings, a dresser and vanity table, had been painted white with gold trim. very elegant and very much appreciated by her highness. A new set of Barbie dolls with a wardrobe sat next to an overflowing toy chest with stuffed animals and toys and building blocks.

Everything a little girl could want. Emma squealed with delight and dove into her treasures. "Mommy, look, Nana bought me books too."

"I see." Abbie chuckled. "We'll have a lot of reading to do." Turning toward her mother, she added, "Mom, you didn't have to do all this."

"Of course, we did." Carlene placed a hand on Abbie's shoulder, slipping up beside her. "Grandchildren are precious, and we want to make her happy."

"You'll spoil her." Abbie couldn't have been more pleased. She circled her mother's waist and hugged her.

Abbie spent a few minutes hanging up Emma's dresses and tucking her shirts, pants, and underwear into the dresser before moving into her own room.

She paused at the doorway to the bedroom. Her mother had decorated in there as well. The walls were white and the bedspreads floral, with various pillows that picked up the colors in the flowers: pink, rose, cream, pale green. a white wooden rocking chair sat in front of a window that looked out over the ocean.

While Emma made herself at home with her toys and dolls, Abbie tucked away her own things in the large closet. The unpacking reminded her of the day she arrived at Margie's. She'd come with little and had left with slightly more. About the only real purchases she'd made had been pillows, linens, and art supplies. In Grand Forks, she'd bought an extra suitcase for those things. They'd planned to rent a trailer, but in the end realized everything she and Emma had would fit in Jake's car.

Abbie sighed. There was something pathetic about a twenty-eight-year-old woman who could pack her whole life into three suitcases. She did, however, have an easel and her art supplies, along with a portfolio of watercolors she'd done at Margie's. She'd had to leave her original equipment along with her portfolio in Iowa when she fled.

Maybe someday she'd go back and get them. Though knowing Leah, they'd have gone out with the trash and been burned. She shoved the unkind thought aside, along with memories of Leah. She was home and it was time for celebration—not despair.

Chapter Eight

After dropping Abbie off, Jake headed straight to the office. He hesitated before opening the door, worried about what might be waiting for him. Then, taking a deep breath, he went ahead.

"Jake!" Sandy eased her bulky frame out of the chair and waddled over to give him a welcome-home hug. "I am so glad you're here. The phone has been ringing off the hook. We have a lot of unhappy clients. Barbara didn't show up for any of her appointments and..."

"You still haven't been able to locate her?" Jake headed for his desk. The office was a single large room with a small storage space, a conference room for meeting with clients, and a restroom. This room held three large executive desks. Sandy's was situated just inside the entrance. Barbara and Jake's desks faced the door as well.

The desks formed a triangular arrangement.

Sandy shook her head. "Not a word. The police are finally starting to take her disappearance seriously. A police officer was here this morning asking questions about you."

"About me?"

"Yes, well, it appears that since Barbara went missing about the same time you left, you are their primary suspect."

Jake ran a hand through his hair. "Great." He paced to the door and back. "So, they're suspecting foul play. Did they give you any particular reason why I might want to get rid of my partner at a time when I needed her to take over for me?"

"Money?" Sandy looked up at him, her brown eyes brimming with tears. "I had to tell them that if something happened to her you would get any commission she might make."

"Wonderful. and I suppose you told them about how great Barbara and I get along." Barbara was a good worker, but they'd had plenty of disagreements. Since he was the senior partner and the broker, he'd gotten on her case a few times for not following through. She worked hard but didn't seem all that invested in the business.

"I told them you got along okay." She grabbed a tissue and blew her nose. "I'm sorry, Jake. I didn't offer them any extra information. I just answered their questions."

"It's not your fault. Sorry for giving you a bad time." He dropped into his leather executive chair and started going through the papers. "I suppose they want to talk to me."

Sandy nodded. "As soon as possible."

Focusing on the stacks of paper in front of him, Jake said, "Walk me through this, will you. Tell me if there's anything urgent I need to deal with this minute."

"I took care of most of the calls, but there are a couple of people you need to talk with. One is Douglas Perkins. He's been working with Barbara on the Cold Creek property. He's saying he put an offer on it before the Grants did."

With elbows on the desk, Jake held his head in his hands. Could things get much worse?

He'd been afraid Perkins would pull something like this. It was true that Barbara had shown the property to him first, but they'd gotten a yes from Lyle Grant before Perkins called with his offer.

Jake didn't feel up to talking with the guy, but he should at least acknowledge him. He stood and took the note to Sandy.

Placing it on her desk, he said, "How about calling Mr. Perkins for me and setting up an appointment for tomorrow—say around ten?"

"Will do." Sandy picked up the receiver and began dialing.

"Did the police officer leave a card?" Jake asked.

"Um, yeah. It's around here somewhere." She shuffled through the stack of papers on her desk, found the card, and handed it to him. "Detective Meyers. He's with the state police and said he had to go back to Portland this afternoon. Said you could just call the local authorities. He mentioned Jeff's name."

"Well, that's something." Jeff Stuart was a long-time friend who worked with the Oceanside Police Department. Jake had sold Jeff and his wife a house up north in road's end. Jake pulled his suit jacket off the back of the chair and flipped it over his shoulder. "I'd better go talk to him. Find out what's going on."

A few minutes later, Jake walked into the police station and asked to talk to Jeff. He spoke briefly to the receptionist and was told to wait. Jeff showed up about two seconds later.

"It's about time you got here, buddy." Jeff clasped his shoulder. "Let's go get some coffee. Have you had lunch?"

"Coffee sounds good. Lunch too, for that matter." He and Abbie had stopped in Portland for a late breakfast. Eating on the road had turned his meal schedule upside down.

He followed Jeff out of the building and into the parking lot. Jeff started toward his unmarked Chrysler. "We'll take my car, if you don't mind."

Jake climbed into the passenger seat. "Sandy told me a Detective Meyers came by the office. She says he asked about my having something to do with Barbara's disappearance. What's that all about?"

"He had to ask, Jake. You left town about the same time she disappeared. How do we know you didn't help her disappear, or maybe you killed her, pushed her car off the road, put her body in the trunk, and buried her somewhere between here and Fargo?"

"I didn't go to Fargo."

"Oh, right, Grand Forks. And what's the deal with a police officer out there calling us to ask about you? Did you get into some kind of trouble?"

"Come on, Jeff. You know I didn't have anything to do with Barbara's going missing. Charlie, he's the officer who called you, just wanted to make sure I was who I said I was. They weren't about to send Abbie off with some stranger with a criminal record. Thanks for giving me a good report, by the way."

"No problem."

"Have you come any closer to locating Barbara?"

"No, but we did find her car this morning." Jeff cast Jake a sidelong look before twisting the key in the ignition. "A tourist spotted it when he walked off the path to get a picture."

"Where?" Jake's gut twisted. From the timbre of Jeff's voice, the news wasn't good.

"At the bottom of a ravine just south of town."

Chapter Nine

Jeff drove out of the lot and turned right.

"She was in an accident? Is she…?" Jake rubbed his brow, bracing himself for the worst.

"She wasn't in the car." Jeff pulled onto highway 101 and headed north.

Jake let the news sink in. "So, where is she?"

"That's what we're trying to find out. We searched the car and the area around it but found no sign of her. No purse, no briefcase, nothing. First, we thought she might have survived and crawled out, but there's no evidence of that. Of course, we've had a lot of rain."

"You think she could have been thrown free of the car and climbed back to the road. Maybe hitched a ride with someone?"

"It's possible. We just don't know, Jake." He sighed. "She may have planned to ditch her car and had someone waiting."

"That seems pretty farfetched."

"Maybe, maybe not. We need to cover all the angles. The gearshift was in neutral, so it looks like someone purposely shoved it over the edge of the cliff."

"Why would she do something like that? She needs her car to get around."

"To be honest, we're stumped." Jeff slowed with the traffic at a stop sign. "You were right having your secretary call us. I just wished we'd taken your concerns more seriously early on."

"Have you found anything else? Any clue as to what happened to her or why she might want to ditch her car and leave town?"

Jeff hesitated, and Jake suspected he had something but wasn't ready to share. "Her parents told us she hadn't been in contact with them." He blew out a long breath. "We asked the police department in Portland to notify her parents about the car. Next thing I know Detective Meyers is on the case."

Jeff pulled into the Oceanside Café's gravel parking lot, and they went about getting seated and ordering before taking up the conversation again.

"Have you checked her apartment?" Jake asked once they'd gotten their coffee.

"We did." Jake met his gaze. "Look, I'm not sure how much of this to tell you. We like to keep evidence close to the vest."

"Sure. I understand that, but I might be able to help if I know what you're dealing with."

"You have a point." Jeff blew on his black brew before taking a sip. He took his coffee straight up.

Jake added a little cream and sugar to cut the bitter taste.

"The only odd thing we found in the apartment," Jeff went on, "was that her closet had been ransacked and her personal items—things like a toothbrush—were gone. There was no suitcase, and it looked as though she might have packed up and taken off."

"Why would she do that?" Jake mused as he tasted the coffee and added a bit more cream. "Barbara seemed to like her job. She had several sales pending."

"Truth is, I'm not sure what to think."

"Have you talked to Travis?" Jake interrupted. "He's been dating her for a couple months or so. Maybe he has some insight."

Jeff nodded. "I questioned him, but that was before we found her car. I'll need to talk with him again."

Jake wiped up a drop of cream from the table. "None of this makes sense."

"You've got that right. So, what can you tell me about Barbara?"

"Not that much. She was quiet. Kept to herself a lot." Jake thrummed his fingers on the Formica tabletop, trying to remember more about the woman.

Jeff nodded. "Travis told me he had a date scheduled with her the night before you left, but she cancelled on him. She told him there was something she had to do."

"But she didn't say what?"

"Nope. He said it might have had something to do with a project she'd been working on, but he couldn't tell me about that either." Jeff stared into his cup before adding, "Detective Meyers considers him a suspect too."

"Huh. Of course, he does." Jake couldn't see Travis doing anything to hurt Barbara or anyone else for that matter.

Jeff was silent for a moment, as if wondering how much to say. "Sandy told me Barbara was thinking about breaking up with Travis. That gives him motive. He also had the means and opportunity. Trouble is, there's no tangible evidence of foul play. Right now, it looks as though she skipped town without letting anyone know."

"I don't believe Barbara would skip town, but if she did, why would she push her car over an embankment?" Jake thought about his statement and backed off a bit.

"On the other hand, even though we've worked together for two years now, you'd think I'd know her better than I do. She rarely talked about her personal life. Kept to herself a lot. The only reason I knew she was dating Travis is because he told me, and I'd seen them having coffee a few times. She's good with people, but not pushy. Barbara brought in a lot of business."

"So, you're saying that you're better off with her alive."

Jake shrugged. "Of course."

"Did you ever date her?"

Jake shook his head, thinking immediately of Abbie and not sure why. "Not my type, I guess. We talked a fair amount, but mostly about business. Like I said, she rarely if ever mentioned family. About all I know is that she had parents living in Portland." He looked up at Jeff. "I wish I could offer more."

He took another drink of coffee thinking about his partner. Something niggled at the back of his mind. "Come to think of it, she seemed jumpy, kind of agitated before I left town."

"Sandy mentioned that." Jeff pushed his empty cup toward the waitress when she came by offering refills. "Did she ever tell you about any previous jobs she might have had?"

Jake pursed his lips, trying to remember. "She used to be a bank teller in Portland. I never checked her references. I suppose I should have, but it didn't seem necessary. When she came to me to apply for a job, she'd just gotten her real estate license and that was good enough for me. She was on a six-month probationary period and passed with flying colors."

Jeff leaned back and studied Jake's face, then, apparently coming to a decision, leaned forward again. "When you clued us in that something might be wrong, I did some digging. Ordinarily I wouldn't tell you this, but there's good reason to suspect foul play and/or the theory that she skipped town. She was a bank teller until five years ago when the bank she worked at was robbed. It didn't go down well. The bank robber took a hostage and got away with half a million in cash."

Jake whistled. "And Barbara was there?"

"She saw the whole thing. The gunman disappeared with the money and a twenty-five-year-old woman who worked with Barbara at the bank. There's been no trace of them since. The hostage was Barbara's best friend, so it was doubly traumatic for her. Her mother said she changed after that. Wouldn't go back to work and sort of shut down for a while. She lived at home and finally went back to school and decided to go into real estate."

"What brought her to Oceanside?" Jake asked as he processed this latest information. Barbara's past experiences shed a whole new light on her disappearance.

Jeff shrugged. "No idea. her parents said she thought it was time to move on and she had always liked this area. The robbery is why Meyers is chiming in on the case. He thinks she may have come here because of some tip they'd gotten about two years ago that the bank robber had been seen out here. About the same time a few bills from the robbery surfaced in Oceanside."

"I'm sorry, I'm not following you. You think Barbara came here to work so she could search for a bank robber? Isn't that up to the police?"

"Yes, but Barbara was apparently obsessed with the case. For a while after it happened, she drove the police nuts calling in with sightings. After a while she stopped calling altogether."

"And now she's missing."

Jake straightened when the waitress brought their orders. The breakfast special for Jeff and a BLT for him.

Jeff and Jake talked while they ate, but not about Barbara. Jeff's wife was pregnant and due in October. They were all friends— Jeff and his wife, Becky, Travis, Sandy, Jake's sister Peggy, and her husband, Brent, Jake's primary carpenter. Jake had known all of them for as long as he could remember.

He had to smile at the weaving of people making up the town of Oceanside. It was like a lot of tourist towns along the Oregon and Washington beaches. There were the locals—people who lived there year-round—and the tourists. But there was also a division between the locals. There were the natives, those who were born and raised Oceansiders, and there were those who had moved in as adults. He and his friends were natives and tended to band together. Not that they excluded others, but they had an unspoken pact. He'd gone through grade school and high school with these people. In a way, their closeness was a good thing. In another, they were like a high-school clique that made outside friendships difficult.

As an outsider, Barbara had never been part of their group, but not because they didn't want her to be. He couldn't ever remember her wanting to be with them. Early on, he'd invited her to a few of their get-togethers and she'd turned him down. Come to think of it, Travis had mentioned inviting her as well. Jake wondered if Barbara had made any close friends in Oceanside outside of Travis. If she had, he didn't know about them.

"Did you talk to any of Barbara's neighbors?" Jake set his empty plate aside, thinking maybe someone at the apartment complex could tell them something about her or people who might have visited her.

"I made a quick run-through. A couple of people know her by sight. None of them remembered seeing anyone come or go from the apartment but her."

"Not even Travis?"

"Apparently not. I showed them photos of both you and Travis, but no takers."

Jake frowned. "You showed them my picture?"

"Well, you are her boss."

"And a suspect, I know."

"Sorry about that."

"What about Travis? No one saw him at her place either?"

Jeff shook his head. "Seemed strange to me, but Travis says he was never invited to her apartment, not even to pick her up. She always met him somewhere."

Jake frowned. It sounded as though Barbara was hiding something. "Come to think about it, I've never seen the inside of her apartment either. I picked her up outside or dropped her off a couple of times when she had car trouble or needed a ride, which wasn't very often." The more Jake thought about it, the more he realized how little he knew Barbara Nichols.

Jeff asked about Jake's trip to the Midwest, so Jake filled him in. Talking about Abbie and Emma raised his mood considerably. His friend apparently noticed. "You like her."

He grinned. "Maybe a little."

"Don't try to deny it, buddy, you've fallen big time."

"It's not like that. I do like her. There's something special about her. She's an artist. I'm not into art, but I appreciate it as much as the next guy does. I care about her. Abbie has been through a lot and I want to help in whatever way I can."

"Oh, yeah. you have all the symptoms." Jeff chuckled. "You're even playing the knight in shining armor."

"It's more than that." Jake wanted to tell him about Abbie's ordeal with her late husband's family but thought better of it. If there was a warrant out for Abbie, Jeff would feel obligated to act on it. His friend was an honest cop, which was one of the reasons Jeff couldn't arbitrarily rule out him or Travis as suspects in Barbara's disappearance.

Jake paid for their lunches and the two walked out to the car. Jake felt more confused than ever. Had Barbara really skipped town? Somehow, he couldn't see her doing that. True, he didn't know her as well as he'd thought, but her leaving town so suddenly and mysteriously didn't seem like a reasonable theory. If he was right, and she hadn't sent her car over the cliff, then someone else had.

Chapter Ten

A few minutes later, Jake returned to his office to take care of the work that had piled up in his absence. He asked Sandy to show a couple of properties and spent the rest of the afternoon returning phone calls and making appointments.

By eight that evening, he'd pretty much caught up. Jake had shown three houses to three of Barbara's clients and taken earnest money on two of them—overall a productive day.

Two things remained outstanding, though. Barbara was still gone, and he missed Abbie and Emma. On the plus side, he'd received an invitation to join Abbie's father for a fishing trip to Bear Lake in the morning.

It was dark when he left the office. He really needed to go home, unpack, shower, and get some sleep. Trouble was, when he entered the gates of the Pacific View Estates, his car seemed determined to pass by his place and go straight to the Grants' home a few blocks away.

Jake might have been able to resist if they lived anywhere but in the housing development where he'd built his own house. He drove past their home, debating whether he should stop. It wasn't exactly late, but he hadn't called. Jake stopped at the lookout, where the earth dropped out of sight on the other side of the guardrail. This was one of his favorite developments. He had bought the property, along with several other properties in the area, after his parents died and left him and his sister, Peggy, a sizeable inheritance. So far, real estate had been the best investment they could have made. He and Brent, Peggy's husband, had gotten together right out of college. They built the house Jake now owned on spec, to be used as a model home, then Jake began selling lots and Brent built the houses.

They made a good team and had earned a lot of money. The development was different from the places where homes were pressed together as close as building codes allowed. Brent and Jake preferred parceling out one- and two-acre lots.

The lookout where he'd parked cut into the coastline, creating a perfect place for a park for residents to enjoy. The view itself had settled the deal for most of the people who bought there. He'd sold forty places, and they had ten more lots to go.

Jake turned around and went back to the Grant home, this time pulling into the driveway. He turned off the engine and was just getting out when he noticed the red glow of a cigarette and two silhouettes on the porch swing.

"Jake!" Abbie's voice drew him forward. Maybe he was imagining it, but she sounded happy to see him.

"Come join us. I was just telling Skye about our trip." He greeted them as he took the steps two at a time.

"What brings you out here?" Abbie asked. "Did we leave something in your car?"

"No, truth is, I missed you and Emma."

"Abbie was missing you too." Skye's raspy voice gave way to a cough. She leaned forward to snuff the cigarette out in the ashtray.

Jake turned to look at Abbie and smiled. "Were you really?"

"Maybe a little." Abbie returned the smile. The soft light from the streetlamp illuminated her face as she tipped her head back to meet his gaze.

"I'm going inside," Skye announced. "Why don't you sit here on the swing with Abs."

"Abs?" When she vacated the swing, Jake followed Skye's advice. He wasn't about to argue with the best invitation he'd had all day.

Abbie laughed as the door closed. "Skye has always called me that."

"It's kind of cute."

"Better than Abigail."

Jake relaxed against the cushion, his arm stretched across the back, almost touching Abbie's shoulders.

"Any word on Barbara?" she asked.

"Quite a lot, actually." Jake told her what he'd learned from Jeff.

"So basically, no one knows what really happened to her." Abbie took his hand. "I'm sorry you're having to go through this."

"You know, Abbie, the strangest thing is, I thought I knew Barbara. It's unnerving to find out I hardly knew her at all."

Abbie nodded. "I know the feeling. I'm finding that out with Skye, and she's my sister." She pulled her hand back and knuckled away a tear. "I've been out of her life for six years." Her voice rose and cracked. "During the most important times of her life, I wasn't there for her."

"It happens." Jake wished he could do something to alleviate her sorrow.

"It wouldn't be so bad if she hadn't made so many wrong choices. If I'd known what she was going through, maybe I could have stopped her."

Jake swallowed back a lump building in his own throat. He didn't know how to respond. "Unfortunately, we can never go back."

"I know. If-onlys are as bad as what-ifs."

Somehow, he had moved closer to her. Or had she been the one to move? His arm easily slipped around her shoulder and he lifted his left to complete the embrace.

They had traveled together for five days and four nights, but he'd never been this close. Jake wanted to kiss her and sensed she wanted it too.

* * * * *

Jake's arms tightened around her and Abbie nestled against him. He was warm and masculine, gentle and understanding. She wanted to stay in his arms. She wanted him to kiss her. All she had to do was tip her face toward his and turn ever so slightly, and his lips would cover hers. But as her desire grew, so did caution. Abbie pulled back. She shivered, not so much from the cold as from what she'd almost done.

She couldn't allow herself to be attracted to Jake, or any man for that matter. She was a woman with a child, not a teenager with a crush. She needed to keep her wits about her. Her past indiscretions were about to catch up with her. She had a criminal record, and tomorrow she'd see the attorney and turn herself in.

Jake moved back; disappointment clear in those incredible blue eyes. "Are you okay?"

"I'm fine," she lied. "I should go in. Did you want coffee or anything?"

"No. I need to get home. He stood and offered her a hand up. I have an early day tomorrow."

"Me too." Abbie allowed herself to relax now that they were back to a safer place. "Can you believe Pops is taking me fishing? He wants to show me the property from Bear Lake." She chuckled. "I tend to be an early riser, but four-thirty? I can't believe I agreed to go with him."

"I'm glad you did." Jake smiled. "He asked me to go too, so I guess I'll see you out there." He paused. "Knowing you're joining us will make the outing much more appealing."

Abbie felt the same way but didn't say so.

He was several inches taller than her and his nearness reminded her of the night they had danced. Being so close to him unnerved her. If he took her in his arms, her head would fit perfectly just under his chin. He'd have to bend slightly to kiss her. And he did.

His kiss was as sweet and gentle as she had imagined. Abbie wanted more, but she couldn't let it go on. She pressed her hands against his chest and it almost hurt when he stepped away.

"Abbie, I'm sorry." Jake seemed as surprised as she was.

"Don't be." she pressed her lips together. "It's as much my fault as yours. I like you, Jake, but we can't afford to act on our feelings."

"Why not?" He smiled and tried again. She turned her head, catching his kiss on her cheek.

"Jake, I can't."

He sighed and nodded. "I understand. We have a professional relationship. I'm your realtor and…"

"There is that. Besides, things are too unsettled."

"Right."

Abbie stepped around him.

"I'll see you in the morning." He smiled, almost melting her reserve. "You'll love it. The fishing is great in Bear Lake."

"I'm looking forward to holding a pole in my hands again."

"And the worms?"

She wrinkled her nose. "I'll leave that part to you and Pops."

"And here I thought you were a true fisherman." He stuffed his hands in his pockets.

"Bye, Jake." Abbie opened the door and stepped inside.

He turned toward his car, whistling *"Strangers in the Night."* Smiling, she closed the door and leaned against it, glad he was no longer a stranger.

Chapter Eleven

"Jake isn't coming in?" Carlene came around the corner.

"No." Abbie moved away from the door after locking it.

"Apparently he's coming fishing with Pops and me in the morning."

"Oh." It was a wistful sound. Maybe a tinge of jealousy.

"Are you really going fishing? I'd hoped...never mind. I know how much your father wants to spend time with you. He can't wait to show you Cold Creek."

Abbie nodded. "And you want to spend time with me as well. Maybe we girls can go shopping in a day or two."

"That would be nice. I'd like that." She continued into the kitchen, filled a glass with water, and proceeded to take several pills. Refilling the glass, she skirted past Abbie.

"I'll be off to bed, sweetheart. Do you need anything before I go?"

Abbie smiled. Ever the nurturer. "I'm good, Mom. sleep well. I'll see you in the morning."

Her mother raised an eyebrow in disdain. "No, you won't. I put together snacks for you. I plan to sleep until at least seven... unless Emma wakes up."

Abbie hugged her. "I have a hunch she'll sleep late. But don't be surprised if she crawls into bed with you."

"I'd love that." She sighed, content as a hen whose chicks had come home to the nest.

After turning off the lights, Abbie lingered for a while, roaming around the large living room, pausing to look out the large picture window toward the ocean. A moonbeam painted a large swath across the water. She imagined herself standing there on the shore with Jake.

Abbie, Abbie, it's much too soon. And you hardly know the man. Still she couldn't help but wonder. Would he appreciate the earth's beauty as she did? Would he think her foolish for wanting to paint a scene like this?

Sobering, she thought about Nate and his family. Nate had appreciated her work in the beginning. He'd told her he would build her a studio when he had time. He never found the time. Nate was a practical and thrifty man—much like his parents.

There was little time on the farm for mooning about, drawing pictures and painting canvases in whimsical colors. Lack of time and demanding work, along with Leah's disapproval, had nearly destroyed her dreams of being an artist. In Grand Forks, she'd regained her dream as well as her abilities.

Abbie shook her head to clear it of the farm and the sorrow it held for her. The moonscape drew her back to what she had become—what she had always been, an artist. She imagined using a wide brush, saturated with color, to wash dark hues of blue across the sky. She would use wax resist to save the moonbeam swath and the white caps. The scene was much too perfect to resist.

Abbie hurried to her room to collect the brushes and paints she'd need, returned to the living room, and sat in one of the cushioned chairs. She sketched out the scene and wrote in soft pencil the names of the colors she would later use. Once the sketch was done, she turned on a light over the table and painted her vision.

When she finished as much as she could, she left it to dry on the wide kitchen counter then headed upstairs to get ready for bed.

Sleep didn't come easily. Perhaps it was the anticipation of seeing Jake again. Or the feel of his lips on hers. Or the vision of her and Jake walking on that moonlit beach she'd captured in her painting. Abbie groaned and rolled onto her side. Punching up her pillow, she tried putting the man out of her mind. She'd begun to like him entirely too much.

Abbie tried to focus on her breathing—on counting to ten with each inhalation and exhalation, but her thoughts shifted from dreamy visions of Jake, to seeing the attorney and facing the possibility of arrest, making sleep even more difficult.

* * * * *

The following morning her alarm went off at four and Abbie would have given anything for another four hours of sleep. still, part of her was excited to see the property, the lake, and the man who'd brought her home.

At four-fifteen, Pops tapped lightly on her bedroom door, making certain she was awake.

"I'm almost ready." She spoke softly so she wouldn't wake anyone.

"I'll be in the car. Got to pack our gear and get our lunch basket." Abbie dressed in jeans and a long-sleeved knit shirt. since it would likely be cool until midmorning, she slipped a sweatshirt over the top. she thought about wearing makeup but decided against it.

She was there to fish, not to impress Jake. Abbie had never worn makeup to go fishing and wasn't about to start now. She pulled her hair into a ponytail and banded it, then, on the way downstairs, grabbed one of her father's caps off a hook near the door.

Their gear consisted of a tackle box and poles along with a couple of rain ponchos. Abbie hoped they wouldn't need the rain gear. In the predawn darkness, the sky gave no hint as to what it intended to do.

By the time Abbie stepped outside, Pops was ready to go. She climbed into his old Jeep and off they went.

They drove through the main part of town until 101 curved to the right, taking them away from the beach. Abbie leaned her head against the seat back, thinking she might be able to catch a few winks.

"I saw your painting," Pops said. "It's amazing."

"Thanks. I got inspired last night. It needs some finishing touches, but I think I captured the mood."

"You did indeed." He glanced over at her. "I can't believe you went for so long without painting. All that time you were married to Nate, did you paint even once?" She shrugged. "I lost my muse."

"Nonsense. Those people took it."

"Pops, don't." Her parents hadn't wanted her to marry Nate. Back then, they had seen something she hadn't. In a way, he was right. They—or she should say Leah—had stolen her muse. Abbie had known early on how Leah felt about her artistic gifts. She'd said that living on the farm would knock some sense into her. Back then, Abbie didn't know how strong Leah was. And how weak she would become.

Abbie blamed Leah for a long time, but during those two years in Grand Forks realized that she shared the blame. She had allowed Leah to rule her life. She hadn't fought back. She'd believed the lies about her short-comings. Like Leah's husband and sons, Abbie gave in too. It was always easier to let Leah have her way.

"I'm the one who quit painting. I'm the one who gave up."

"But you're back."

"I am." Abbie sighed. "I loved Nate, Pops. And in a way, I love Leah. I just don't like her very much."

He chuckled at that. "I have a feeling God would agree."

"I'm afraid of her, Pops. I'm terrified at what she could do to me. At what she's already done."

"God is with us, Abbie. No matter what happens, you need to believe that. The promise of light, of abundance, of hope, is ours."

Abbie swallowed hard. "What if I'm arrested?"

"We'll pay the bail."

"I'm a flight risk. I've proven that."

Pops didn't respond. Instead, he eyed the road signs and slowed down, turning off the main highway onto Bear Lake Road. "Almost there."

The road, barely two lanes, wound on for about a mile. Abbie felt fearful and excited all at once. The thought of buying over two hundred acres could do that to a person—especially someone like her. Her heart skipped as they passed the carved wooden sign, Welcome to Cold Creek, est. 1882.

She turned to look at her father. "I love the entrance. Makes you feel like you're in another world." Her excitement ebbed and, in its place, came a feeling of dread. Hairs rose on the back of her neck as they drove past the overgrown scrub maples that crowded the narrow road. A premonition of sorts? A warning that something dreadful was going to happen? As she peered into the dense shrubbery a branch reached into the open cab and brushed against her arm.

Abbie shivered and pushed the worrisome thoughts aside, attributing them to nerves and the eeriness of dawn. Instead, she focused on the smell of fresh air and the abundance of leaves fluttering in the wind.

"Here we are." Pops stopped at a junction in the road and pointed ahead. Cold Creek.

Abbie felt a flood of disappointment. Three mismatched streetlights lit several boarded-up storefronts. The town looked as though it hadn't seen much activity for a long time. Jake had warned her about that. Still, it was emptier and more rundown than she'd imagined.

"I know it doesn't look like much now." Pops peered out the windshield. "We'll come back later when it's daylight."

It didn't look like there'd be much to see, daylight or otherwise. As he turned to the left, bypassing the main part of town, Abbie switched out her disappointment for optimism. She'd hold off on her critique until she had time to make a full assessment in the daylight.

They continued through town and at a Y in the road, made a left. This, Pops told her, went around to Bear Lake and the fishing dock.

They parked in the small gravel lot, and while they were pulling out their gear, Abbie looked around to get a feel for the place. A path led from the parking area to the dock, where two rowboats floated. Another path went from the dock to a doublewide trailer that sat atop a knoll. A large picture window gave the occupants a beautiful view of the lake.

"This could be a wonderful place for a retreat center, Pops," Abbie said. "Is the house and land here part of the property?"

"It is, and I was thinking the same thing." Pops leaned into the trunk and pulled out the cooler that held their lunch. "It's a rental, like a lot of the places here. Travis Jennings lives up there. He's the caretaker slash security guard. He stays rent-free and keeps tabs on the place."

Abbie glanced toward the house. "Jake mentioned that Travis was a good friend." He'd also mentioned that the police considered him a suspect. This Abbie kept to herself.

The doublewide looked like it had been around for a while and Pops suggested they might want to get rid of it and build the retreat center in its place. They would need a large area for classes, and this seemed perfect. Abbie envisioned a dozen Adirondack chairs sitting on the slope and artists setting up easels, preparing to paint the sunset. The retreat center would have a glass front to take advantage of the view.

The prospect excited her. Slow down, she told herself. As her father would say, she was putting the horse before the cart.

"I wonder how Travis would feel about moving," she said as they made their way down to the dock. "Free rent is a great deal for a place like this, and I can't imagine a nicer view." She smiled. "Except for your place, of course." She'd have to talk to Travis and Jake about the possibilities.

Pops chuckled. "If I had my druthers, I'd build a log cabin right here on the lake so I could go fishing every morning right off my deck."

Abbie laughed. "I'll bet you would. If we buy it, you can do just that."

When Pops stopped in front of the two boats tied at the dock, she set down the heavy tackle box. "This is it." He pointed to the larger boat with oars and a small motor. "Did you know he built this dock? I'm thinking we might want to keep him on as caretaker."

"Have you talked to him about that?"

"Not yet. I thought we'd check with Jake first. Get his take on the situation." He nodded back toward the parking lot. "Speak of the devil."

Looking up, she spotted Jake driving into the lot. He parked his white caddie beside the Jeep, grabbed some gear, and jogged toward them.

He was wearing shorts and a sweatshirt, Abbie noticed as he passed under the yard light. His legs were muscular and as tan as his face. During their trip from North Dakota, she'd only seen him in slacks and sport shirts. Considering that the northwest was just coming out of the rainy season, she suspected that Jake had recently spent time in a sunny climate. She could imagine him lying on a beach on some exotic shore.

And you lying beside him.

The thought vanished when Travis came out of his house and waved. "Hey, Jake, got a minute?" Travis jogged over to meet him. She couldn't hear what they said, but Travis sounded upset. Travis helped Jake with his gear, and they began walking down the dock toward them. It was then she heard Travis say, "I know Jeff is just doing his job, but come on. He should know better than to think you or I could have anything to do with Barbara's disappearance."

"I know it's frustrating, but we need to face facts. We probably knew Barbara better than anybody around here, and that's not saying much."

Travis sighed heavily. "You're right, but how am I supposed to know why my ex-girlfriend's car went over a cliff?"

"They need to ask." Jake stopped a couple feet from where Abbie stood. His knowing smile reminded her of the kiss they'd shared the night before. She felt the warmth of a flush creep into her cheeks.

"Have you met Abbie yet?"

Travis managed a smile. "Haven't had the pleasure. Hi Abbie, I'm Travis. Welcome to Cold Creek." He held her hand a little longer than necessary—probably checking her out. "I'm glad to finally meet you. Your dad's been talking my ear off about this artists' retreat idea he's cooked up."

"It's nice to meet you, Travis. Have you lived out here long?"

"In Oceanside all my life. Out here for about ten years. Isabelle hired me to keep an eye on the place." He chuckled. "Tough job, but somebody's got to do it."

"You all can chit-chat later," Pops said. "We'd better head out before sun-up if we want to catch some trout." He had already loaded the boat; now he stepped in and took the seat in the bow.

"Aye, aye, sir." Abbie climbed in behind him and Jake untied the boat before boarding.

Jake told Travis they'd talk later. Turning to Pops Jake said, "Now I know why you invited me. You need some muscle to row this thing."

"Would you mind?" Pops asked. "My back is giving me fits this morning and I need to save it for reeling in the trout."

"I don't mind. I was planning to work out today anyway." Jake settled onto the seat beside Abbie. "Unless you plan to do the rowing, Abbie, you might want to sit aft."

She'd never rowed a boat in her life and should have simply moved, but something in her nature resisted. "Why not? How hard can it be?"

"Okay. Have at it." Jake moved to the bench behind her. Abbie didn't miss the winks he and Pops exchanged. She should have given in and let Jake take over, but no. She was not the type to give in without a fight—not anymore.

She studied the oar, noting a ring with a sort of spike protruding from it. Abbie surmised that the spike might fit into the hole on the side of the boat. She picked up one of oars, slid the ring up slightly, and placed it into the hole, letting the paddle part of the oar rest on the water. When it fit perfectly, she did the same to the other side. Pleased with her progress, Abbie dipped both oars into the water in front of her then pulled them back as she'd seen rowers do. Up, forward, and back. The boat moved ahead a bit and then rotated slightly to the right.

She repeated the movement several more times, beginning to get the hang of it. But her arms were already starting to hurt, and she was only about twelve feet from the shore.

"Not bad," Pops said. "Let us know when you've had enough." The harder she rowed, the more the boat listed to the right. "Your right arm is stronger than your left," Jake offered. "So, you need to compensate." She raised the right oar out of the water, using only the left.

After a few minutes, her arm muscles not only ached, they became so weak she could barely bring the oars out of the water.

Jake came forward and sat beside her. "You're doing great, Abbie, but do you mind if I give you a few pointers?"

"Sure." Too achy to argue, Abbie moved back to the seat he'd vacated.

Jake turned to sit facing her. "First, you want to face aft. This allows you to put more power into the stroke." He dipped in the oars, almost parallel to the boat, then with one swift move pulled them nearly to his chest. The boat must have sailed forward five feet. He repeated the process several more times until they were near the center of the lake. Pops directed him a little closer to the far shore to his favorite fishing hole.

A few minutes later, the boat drifted peacefully atop the still water. Jake set the oars in the boat and the three sat quietly, soaking in the predawn stillness.

An owl hooted and a frog croaked as morning began to break. The sounds reminded Abbie of early mornings on the farm when she'd wake up early and amble out to the henhouse to gather eggs. She often stopped at the pond and listened to nature's symphony, absorbing the beauty around her as the sun began its slow and colorful rise over the vast expanse of farmland.

Here, evergreens towered around them. Abbie drew a long breath of fresh, crisp morning air.

Her father broke the silence with a cough. "What do you think, Abbie?"

"I can see why you fell in love with the place. Sitting here fills my senses and makes me want to capture it all on canvas."

"I knew you'd like it." He chuckled. "Now let's catch us some trout."

They took a few minutes to bait their hooks and drop their lines into the water.

Pop leaned forward, resting his arms on his knees. "I'll let Jake here tell you about the lay of the land." Turning to Jake he added, "It was too dark to see much when we got into the town itself, but I figured she could see all that later. The buildings can be repaired or torn down. This…" He waved an arm. "This is what's important."

"I couldn't agree more." Jake agreed. "The place has a lot of potential."

"I can see that. How large is the lake?"

"About twenty-five acres. It's about a mile wide here and then cuts in. I have a map that shows the lake and the town, so you get an idea of proportions."

"Is there another way in?"

"By car, no. There is a trail from town. Isabelle doesn't like having a lot of people driving in, so we don't usually direct non-locals out this way. We encourage tourists to hike in, and most are willing to do that. They come out to an area of the lake you can't see from here. There are a couple of docks there and some places to fish from the shore. This is a fresh-water lake with nutrients, which means it can sustain fish and other wildlife. So far, we have plenty of trout. We've never had to stock it. This is as pristine as it gets. We don't even allow motors except in emergencies."

"Yet there is a motor on this boat."

"I've never used it," Pops said. "I just take the boat out the old-fashioned way."

"One of the things locals are worried about," Jake added, "is what property development could do to the lake. Isabelle doesn't want to sell to anyone who plans to cut down the timber."

"We certainly wouldn't need to do that. I love the woodsy feel." Abbie hesitated. "We'd have to improve the road in, though."

Jake nodded.

Abbie asked about Travis's place. "Pops and I were talking about Travis and how he might feel if we eliminated his house and built the retreat center there."

"We were thinking he might stay on," Pops added. "We're going to need someone to keep an eye on things."

"Travis knows there's a good chance the mobile home will have to be moved. I'll bet he'd be happy to stay on—at least for a while."

Jake's line jiggled, and he jerked the pole back to snag his catch. A wide grin stretched across his face. "I got him."

"You sure do. I'd say from the bow you got on that rod he's a big one." Pops lifted the net, ready to scoop up Jake's catch.

"Four pounds, I'm guessing."

Abbie watched, fascinated, as Jake let the fish play, reeled it in, and let it play again. The rainbow trout lived up to its name, colors flashing just under the surface.

Abbie rooted around in her bag for her camera and just as the sun began its brilliant ascent, she snapped off the lens cover and shot what might become her next painting. The trout fought hard, but Jake expertly reeled it in and held it above the water just as Pops raised the net and drew it into the boat.

The colors in her painting would be vibrant. She could hardly wait to have the film developed. While Abbie had the camera out, she snapped a dozen or so photos of the exquisite sunrise and the lake, the tall firs and cedar.

As she turned back toward the dock and the house, she noticed Travis sitting on his deck, legs stretched out, drinking from a large mug. She switched up the settings, zoomed in for a close-up, and snapped another couple of photos.

Abbie already loved it here. Her parents were right. This was the perfect place for an artists' retreat. She imagined guests imitating Travis, serenity evident in their faces. She scanned the shoreline, snapping photos of fallen logs, interesting inlets, and inviting fishing spots carved into the landscape at intervals.

Abbie only hoped that their visit to the attorney that afternoon would allow her to move on with her plans and not lead to her arrest for abducting her own child.

Don't go there, Abbie. God wouldn't be showing you something so perfect and beautiful of he meant to snatch it away. Would He?

An hour later, the threesome, with their six sizeable trout, headed back to shore. Jake hadn't rowed far when Abbie spotted something red floating in the water near a fallen tree.

She pointed it out. "It looks like a piece of cloth or plastic."

Pops mumbled something about littering.

Jake nodded and rowed in that direction. "We should pick it up. Travis tries to keep the place pristine, but not everyone follows the rules."

They pulled up alongside the snag and Pops fished what looked like a piece of loosely woven fabric out of the water. He wrung it out and shook it open. "Looks like a woman's scarf."

"It is." Jake paled as he examined it and then peered into the water below.

"What's wrong?" Abbie eyed the beautiful fabric, woven with various shades of red and gold threads with tassels on each end. A woman's shawl. It looked handmade.

Jake's eyes, filled now with dread, locked with hers. He took the scarf from Pops and placed it on the seat beside him. "It's Barbara's."

"Are you sure?" She, too, studied the water, fearing the scarf's owner might be there as well. It was shallow and clear. The fallen tree rested on the bottom. several fish zipped in and out between the branches.

Jake lifted the oars and began rowing again. "Not definitely, but she had one like it. I'll check with Travis and call Jeff."

"I think he's right, Abbie," Pops said. "I recall seeing her wearing a red scarf like this last week when she met us out here."

"Maybe she lost it—did she ever come out here on the lake with Travis?" Abbie wasn't sure why she'd asked. The woman's scarf being in the lake didn't mean anything, did it?

Jake shook his head. "Maybe, but I have a feeling there's more to it than that." He gripped the oars and began rowing back across the lake as if he were in a race.

Abbie shivered and tucked her hands into her sweatshirt sleeves and stared at the scarf for a long moment as if she expected it to reveal its owner's story.

It didn't, of course. *It's just a scarf,* she told herself, but she couldn't shake the sense of urgency she seemed to share with Jake.

Chapter Twelve

Face deeply etched with concern, Jake rowed back to the dock. He pulled alongside so Pops could get out and tie the boat up, then, after helping Abbie onto the dock, grabbed the scarf off the seat.

"Like I said, I don't know if it means anything, but I need to call Jeff. You guys can follow me up to the house. I'm sure Travis will have coffee on."

With that, he jogged on ahead of them, the red and gold fabric furling like a flag in the light breeze. "Why don't we pack up our stuff before we go to the house?" Pops suggested.

He hadn't said much since they'd made their discovery. Abbie suspected that he, too, feared the worst—that if Barbara Nichols' scarf was here in the lake, her body might be there as well.

One did not necessarily follow the other, Abbie reasoned. After all, Barbara and Travis were dating. He could have taken her out on the lake for a romantic sunset picnic, where she'd accidentally dropped it. Besides that, her car had been found over forty miles away at the bottom of a ravine. Even so, Abbie's stomach churned with worry as they loaded the car and settled the fish into a cooler then hurried up to the house.

The door was ajar, and Abbie stepped inside. The mobile home was larger and homier than she'd expected. Double glass doors and a large window framed a perfect view of the lake. A deck beyond the patio door sported several Adirondack chairs. Several expensive-looking woodcarvings were artistically displayed around the living room. Travis obviously had money and good taste. He sat on a leather couch; head buried in his hands. The scarf was draped across his lap.

Without speaking, Jake came forward to usher them in and close the door.

Travis looked up when she and Pops entered. For a moment his eyes flashed with anger. Or had they? Perhaps she had misread him because in the next moment, he seemed to look straight through her. "Jake tells me you found her scarf."

"Is it Barbara's." The words caught in her throat.

He nodded. "I was with her when she found it at the art gallery in Depoe Bay. She…it made her happy and I bought it for her. I— I can't imagine how it got out here." He gently ran his hand over the fibers and fingered the satiny label bearing the artist's logo.

Are you sure? The question remained unspoken. Of course, he was sure. A hard knot formed in her chest.

Perhaps it was Jake's expression that zapped her of the hope that the woman would be alive. Then, too, came Travis's revelation that Barbara, to his knowledge, had never been to the lake other than to show the property to a prospective buyer.

Of course, sometimes you just knew that something was terribly wrong.

Abbie wished she could walk away from the aura of despair emanating through this place. Though she hardly knew these men, their pain became hers. "I'm sorry." The words seemed empty and hung in the silence like worthless particles of dust.

Travis stood then and walked the few feet into the kitchen area. From the freezer compartment of the refrigerator, he withdrew something wrapped in aluminum foil and set it on the counter. "Zucchini bread, in case you want something to eat.

Coffee's on. I made a fresh pot." He reached into the cupboard to the right of the sink and pulled down a couple of hand-thrown pottery mugs.

She could see that Travis appreciated art. Perhaps that, in part, explained why she felt drawn to share his grief. Sadly, the thought that she was drawn to him at all disturbed her. This man, she realized, could be lying. He could have killed Barbara.

If she's dead. Please, Lord, let her be alive. Even as the prayer flitted through her mind, intuition told her it was too late for prayers.

******

Half an hour later, Abbie poured herself another cup of coffee. She paced across the olive-green shag carpet, staring out the plate-glass window at the two boats and the four men looking intently into the water. Travis and Jake worked alongside the sheriff and two deputies as they scanned the lake, beginning at the dock and spreading out toward the old tree that had caught and held Barbara's scarf. Pop stood on the dock holding the bag of trout he'd just cleaned. Since they had no idea how long they'd be at the lake, he decided to wrap them up and put them in Travis' fridge.

While she watched them, another reality forced its way into her mind. She had been with Jake and had spotted the scarf. What if the sheriff wanted to question her? What if he recognized her name or went to check her out? He'd find out soon enough that she was a fugitive.

She should leave. Now. Hauling in a long breath, she willed her heart to stop slamming against the wall of her chest. He wouldn't need to question her, would he? Her name might go into his report, but he wouldn't consider her a suspect. He wouldn't need to look up her name in his files. She folded her arms across her chest.

Maybe Jake wouldn't mention her name. He knew her situation. Knew she needed to avoid the police.

Coming home had been a terrible mistake.

No, it hasn't. This is what you needed to do, Abbie reassured herself. *Regardless of what happens, you couldn't keep running.*

Jake had assured her that everything would work out. Somehow, she had to keep believing that. Soon, once he'd gathered the information needed to assess her case and advise her, she'd be hearing from the attorney.

God, please let the news be good.

They had been scheduled to meet with the lawyer, but that wasn't going to happen today.

Chapter Thirteen

Having come inside a few minutes before, Pops sat at the oval table covered with an ivory linen cloth. "Why don't you sit for a spell? All that pacing is gonna wear out the rug." He reached for another piece of zucchini bread.

Abbie didn't feel like sitting. Instead, she pulled her gaze away from the lake and began to examine several pieces of exquisitely carved animal figures. Elk, deer, a ram, a wolf, each one carved into a true-to-life scene. had Travis sculpted these? If so, would he be interested in selling them? Perhaps he already did. She turned toward her father, her fingertips following the curvature of a wolf's back.

"Did you notice these carvings?"

He nodded. "I certainly did. Travis is quite the artist."

"We'll have to talk to him about showing his work at the retreat center. That is if this idea of ours pans out."

"It will."

"Not if I end up in jail."

He gave her a sharp look. "You won't, Abbie. I'm not going to let that happen." Abbie wished she could share his and Jake's confidence. She wished she could stop thinking the worst. "I hope you're right. But the sheriff is out there right now. We're here."

She frowned. "By the way, why are we still here? Why don't we go home? We're not helping and there's no reason other than curiosity…"

"We can't. The sheriff asked us to stay in case they found something. And they're going to need to eat soon. I thought we could help that way."

Abbie closed her eyes and willed herself to relax. They were here for the duration. *Lord, please let this be a false alarm. Don't let them find Barbara's body. Please, please, don't let them find out about me.*

Feeling somewhat selfish for thinking of her own needs, she added, *Please, let Barbara be alive and well and not at the bottom of that lake.*

Abbie forced herself to accept the situation in which she now found herself. She sank onto the chair opposite him and after serving herself a slice of the zucchini bread, reached for the butter. "Looks good."

"It is." Pops winked. "'Course, not as good as what your mama makes."

The bread was moist and nutty and likely absorbed a good deal of the acid rolling around in her stomach. She'd lost track of the number of cups of coffee she'd had. "I hate sitting here, doing nothing."

"I know." he leaned forward and patted her hand. "But I figure they can manage the job better without an old man and a woman being underfoot." Abbie bristled a bit at being classified as practically useless. Neither she nor her mother fit the traditional, tidy homebody type of women. Her mother had been raised that way, but her beautiful alto voice had pulled her out of the home and onto the road as a blues and folk singer.

Abbie had never seen herself as a leave-it-to-Beaver mom or a Donna Reed type. She could have been out there helping the men look—but then again, maybe it was better that she not be.

The farther away she stayed from the authorities, the less likely they were to realize that she was a criminal.

One thing she could do was make another pot of coffee and cover the rest of the zucchini bread to keep it from drying out. She glanced at the carved wood clock on the wall above the fireplace.

"You're right about one thing, Pops. The men will need lunch before long. Maybe I'll root around and see if Travis has something edible."

Pops nodded. "Good idea. You might want to fry up that fish." His gaze shifted back to the lake, worry lines making him look older than his sixty-two years.

After taking their dishes to the sink and rinsing them, Abbie focused on cleaning the nearly empty percolator and refilling it with water. She rinsed out the basket and set it onto the stem and into the pot. Opening the can of Folger's, she filled the basket, capped it with the lid, and turned on the burner.

While she waited, Abbie looked through Travis's cupboards and fridge. He had plenty of staples, and Abbie set about boiling eggs then scrubbing, peeling, and cutting up potatoes for a potato salad. She also took the trout out of the of the refrigerator and made a flour coating. While she worked, she felt a bit guilty for making herself at home in this Tavis's kitchen. She hoped he wouldn't mind too much.

A little later, while looking for a fork to test the doneness of the potatoes, she pulled open a drawer. Right on top she spotted a yellowed newspaper clipping. It contained information about the bank robbery Jake had told her about. Why would Travis have the article, especially since he'd told them that Barbara had never been in his home.

Maybe Barbara had given him the article to solicit his help. Maybe she'd ask him about it or mention it to Jake. She wondered how long Travis had known about the robbery. Jeff thought that perhaps the bank robbery was somehow connected to Barbara's disappearance. Had Barbara told Travis about it?

Pops rose from his chair and went to stand in front of the window. "Looks like they've found something." He dragged his fingers through his thick graying hair.

She stuffed the article back into the drawer and hurried toward the window.

"You don't want to see…." Her father turned toward her, but it was too late.

Abbie watched in horror as Jeff and another man pulled a body out of the water and into their boat. Jake waited until the men were seated, then began rowing toward the dock. Jeff signaled the other boat and they too headed for shore. They had found her only about fifty feet from the dock, near a patch of water lilies.

You don't know that it's her, Abbie reminded herself. She shuddered and tried to rub away the goose bumps on her arms.

Pops placed a comforting arm around her shoulders, and she leaned against him. "This won't look good for Travis," he murmured.

Abbie straightened. "Because they found the body here?" She shook her head. "It might not be her." Even as she said the words aloud, she knew better.

"Safe bet it is. Whoever they hauled into that boat is wearing a dress."

Chapter Fourteen

Abbie turned away from the window and went back to the stove, where she drained the water off the potatoes and eggs. She rinsed both in cold water and set them aside.

Moments later, the front door banged open and Travis barged in. Jake came in right behind him. "Travis, for crying out loud, settle down before you get yourself arrested."

"They think I did it." Travis sank onto the couch and covered his face with his hands. "They think I killed her."

"The sheriff is speculating—he has to ask questions."

"You heard what he said. I'm a suspect."

"So am I." Jake lumped his hands into fists and rested them on his hips.

Abbie filled two mugs of the freshly brewed coffee and brought them to the men. "Sounds like you could both use some."

The men stared at her as if she'd grown horns. They'd obviously forgotten that she and Pops were there.

"Thank you." Jake lifted his cup in a salute of sorts. Travis thanked her as well.

"It was Barbara then?" Abbie swallowed back a lump in her throat. The enormity of the situation pressed itself into her chest, making it hard to breathe.

Jake nodded. "No doubt."

"She drowned?"

"No. She was murdered." Travis barked out the words as though each took every ounce of strength. He leaned back into the couch.

"How?"

"She was shot, Abbie." Jake took a seat beside his friend. "There's no way to tell where it happened. The coroner might be able to give us a time of death once he's examined her body and runs tests, but that's going to take time."

Abbie's only connection with solving crimes came from mysteries she'd read as a teenager. But her mind reeled with possibilities and questions.

"What about her car?" Abbie asked. "Didn't you tell me it had gone over a cliff near Oceanside?"

Jake nodded. "There has to be a connection between what happened to her car and her disappearance. It looks as though whoever did it wanted to throw the cops off track."

"I'll tell you what happened." Travis warmed his hands around the cup then took a tentative sip. "Whoever did this dumped her body in the lake to throw suspicion on me."

Abbie thought about the article in the drawer. "Jake, earlier you'd mentioned that the bank robbery might be connected to her disappearance."

"What bank robbery?" Travis leaned forward. He genuinely seemed not to know. But that didn't make sense. Why would he have the article in his kitchen drawer and not know about it?

Jake told him about Barbara and her friend and that the friend had been abducted by the bank robber and never found.

While he spoke, Abbie watched the ambulance driver load Barbara's body into the back and close the door. she hadn't met Barbara, but they were connected by this property and Jake.

"I had no idea," Travis said, once Jake finished the story. "I suppose it explains her preoccupation." He offered his friend a wry smile and shook his head. "Here I thought I wasn't interesting enough for her."

Chapter Fifteen

More than anything Abbie wanted to get away from Bear Lake and Cold Creek. She wanted to go back to Grand Forks to familiar ground. Back where she and Emma had at least known a modicum of safety.

The sheriff entered the house and Travis introduced them. Sheriff Moore already knew her father and seemed to like him. He verified that Abbie had seen the scarf and pointed it out to Pops, who had fished it out of the water. Then he seemed to be finished with her.

Abbie didn't know whether to be upset or relieved. A bit of both, she supposed. Jeff wrote some notes in a small black notebook and then tucked it away in his shirt pocket.

Travis thanked her for making lunch and finished the job, taking out paper plates, napkins, and silverware. Abbie busied herself with pouring coffee for Jeff and Sheriff Moore.

"We should go, Pops," Abbie said as she set the coffeepot back on the stove.

He nodded. "Good idea. I imagine your mother is fit to be tied."

"I should have called her." Abbie opened the door and came face to face with a man she'd known since childhood but barely recognized.

"Hey, Abs." He swept her into his arms and whirled her around. "Mom said I might see you two out here."

Her little brother had turned into a hunk of a man, over six feet and sturdy as an oak. She hugged him back, reluctant to let him go.

"I had no idea you were coming out this way or I'd have stayed home."

"Did Mom tell you I was moving back home?" Tim asked.

Abbie nodded, still in shock over how much her brother had changed.

He was all dressed up now, wearing slacks, a white shirt, and a sports jacket. "She said you were looking for a job out here."

"Was looking. Got hired by the Oregon State Police this morning, and I'll be working with Detective Meyers." He stepped aside and motioned to the man beside him. The detective was about a head shorter than Tim and much older—maybe in his fifties. He wore a suit as well.

"Are you kidding me?" This from Jeff, who reached out to shake Tim's hand. "Man, I thought we got rid of this troublemaker for good." Jeff winked at Abbie. "But they always come back." In explanation, he added, "Your brother used to spend hours at the police station before he decided to become a cop."

Tim laughed. "Good to see you too." Glancing at his sister he said, "That's not quite accurate. I got arrested once for underage drinking when the cops raided a party I happened to be at; it scared the you-know-what out of me."

Pops joined the cluster and clapped Tim on the back. "Good to see you, son." Once the introductions had been made, the momentary joy of seeing her little brother slid into the background as Jeff and Sheriff Moore filled Meyers in on the morning's activities.

"I appreciate the heads-up on the Nichols woman, Jeff." Meyers looked up from his notebook. "I'd have been here earlier, but I was assigned to train our new rookie here and had some things to take care of in Portland before we could be on the road."

* * * * *

While the men talked about the murder case and speculated as to motive, means, and opportunity, Abbie slipped out through the patio doors onto the deck. She rested her arms on the railing and breathed in the fresh clean air, watched an egret stand on one leg in the marshes.

What a painting this would make. And how pristine. No one would ever guess that a murder victim had been stowed away in the lake's depths.

Abbie tried to pull her mind away from the horror of what they had witnessed. Instead, she focused on the beauty and tranquility of the lake and the trees. She'd only been out there a few minutes when she heard someone come up beside her.

Funny, but she knew without turning who it was. Had they formed that close a bond in so short a time?

Jake stepped up beside her. "Are you okay?"

She nodded. "Just processing."

"I'm sorry our outing took such an ugly turn." Jake rested his arms on the railing as well.

"Me too." Abbie turned toward him. "I'm sorry she's dead, Jake, but I'm glad you guys found her."

He pressed his lips together and stared out at the lake. "I still can't wrap my mind around this. As far as I know she didn't have any enemies."

"Unless her death is tied into that bank robbery. Maybe she found the man she'd been looking for. The one who kidnapped her friend."

He gripped the porch railing. "That's what detective Meyers is thinking. Unfortunately, the sheriff is ready to arrest Travis

101

because he was supposed to have had a date with her just before she disappeared. Plus, her body was found here in the lake."

Abbie thought about the grief she'd seen in Travis's face. He hadn't known about the robbery either, she was certain of that. Yet, the article had been in his drawer.

"The only reason the sheriff hasn't arrested Travis already is that there isn't any concrete evidence."

She considered telling Jake about the article but didn't. Abbie couldn't say why she decided to remain mute about the article except that she hoped to have as little to do with the police as possible.

Besides, if Travis was a suspect, wouldn't the police search his house, looking for clues? The less attention she drew to herself, the better.

"Travis is quite the artist," she said, hoping to change the subject.

"He is. I bought one of his carvings some time back. An eagle scooping up a salmon in its beak. The detail is phenomenal."

"Do you think he'd consider being part of the artist community?"

Jake straightened. "You mean you'd still consider buying the place? I thought you'd probably take the next train back to Grand Forks."

"I meant what I said about not running anymore. I don't know about buying the town, but I'll consider it." She closed her eyes for a moment. "I need to settle my accounts and be here for Skye."

"I'm glad."

She smiled. "Though with Tim coming back, the house is going to be a bit crowded."

"You could always stay at my place." He winced at his audacity. "But I don't suppose that's an option."

She shook her head. "It's an option. Just not a good idea."

"Right."

They stood for several long moments in silence before Jake offered a suggestion. "I don't know if you'd be interested, but you could consider staying at the bed and breakfast here in Cold Creek for a few days. It would offer you a chance to get a feel for the place. If you decide to stay, you'd probably want to move into one of the houses eventually—of course you'd need to remodel. Or build a new place."

"I'll think about it."

Chapter Sixteen

The more Abbie thought about Jake's suggestion, the more sense it made. Living out here prior to making the final decision on whether or not to buy the property, would be a logical solution.

Still, there was the matter of Barbara's murder and her body turning up in the lake. Was her murder related to the bank robbery or were they dealing with something else entirely? How did it affect Cold Creek and the possibilities it offered for her and Emma?

Abbie mentally stepped away from thoughts of the murder. She needed to see the property and its possibilities as an entirely separate entity. Yes, Barbara's death was tragic, but it shouldn't factor into her plans to build an artist community here.

Regrettably, her attempt to separate the two proved impossible. Still, she managed to spend two hours of the afternoon exploring at the town and counting the costs of the purchase and the remodeling that would have to be done.

That evening after dinner, with her family, Abbie announced her plans to stay in Cold Creek for a few days.

"Good idea." Pops forked the last piece of his apple pie. "Give you a chance to get to know the place inside and out."

"I agree." This from her mother.

"Really?" Abbie had expected an objection.

"Don't misunderstand. I would love for you to stay here with us, but you do need to spend some time there. You're the artist, after all. Your father and I love the place, but you're the one who'll have to live there and run it. You'll need to decide if it's feasible or not. And after what happened at Bear Lake today, I would understand if you gave up on the whole thing."

"Can I come too, Mommy?"

"Abbie and her mother exchanged glances. It was one thing for Abbie to explore this unknown territory on her own, but quite another to bring Emma. "Not right away. I'll need to find a place to stay and have a look around. Maybe in a couple of days."

Tears filled her daughter's eyes. "But I need to be with you."

"Oh, honey." Abbie leaned over and gathered Emma into her arms. Maybe this wasn't such a good idea after all. Emma had had too many changes in the last few days. It wasn't fair to leave her. "I won't be going for a couple of days."

"Emma—did you forget about our shopping day?" Carlene rose from her chair and came to kneel between them. "We can let Mommy do her work and we'll go play. And then, when Mommy's done working, we can go see her."

"Can we play on the merry-go-round?"

Carlene clapped her hands. "Yes! We can ride on the carousel! And go swimming!"

Emma's sadness evaporated. "Can we go now?"

Carlene laughed. "It's too late to go tonight."

"Okay. Let's go to bed now."

Abbie explained that the next day was Sunday and that their shopping day was on Monday. She felt a stab of jealousy coming on and wished she could join them. The adventure sounded like fun. The Oceanside amusement Park offered rides, roller skating, swimming, and all sorts of things that would take her mind away from Barbara and the murder. Maybe she should forget about Cold Creek and all that it entailed. After all, no one would blame her for backing away from the deal.

* * * * *

Abbie spent Sunday with her family and Jake in church and then picnicking at the beach. They had all needed the respite, and after hiking on one of the coastal trails, she loved the area more than ever. Even with everything going on, she managed to enjoy herself. Of course, Jake had a lot to do with that.

By Monday morning, Abbie had reverted to her original plan to drive out to Cold Creek and see about staying there. She pulled her thick chenille robe over her flannel pajamas and padded downstairs.

She found Pops in the kitchen running water into the coffeepot. He assembled it, spooned coffee into the basket, and set it on the stove. When the coffee bubbled up rich and brown in the glass lid, Pops poured while Abbie set cinnamon toast on the table along with a couple of plates. They began talking about Cold Creek, and Abbie jotted down ideas for the artist community.

Several minutes later, they heard a sharp knock at the door. Father and daughter simultaneously pushed back their chairs. "I'll get it," Abbie offered.

"Expecting anyone?" Pops asked.

Abbie shook her head and opened the door then stepped back in surprise.

"Hey." Jake stood on the porch, grinning and looking much better than anyone had a right to at six-thirty in the morning. "Are you ready?"

"For what?"

"For our walk on the beach."

"What are you talking about?" Abbie struggled to recall him saying anything about a beach walk but couldn't. "You never…"

He chuckled. "I sent you a telepathic message. You didn't get it?"

Abbie grinned and motioned him in. "Sorry, Jake. My brain doesn't pick up telepathic messages until after I've had my coffee."

By the time Jake had come in and settled into a chair, Pops had poured him a cup and set it on the table.

"Thanks." looking over at Abbie, he asked, "Well, what do you think? Are you up to a walk on the beach?"

"I'd like that." Abbie took a final sip of her lukewarm coffee. "While you finish, I'll go get ready."

Pops laughed at something Jake said as she headed for the stairs. Abbie supposed she should have said no to the walk. She had a to-do list a mile long. But a walk on the beach sounded perfect, and a walk with Jake filled her with an anticipation she couldn't explain.

* * * * *

By one that afternoon, Abbie was packed and ready for a stay at the B&B. At Jake and Pops' insistence, she'd called for reservations. Dawn, the woman who ran it, sounded delighted to have her there and was anxious to meet her. She'd met Abbie's parents already and wanted to hear more about their plans for Cold Creek.

Earlier, around ten, she'd shared a tearless good-bye with her mother, Emma, and Skye, who had gone seeking adventure in Oceanside.

She planned to have her father drive her to Cold Creek, but he stopped her on the way out to the car.

"Decided it would be best if you drove yourself."

"But you'll need your Jeep."

"I wasn't planning on giving you the Jeep." Gesturing with his arm, he grinned. "Come on over to the garage. Got a surprise for you." He swung open the double garage doors, revealing a vehicle covered with canvas. Pops pulled off the cover and

Abbie's jaw dropped. It was her old '52 Mercury—the one Pops had bought for her when she went off to college. When she married Nate, she'd insisted Pops take it back and maybe give it to Tim or sell it.

"Pops…" Tears clouded her vision. "I don't understand. Why would you keep this old thing?"

He shrugged. "Figured you'd come back one day."

Abbie hugged him. "I can't believe this."

He dug in his pocket, pulled out a set of keys, and tucked them into her hand. "She still runs good. I checked her out, took her out for a spin, and gassed her up before you came."

Abbie shook her head. "I thought Tim would have it, or Skye."

Pops sighed. "Tim didn't want it. Skye didn't meet the criteria. Grades weren't up and…well, you know the drill. 'Course, Tim's doing good, but you're here now and the car is yours if you want it."

"I do." Abbie nodded. "I'm sorry I wasn't here for them, Pops, especially for Skye."

"Don't even think about blaming yourself. Your mother and I have done more than enough of taking on the blame. Does no good at all." He picked up Abbie's suitcase and set it behind the car. "We weren't the best parents, but not the worst either." Taking the keys from her, he opened the trunk.

"You were wonderful parents." She placed a hand on his shoulder. "I can't imagine having a better childhood."

He smiled. "You were an easy kid to raise. And, maybe retiring from the music scene changed us. We went through a rough transition for a while there. Seemed like some of the fun went out of our lives—mine at least. Your mother loved being a homebody. I was a bit lost."

"Oh, Pops." Abbie understood being lost. Giving up her art had nearly destroyed her.

"We thought settling down and giving you kids more stability would be a good thing. We finally realized we couldn't give up the music altogether, but by then, Skye had gone."

"Like you said, kids made their own choices. Besides, Tim is okay. And Skye is here and safe."

"For now." He pressed his lips together. "We'll see."

He was right of course. They had no guarantee that Skye would stay clean. Abbie promised herself that she would do her best to keep her sister out of trouble.

He handed back the keys. "Call me when you get there so I know not to worry."

She chuckled and kissed his cheek. "I will. And thank you." He stuffed his hands in his pockets and watched as she maneuvered the once familiar vehicle down the driveway and onto the road.

* * * * *

A short while later, Abbie turned off the main highway onto a narrow two-lane road that led to the old logging town. Leaves made brilliant green by patches of sun, quivered in the wind. She swallowed back her fears as images of Saturday morning forced themselves into her mind.

Abbie pushed the disturbing thoughts aside and instead tried to concentrate on how the area might look to a tourist coming to the artist colony and the monthly art fair they would have. Not an easy task when Barbara had been killed and her body found not more than a mile away.

Don't think about it. Yes, Barbara's death is disturbing—tragic, but there's nothing you can do about that.

Besides, her death had nothing to do with this town. Or did it? The town was a piece of real estate, and Barbara had been a realtor. Jake had mentioned that she'd even had a client who wanted it.

Earlier, on their walk, Jake had told her about a client of Barbara's who was irate about the property being sold out from under him. He insisted that he'd made an offer on it before Pops put the earnest money down. Jake had paperwork to disprove him. What if this client had taken his revenge on Barbara?

109

Abbie shook her head to dispel the idea and focused on the carved wooden sign she and Pops had seen the day before. She wondered if Travis had carved it and made a mental note to ask him.

The sign, worn by wind, rain, and heat, needed a good cleaning. The vine maple and wild rhododendrons would have to be trimmed. Potholes fixed.

In another few minutes, she reached what looked like the main street and felt the same letdown she'd experienced before. The town, if you could call it that, looked more rustic and beaten down than she remembered. Main street was about a block long and had a library, a post office and small store, and a gas station. Across the street stood what used to be a small café and used bookstore. An Out-of-Business sign hung in the window, but books still sat on the walls of shelves, and several lay in a fan as a window display. The hours on the post-office/store told her it would only be open from noon until two, Monday through Friday. According to Jake, lack of funding had forced the community to close the school and bus their kids into Oceanside.

Off the main road stood older homes in varying stages of disrepair. Abbie forced herself to look beyond the destruction and neglect and to see it all restored, filled with artists and students, and, eventually, tourists who came for shopping, retreats, and a good time. Even with her ability to see the potential, she found it difficult.

Cold Creek Bed & Breakfast was located at the end of the street near the woods. Jake had been concerned that news of Barbara's death would bring reporters and that they might take up all the rooms. The B&B offered the only overnight option in town. Thankfully, that was not the case. Dawn had thanked her for calling but told her things were as slow as usual. The lack of cars in the small gravel parking lot attested to the fact.

Two blocks west of the B&B sat what looked to have once been a stunning Victorian. The house, with its gables and turrets and stained-glass windows, beckoned to Abbie, challenged her to come closer and explore the grandeur that had once been.

Farther up the road, Abbie spotted what could only be described as a mansion. It rested on a knoll, looking down on the town. From what Jake had told her, this incredible place had to be the Johansson estate. A black wrought-iron fence surrounded it. Abbie could hardly wait to get a closer look, but first, she wanted to settle into her room.

As Abbie stepped out of the car, a woman with carrot-red hair and glasses hurried down the stairs. A wide smile rounded her face and brightened her brown eyes. She wore jeans and a red-and-white flannel plaid shirt and looked as though she'd been cleaning. "You must be Abbie."

"I am. You're Dawn?"

"What gave me away?" She chuckled. "Here, let me get that for you." Dawn hefted the heavy suitcase out of the trunk as if it were a pillow. "Do you have more?"

Abbie nodded "Just one. It's in the backseat."

Dawn insisted on carrying both bags. Once inside, she deposited them in a room on the first floor at the end of a hallway. "What a beautiful room." Abbie let her gaze linger over the Victorian furnishings and the decorative floral trim on the walls.

Dawn pushed aside the drapes, revealing a large picture window and a sliding patio door that led to an aggregate deck bordered with colorful geraniums. A white café table with two matching chairs sat in the center, and off to one side was a chaise lounge. The patio offered a stunning view forest and a lake. "This is really nice."

"It's one of my favorite rooms." Dawn opened the patio door, letting in the scent of fresh mountain air mingled with that of a forest—moldy and woodsy.

"I wasn't expecting a view." Abbie peered outside. "Everything is so lush and green."

Dawn laughed. "Thanks to the rain. We've had one storm after another for the past three weeks. Flooding in a lot of places. That *lake* you're looking at is a wetlands area. It fills with water every winter."

"Could have fooled me." Abbie stepped back and set her purse on the bed."

Hey, listen, I'll leave you to unpack. When you're done, come on into the kitchen and have a cup of coffee or tea. I made some cookies this morning."

"Yum. Tea and cookies sound perfect."

Abbie stepped out onto the patio and inhaled several deep breaths of the fresh air. Sunlight glistened on the wet grass and leaves. The air was nippy, but wonderful. After putting her clothes away and placing her bags out of sight in the small closet, Abbie went in search of a phone so she could call her father, as promised, to let him know she'd arrived safely.

"You were right, Pops." Abbie stood in the entryway. "The town has a lot of possibilities if you look beyond the damage."

"Your mother and I knew you'd feel that way. Should I call Jake and have him bring papers for you to sign?"

Abbie laughed. "Not just yet. I'd like to look around a little more. Maybe get a feel for how much it's going to cost to get it up and running."

"Don't worry too much about that. Jake and I figured we could renovate a little at a time. Besides, we have the money."

"I know." Abbie had money as well—from her trust fund, and the settlement from the insurance company after Nate's accident. She hadn't touched a dime of it during the time she'd been in North Dakota. She'd been afraid that any activity in the account would alert the authorities. The thought brought her up short.

She still needed to talk with the attorney. With all the business at the lake, Jake had suggested they reschedule the appointment. She'd have to talk to him about that.

Minutes later, Abbie was sitting on a stool at the counter admiring the remodeled kitchen and biting into a chewy chocolate chip cookie. The distinct aroma of Earl Grey tea drifted from the floral English teacup. Abbie sighed. "I've died and gone to heaven."

"I got the recipe from my friend Jeanette. You'll meet her soon." Dawn picked up a cookie and examined it a moment before taking a bite.

They talked about the delicious scents coming out of Dawn's kitchen and about how she and her husband had taken over the place four years ago, staying rent-free and managing it for Isabelle Johansson. "The place was a mess," Dawn told her, "but Keith is a builder, so we lucked out. We did most of the work ourselves." Abbie noticed the strands of ivy decorating the arched entry to the dining area.

"Did you paint that ivy trim?"

"I did." She flashed Abbie a knowing smile. "With the help of some stencils."

"Well, stencil or not—it's lovely."

"Thank you."

"I was just telling my dad I wished I'd brought my paints out here."

"What do you do? Watercolors, oils, acrylics?"

"All of the above. I majored in art, so I've worked in all mediums."

"Which is probably why your parents want you to run the artist colony."

"You know about that?" Abbie took a sip of tea.

"Everybody in town knows about it going on about meeting the famous Grants."

Abbie bit her lip, a mixture of pride and embarrassment warming her cheeks. Being on the farm for so long, she'd forgotten what it felt like to be the daughter of famous parents.

Dawn didn't seem to notice. Her gaze was focused on the clock. She took another tray of cookies out of the oven and after setting them aside to cool, washed her hands. "Hey, listen. I'd love to stay and chat, but I need to pick up Cassie—my daughter. She's part home schooled and part private."

Abbie brightened. "How old is she?"

"Eight." Dawn beamed. "She's the light of our lives. Make yourself at home. I should be back in about an hour."

"No problem," Abbie said as Dawn grabbed keys off a hook in what looked like a mudroom off the kitchen and opened the back door.

Abbie took advantage of the quiet and the sunshine and daylight to walk around town with a map Jake had sketched for her so that she could determine which of the buildings were included in the Johansson property.

She was excited to see that most of the buildings would be theirs as well as the dilapidated Victorian that had captured her attention earlier. Abbie walked to downtown Cold Creek.

She had seen no one except Dawn since she'd arrived. The town looked abandoned except for a bike propped against the stone wall of the library near the door.

The gas station and store had a closed sign in the window. The three-story building with a saloon sign hanging vertically on one corner was boarded up and looked as though it had been that way for a hundred years. Her artistic self could see the brick monstrosity restored into a restaurant and gift shop and hotel for visitors or apartment units for artists.

The artists would include painters, sculptors, ceramicists, writers, quilters, and gourmet chefs. She'd bring in big names to teach classes at the retreat center. There would be a gift shop with numerous themes and art galleries where the artists could display and sell their wares, a bookstore featuring local authors, and a café with a bakery and a museum. Of course, they'd need a grocery store. Ideas flowed as the dream carried Abbie on its current.

All too quickly, her business side reminded her of the logistics of such a venture. "Do you have any idea how much money it would take to accomplish what you want to do?" She spoke aloud, frustrated with the direction her thoughts had taken.

She'd brought up the expense and the feasibility when she and her parents had talked the day she'd arrived. "We have the money, Abbie," her father had reminded her. "We can do this."

They could, but was it feasible? Abbie lowered herself to a worn wooden bench in front of the old saloon. "Oh Pops, I wish I had as much faith in myself as you do." She pulled away from the negative thoughts.

You can do this, Abbie Campbell.

A woman and a young girl stepping out of the library across the street caught her attention. "I'll see you tomorrow, Krystin," the woman said. "Remember to bring your math book."

"I will." Krystin, whom Abbie judged to be around twelve, glanced in Abbie's direction, hesitated for several seconds, then jumped on her bike and pedaled away. She turned off the main road near the Welcome to Cold Creek sign and disappeared into the woods.

"Hi." The woman waved at Abbie. She looked to be in her twenties, attractive with mahogany brown hair held back with a barrette. "You look kind of lonely sitting out here all by yourself. I don't mean to interrupt, but..."

"You're not interrupting anything." In fact, Abbie was glad for the distraction. She rose and walked across the narrow street, smiled, and extended her hand. "Abbie Campbell."

"Sam...Samantha Willis. I run the library here." She nodded toward the girl who'd bicycled out of sight. "And, I help the homeschooled kids when their parents need me to."

"I heard about the school closing. Do you have a lot of students?"

"It varies. There are ten families who still refuse to bus their kids into Oceanside. All of them use the library on a regular basis."

"I'm glad to see the library has remained open."

"That's only because my grandmother and I own and maintain it." She smiled. "I'm the custodian, the librarian, the teacher. You name it, I do it."

Abbie sensed a kinship of sorts with Samantha. "Have you lived in Cold Creek long?"

"I sort of grew up here. My family build the town. Long story." She opened the heavy wooden door ushered Abbie inside.

The place reminded Abbie of a used bookstore she'd frequented in Grand Forks. There were two floors and a grand staircase that looked like oak. The hardwood floors showed their age but had been well maintained.

Near the entrance stood an ornately carved desk. A large study table occupied a back corner, the stack of papers on top testifying to recent use. Unlike more modern libraries, this one boasted all wooden shelves. Abbie took in the familiar scent of books and wood as Sam continued. "My mom and dad moved to California before I was born. But I spent a lot of summers here and moved back two years ago…abusive marriage and all that. Now I live with my grandmother, Isabelle Johansson."

Sam's revelation took Abbie by surprise. "Jake told me about your grandmother."

"At one time my grandmother owned the entire town and a thousand acres around it." Abbie lowered herself into one of the stuffed chairs in the center of the enormous room as Samantha took the other one and continued her narrative.

"As you may have noticed, things are kind of dead around here. Money is in short supply, and Grandma has had to sell off some small parcels of the land. Now the whole thing is on the market. I'm not sure selling such a large chunk is necessary, but Uncle Steven, Grandma's son, is overseeing all her finances. Grandma has agreed to everything. I think she'll be fine as long as he doesn't try to sell her house. It's the big monstrosity on the hill."

Abbie nodded. "Looks like a grand place."

"It is, but it takes a lot of money to maintain. Steven is trying to talk her into moving to a retirement home in Oceanside." Sam shook her head. "Gran is holding firm. She loves that old house and the gardens. I think taking care of it keeps her young."

"I'd like to meet her."

"She'd like to meet you too. She didn't want to sell—not at first. She was afraid some developer would scoop it up and raze the town. But when your parents came around to look at it and told her about the plans for the artist colony, she was delighted."

Sam stood. "Say, I'm getting ready to close up for the day. Would you like to head up to the house with me?"

"Sure. I'd love that." Abbie could think of nothing she'd rather do. Sam and Isabelle were the perfect pair to fill her in on Cold Creek and Bear Lake.

Abbie waited for Samantha to lock up and the two of them went back the way Abbie had come, past the B&B, past the Victorian that Abbie had already claimed for herself and Emma—and hopefully Skye.

"What can you tell me about this place?" Abbie stopped in front of the old Victorian.

"It's been vacant for as long as I can remember. It used to belong to a doctor. It has a reputation for being haunted."

"Really. Good thing I don't believe in ghosts."

Sam raised an eyebrow. "I'm not sure I do either, but how else do you explain the fact that everyone thinks it's spooky."

"Hmm. Old places like this often get that reputation." As Abbie glanced up at the house, a curtain in the third-story window moved. At least she thought it did. The hairs on the back of her neck stood on end. She chastised herself for being so vulnerable to suggestion.

"Are you okay?" Sam followed her gaze.

"Fine." Imagination, she told herself again. Even so, she stepped up her pace.

Chapter Seventeen

By the time they had trudged up the hill and climbed the steps leading to the house, Abbie had to struggle to catch her breath. She'd worked hard on the farm but wasn't used to climbing anything except stairs to the bedroom and basement three or four times a day. In Grand Forks, however, everything had been level.

Samantha led her through an ornate iron gate and around the side of the house. "We never use the front entrance," she explained. "Gran says there's no point tracking dirt into a living room we hardly ever use."

They found Isabelle in the garden pulling out withered tomato vines. The knees of her jeans were soaked and caked with mud. A streak of dirt ran the length of one weathered cheek. Isabelle was a tall, thin woman with a ready smile. She wore her salt-and-pepper hair in a serviceable cut. Sam introduced Abbie and after chatting about the gardens for a few minutes, the three women went into the house. Isabelle excused herself. "Samantha, would you put water on for tea while I shower and change?"

"Be happy to." Sam filled a kettle. Turning to Abbie she asked, "Would you rather have coffee? I can make you a pot."

"Tea's fine. In fact, I prefer it to coffee in the afternoon."

"Gran and I have a cup whenever I get home from work." She set out porcelain cups and saucers. A lazy-Susan in the center of the table held sugar and small packets of creamers. The large kitchen had apparently been upgraded recently to the more modern linoleum floors, Formica countertops, and oak cupboards.

"Who did the kitchen?" Abbie asked. The job looked professional, and if everything went as planned, she'd need a contractor soon.

"Keith Morgan and Travis Jennings."

"Keith—as in Dawn's husband?"

"The same." Sam opened a cookie jar and took down a plate. "He did such an excellent job on the B&B that Gran hired him to do her kitchen. He and Travis do a lot of jobs in Oceanside for Brent O'Brien."

While Sam busied herself in the kitchen, Abbie took a seat at the table in the bay window and admired the view. From this hilltop home, she could see most of Cold Creek. Between the B&B and the possibly haunted Victorian was a path that led into the woods, probably to Bear Lake. On the other side of the lake was Travis's mobile home. "Nice view," Abbie said. "I love that you can see so much of the lake from here. I was over there on Saturday."

"Travis told me you were the one who found Barbara's scarf." Sam said. "So sad. I'm sorry you had to go through all that."

Abbie nodded. "So am I. But at least we know what happened to her."

Sam sat down and, placing her elbows on the table, cupped her chin in her hands. "The lake is much bigger than it looks. We get a few fishermen out here, but it's still relatively unknown."

Abbie watched as someone, probably Travis, jumped out of a red pickup and went into the house. She couldn't see well enough to distinguish his features. "I'm assuming that's Travis."

Sam had a wistful look in her eyes. "Hmm. Wonder what he's doing home so early. He and Keith were working in Oceanside today on a hotel project."

"Are you—I mean—the way you were eyeing at him just now…"

"I'm not looking, but if I were, he'd be on my list. actually, he's… he was dating Barbara Nichols."

Isabelle entered, having changed into burgundy sweats that hung loosely on her slender frame. "Much better."

Sam placed the cookies on the table and went to rescue the whistling teakettle, which she brought to the table along with cups and a basket of assorted teas. Abbie took one of the now filled cups, and selected lavender-infused Earl Grey.

"Tell us about yourself, Abbie," Isabel said. "Jake mentioned that you were a widow and that you have a little girl."

"Yes." Abbie dunked her teabag, wondering how much detail to go into. Even now, two years later, thinking about Nate and the subsequent loss of her unborn baby often reduced her to tears. "Nathan, my husband, was killed in a farming accident two years ago." She sipped at her tea, hoping that was enough of an explanation to satisfy their curiosity.

"I'm sorry." Isabelle stirred a minuscule amount of sugar into her tea and poured in some cream. Her sky-blue gaze lingered on the tea. "I understand what you're going through. I lost my husband in a logging accident when I was about your age. All those years ago and I still miss him terribly. Leaves a hole in your heart that can never be filled. Oh, I managed to go on—I had two children to care for. Samantha's mother and my son, Steven."

Abbie nodded. The hole in her own heart could be likened to the Grand Canyon. She didn't want to talk about her losses, and Isabelle must have sensed her reticence, because she asked about the artist community and for Abbie to share her vision.

Abbie was more than happy to oblige. An hour later, having enjoyed a wonderful afternoon tea with sandwiches and desserts, Abbie thought it might be a good idea to go back to the B&B before darkness settled in. She liked these women and hoped they'd be living in Cold Creek for a long time. By the end of the visit, Abbie counted Samantha and Isabelle as friends.

After saying good-bye, Abbie made her way down the hill and through town to the B&B. Darkness descended and along with it an eerie sense that she was being watched. She looked around but saw no one. This time when she passed the Victorian, there was no movement in the upstairs window. She shuddered anyway and pushed aside the scary thoughts she considered juvenile. Once safe in the B&B, she relaxed a bit.

"Are you okay Abbie?" Dawn asked when Abbie entered the kitchen. "You look pale." Abbie released a nervous laugh. "I'm fine. Just spooked."

"I know what you mean." Dawn hesitated. "I used to feel safe here."

"What do you mean?"

"Well, I hate to think that Barbara's death is a forerunner of things to come, but… hopefully the authorities will catch her killer and Cold Creek can go back to being like it was." Dawn gestured toward the stove. "I'm making stew for dinner. You're welcome to join us."

"Thanks, but I had sandwiches and snacks with Isabelle and Sam."

"Okay," Dawn said, "if you change your mind let me know."

"Thanks, I will." Abbie headed for her room.

When she stepped in, she felt a chill and noticed that the sliding patio door stood open. It was then she saw a note lying on the dresser. It read simply, *Leave while you still can.*

Chapter Eighteen

Abbie threw the note to the floor as if doing so would negate the fear its words had burned into her. A scream caught in her throat and exploded in a muffled sob.

Who could have left the note and when? Obviously, whoever had left it had come through the sliding glass door. Had she left it unlocked earlier? Abbie didn't think so.

Hoping to recapture a semblance of calm, she took several deep breaths. Part of her wanted to run—to do exactly what the note said. Leave. Maybe she should. She'd run away before.

But not this time.

Abbie hurried out to the phone in the entry and dialed for an operator. When one came on the line, she asked for the sheriff's department. After telling him an intruder had left a threatening note, she dialed the operator again and asked for Jake's number.

Once her calls had been made, Abbie turned, to find Dawn standing behind her. "I couldn't help but hear. What's going on?"

"I'm not sure." The familiar scent of the stew emanating from the stove and Dawn's presence settled Abbie's frazzled nerves a bit. Almost brought her back to a sense of normalcy. Almost.

"Abbie." Dawn set a plate in the sink. "Are you all right?"

"Not really." She told dawn about the note.

"Where is it?"

"On the floor in my room. I thought I should leave it for the police."

"That's probably a good idea. Oh, my word. Abbie, I'm so sorry. I can't imagine how someone could have come in without my seeing them unless they came when I went to pick up Cassie."

"I left then too." Abbie shivered and rubbed her arms. "But I was sure I locked my door."

Dawn sighed. "I didn't lock up the B&B. I usually don't. No one around here worries about locking doors. It's not like we live in a big city."

"I locked the doors to my room. Who would do this?"

"I can't imagine." Dawn came around the counter and placed an arm across Abbie's shoulders to guide her to the table. "Come on, have a seat and I'll get you some tea."

Abbie complied and, several minutes later, warm mug in hand, she said, "I don't understand. It's obvious someone wants me to leave, but why?"

Dawn set her mug on the table and lowered herself into the chair across from Abbie. "I'm guessing whoever left the note doesn't want you to buy Cold Creek."

"You may be right. Jake told me that Barbara had been talking to a developer who wasn't too happy about my offer coming in ahead of his."

"I suppose he could have written the note." She frowned. "I met the guy. He's a pompous you-know-what. We might want to mention him to Ted."

"Ted?"

"Sheriff Moore."

"Oh, right." Abbie's fears escalated again, but this time it wasn't from the danger posed by the note writer. This time she worried about one of the police officers discovering her secret.

"Speak of the devil. Here he comes."

"Good evening, ladies." The sheriff tipped his hat as dawn ushered him in.

"What's this about a threatening note?" He sounded more annoyed than concerned.

"It's back here. I found it on my dresser when I got back to my room tonight." Abbie walked with him to her room as she told him about the note and where she'd found it. "I left the patio door ajar like it was when I found it in case you want to dust for fingerprints."

"Huh." He gave the note a cursory glance and ignored the patio door. "My guess is that someone is playing a prank. Not everyone in these parts is happy about Isabelle selling out."

"Aren't you going to bag the note as evidence?" Abbie had read enough mysteries to know how the police worked.

He waved her off. "No need. If this threat is real, I'm guessing the only prints we'd find would be yours."

"What's going on?" Jake came into the room with Jeff following close behind.

"Nothing much. Apparently, somebody's trying to talk Mrs. Campbell here into leaving town." He shrugged and hooked his thumbs in his belt. "Far's I know, writing someone a note isn't a crime, regardless of what it says."

Abbie bristled. "As far as I'm concerned this note is a clear threat."

She felt a hand on her shoulder and knew it was Jake.

"May I see the note?" he asked.

"Sure, why not." She handed the note to Jake. "Apparently the sheriff isn't interested in trying to get prints off of it."

"No need to get upset, little lady." Sheriff Moore folded his arms. "There's been no crime committed here. Leastwise, not that I can see."

Abbie wondered if maybe the sheriff was one of the folks Dawn had talked about who didn't want Cold Creek sold. Why else would he be so blasé?

Jake passed the note to Jeff. While he didn't comment, Abbie thought she saw a muscle in his jaw twitch.

Abbie turned to face Sheriff Moore, who was now talking into the static-ridden radio he'd lifted from his belt. When he lowered the radio, she confronted him. "What you're saying, sheriff, is that until this person acts on his threats you aren't going to try to find him?"

"That's about it, Abbie," Jeff answered as he folded the note and tucked it into his shirt pocket. "No disrespect intended, Ted, but in light of Barbara's murder, maybe we should take this more seriously. Could be the same person who killed her is coming after Abbie."

Abbie sucked in a sharp breath. Up until now, she hadn't connected Barbara's death with the menacing note or her presence in Cold Creek.

The sheriff shrugged. "Maybe. If you all want to print the place, be my guest. You guys are better equipped to do that anyway." He raised a hand and made for the door. I've got some business to deal with out in east county."

Abbie watched him go, anger competing with the terror Jeff had just instilled in her. Barbara's killer? After her? She turned to Jeff. "Do you really think there might be a connection?"

"It's possible. We don't have a clear motive for Barbara's murder yet. What we do know is that she was involved in this property and so are you."

"I am as well, so why not target me?" Jake placed an arm around Abbie's shoulders. She leaned into him, taking refuge in his nearness.

"We'll check for prints, Abbie, but the sheriff is probably right— whoever did this probably didn't leave anything behind."

Abbie nodded. "Thank you for taking the threat seriously."

Jake pulled her closer. "Why don't we leave Jeff to check the place for clues while we have dinner in town?"

"Oh, um…" Abbie glanced at Dawn, who'd been standing just inside the doorway. "I ate earlier with Sam and Isabelle."

Dawn moved away from the wall. "Even so, it might be good for you to get out of here for a while. Take your mind off that note."

Abbie frowned. "And whoever wrote it."

"I have to agree," Jake said.

"You've convinced me." Abbie snatched up the jacket she'd tossed on the bed when she first came in. Turning back to Jake, she asked, "Do I need to change?"

He shook his head. "You're perfect."

The double meaning wasn't lost on her—nor apparently on Dawn. Abbie's cheeks warmed as Dawn winked and offered a knowing smile.

"You kids have a nice time. I won't wait up. I will, however, lock the place up. Abbie, I'll get you a key to the front door."

"Thank you."

Abbie and Jake followed her to the entryway, where Dawn rummaged through a drawer in the curio cabinet.

Abbie tucked the key into her bag along with her room key and preceded Jake out to his car. Memories of their cross-country trip eased into her mind and brought an element of calm. She felt safe with him and almost wished he'd stay at the B&B tonight—in his own room, of course.

As it turned out, Jake, Tim, and Jeff all spent the night at the B&B taking shifts on the patio just outside her room. With her own personal guards, she should have felt safe, but the intruder had her just about ready to give up the entire project and go back to Grand Forks.

By morning, she'd gone back and forth a hundred times and in the end decided to move forward. Except for Leah, she had never tolerated bullies. Leah could make anyone's life miserable, but Abbie had been free of Leah's bullying for two years now and was determined that she wouldn't be so easily intimidated again.

Still, she might have bent to the threat had it not been for Jake, Tim, and Jeff. At dinner the night before, Jake had made her promise that she wouldn't go anywhere alone. He hadn't had to ask twice.

Abbie tossed aside the covers and hurriedly washed up and dressed in a pair of capris and a white shirt. The men were gone now, Abbie saw as she opened the curtains to the patio.

The terror of the night before faded in the light of day. The water lapping at the edges of the sloped yard calmed her. Oddly enough, she'd begun to feel at home in this little town. Abbie straightened her bed and finished just as Dawn called her for breakfast.

Tim and Jeff had gone to work and only Jake remained. He sat at the dining room table now, waiting for Abbie to join him. "Where is your family?" Abbie asked of Dawn as she settled into a chair.

Dawn poured hot water into her cup. "Already gone. We have a kitchen in our living quarters, so we don't usually eat out here."

Dawn served them a wonderful breakfast of coddled eggs and English muffins topped off by a Dutch waffle with strawberries and whipped cream. She then excused herself to do chores, leaving Abbie and Jake to linger over their coffee. Being in the lovely room with Jake made Abbie's world seem right again.

"I suppose you're ready to ditch the entire project." Jake set his empty cup on the table.

She hesitated several moments before answering. "Is that what you think I should do?"

"I like the idea of turning this place around, but not if there's a chance you could be hurt."

"Thank you." She sipped at the now lukewarm coffee. "Last night I was ready to pack up and go home. But I don't want to back out. When I met you, my biggest fear was being arrested. I still don't know why that hasn't happened, but...."

"I can answer that." Jake leaned forward, arms on the table. "You can breathe easy on that score. Yesterday when I talked to Leo, I asked him to check on your status. I talked to him again this morning. He says there are no outstanding warrants. Apparently, Leah never brought charges against you."

"She never..." Abbie couldn't believe it. "So, all this time I've been in hiding for nothing."

Jake covered her hand with his. "I wouldn't say that. If she had legal guardianship of Emma, then unless you filed to oppose her, she would still have it. She could take Emma away if she discovered your whereabouts."

Abbie closed her eyes. "What do we do now?"

"Leo is working on the situation. Discreetly, of course. He'll find out where you stand and do whatever needs to be done to make sure you regain custody."

"Thank you." Feeling the need to step back, she withdrew her hand from his. Poor Jake, he had enough to do without babysitting her. Having him manage her affairs and deal with the attorney reminded her too much of those times she had allowed Leah to handle things like the funerals—and Emma's care. True, she'd been grief-ridden then and needy, but she should have known better.

"I appreciate all you've done for me, Jake, but I've come to depend on you too much. I need to stop relying on you to fight my battles for me."

He frowned; his eyes full of concern. "That sounds like a dismissal."

"Please don't be hurt. It's just that I shouldn't expect you to feel you have to protect me or deal with the attorney in my stead. I'm more than capable of taking care of myself and Emma."

"I never thought you weren't." He smiled. "Besides, I like looking after you."

Abbie touched his arm. "You've done more than your share." She liked having him look after her, but it wasn't right. She could easily fall into the same pattern she'd had with Nate. He along with his father and brother had allowed Leah to rule over all of them. How different things could have been if Nate hadn't been so passive. If he'd taken the initiative and moved them into a place of their own.

Stop it, Abbie, she told herself. *It does no good to blame Nate. You could have insisted. You could have walked away.*

Abbie brought her thoughts up short. It hadn't been that simple. She would never have left Nate. And if he hadn't died when he did, she'd probably still be on the farm.

She squeezed Jake's hand. "I've made a decision. I'm going to buy this place. I'd like to sign the papers today. I want to meet with the attorney and find out exactly what I need to do to gain custody again."

* * * * *

Perhaps Abbie hadn't meant to cut him off as she had, but Jake felt like a man who'd been set adrift. He understood her wanting to be independent, but he'd begun to settle nicely into the role of her protector or knight in shining armor, so to speak. He supposed he should be happy. After all, she'd just committed to buying the largest piece of real estate he'd listed in years. And yet, he couldn't help but be concerned. Abbie had been threatened. Barbara had been murdered.

"Are you sure?" following Abbie's lead, Jake pushed back his chair and walked into the large common living room. He could hear a vacuum cleaner running somewhere above them.

"No. Abbie lifted her chin in defiance. But I won't be bullied into running away."

Jake nodded. "I can understand that.

"There is one thing you can do for me, Jake." Her tone was as determined as the stern look in her eyes.

"What's that?"

129

"Help me buy a gun."

Chapter Nineteen

That evening after dinner, when Jake dropped Abbie off at the B&B, they were met by half a dozen women who were seated in the living room.

Abbie hadn't planned on going out with him again except that he'd brought her the weapon she'd asked for and she had questions about the property. She wanted specifics about the people who still lived there and needed to know which properties in town belonged to private individuals. Fortunately, all the land already sold lay along the north side of Cold Creek, none on the lake or along the creek. She appreciated that the property she would buy was intact—one large piece that included all of Bear Lake.

He'd been reluctant to help her buy the weapon, but after she assured him that she'd learned about firearms and had used them on the farm, he relented. She'd never liked guns and didn't especially want one around, but she would do what she had to do to protect herself.

Jake ducked out after greeting the women, saying he needed to get back to the office to make some calls. He'd seemed unusually sullen, and Abbie suspected the reality of Barbara's death had hit him full force. And she felt certain her own dismissal hadn't helped.

He bid her a hasty good-bye and left her in the entry to fend for herself.

"Come on in and join us," Dawn insisted. Abbie wanted nothing more than to take a long hot bath and fall into bed, but on seeing Isabelle and Samantha, she decided to stay.

The group, she learned, was Cold Creek's monthly book club meeting and prayer group.

"You've already met Isabelle and Samantha," Dawn said. She gestured toward a woman sitting on the sofa next to Isabelle. "This is Jeanette Tremont." Jeanette gave Abbie a finger wave. "She's a retired teacher turned chef."

"Chef?" Abbie grinned. "What an interesting transition."

Jeanette raised her shoulders in a shrug. "I've always loved to cook, so when I retired from teaching, I went to a culinary arts school in Paris."

"Wow. So, you're a real chef?" Abbie's mind was already reeling with questions and she could hardly wait to talk with Jeanette about possibly teaching culinary classes once the artists' retreat was in full swing.

Samantha chuckled. "Jeanette is responsible for those double-decker chocolate brownies on the dining room table. you'll get to try them when we take our break."

Dawn went on to introduce Fannie Snow, who ran the small sundries-and-bait store in which the town's post office was situated. The store catered to hikers, fishermen, and hunters. Then there was Elsie Hunter—she and her husband Floyd spent winters in Arizona and summered here in Cold Creek.

Abbie settled into the one empty chair in the large grouping. "I feel a little silly intruding into your group. What book are you discussing?"

"Actually," Sam told her, "we're reading a P. D. James mystery, but we're not discussing it yet. I'm afraid Barbara Nichols' death has taken center stage. Who wants to talk about a fictional mystery in England when we have a real one in our own backyard?"

Abbie thought the fiction was a much safer topic but didn't comment.

"Just before you came in," Jeanette said, "we were saying that Barbara is the third woman to be murdered in this area in the last three years."

Abbie gasped. "Three murders? here in Cold Creek?" Maybe she should reconsider buying the property.

"Not exactly," Isabelle offered. "We're talking about Oceanside County. And the last one happened six months ago. I doubt there's a connection. Besides, Oceanside has an exceptionally large tourist population and is bound to attract some unsavory people."

"True." Jeanette agreed. "There's not much crime around here except during tourist season. What little happens is rarely attributed to the locals. And, Barbara lived in Oceanside—not in Cold Creek."

Dawn nodded. "It's frightening to think that Barbara's body was found so close by though. Abbie, tell them about the threatening note you found in your room last night. I've always felt that Cold Creek was a safe place, but now I'm not so sure."

"Someone threatened you?" Samantha asked.

Abbie nodded. "When I got home from visiting with you and Isabelle, I found a note waiting for me."

"What did it say?"

"Leave while you still can." Abbie gave them the details about the note and her talk with the authorities. "I admit I was having second thoughts about buying Cold Creek, but I don't want my decision to be fear based. I told Jake today to go ahead with the paperwork."

Elsie shook her head. "I don't like it. Isabelle, I wish you'd take Cold Creek off the market. You can keep selling small parcels, but not the whole town."

"I know it's a big step, Elsie, but Steven thinks we should sell while the market is good."

"Humph. He's a greedy one, that son of yours."

Samantha pursed her lips and looked as though she was going counter, when Elsie continued.

"No offense to you, Abbie," Elsie said, "But we don't want our town turned into a tourist Mecca. We want it to stay like it is."

"That's not going to happen," Isabelle told her. "as much as I hate to do it, I have to sell. Would you rather I sell to Abbie or to that developer from California? He'd come in and raze the entire town. Abbie plans to restore the buildings and keep the flavor of our Cold Creek."

"She's right, Elsie," Abbie said. "It wouldn't be open to tourists all the time. My idea is to turn it into a quiet community of artisans and locals. One weekend a month we'd open it to tourists who would come and buy goods produced by our own people."

"And," Isabelle said, "You'd be able to sell all those wonderful doilies you make for the Christmas bazaar."

"Humph. I still don't like it. Just so you know, Floyd is looking into zoning laws. We've lived in Cold Creek for twenty years; we should have some say. The last thing we need is more people."

Samantha gave Abbie an apologetic look, and she heard several groans. Apparently, Elsie was the only dissenting vote among the women, and Abbie got the idea she and her husband opposed anything new.

"Now, Elsie." Isabelle's tone was both soothing and firm. "It's a free country we live in. I know things have been relatively quiet around here, and I'd never sell if I didn't have to. You and Floyd will still have your land, and no one can build there unless you want them to."

Elsie mumbled something about changing times and the conversation went back to speculating about the mystery in their own backyard.

When they broke for brownies, coffee, and tea, and everyone had raved about Jeanette's new recipe, Elsie took Abbie aside. "Is Isabelle right—that you won't tear down our buildings and put in apartments and malls and such?"

"Yes. Rest assured that at this point the only new building I'm considering would be a retreat center on the lake where Travis has his trailer. It will be a place where artists can come to take classes and improve their skills. Otherwise, I'll remodel and try to keep the town's original flavor."

"Well, you might want to get together with those of us who own land here and show us your plans. Not that we'd have a say. According to Isabelle, we have to take whatever you dish out."

"I'd be happy to show you and the others my plans before they are implemented. After all, you know more about the area than I do."

"You're serious about buying the place then."

"I think so." Abbie wondered how many of the townspeople were against the sale. She wondered too how many of them would threaten her.

Samantha came up beside them. "Sorry to interrupt, ladies, but we should probably get around to the prayer portion of our meeting. Gran is feeling tired tonight—too much time in the garden lately."

Dawn called the group together again and Abbie thought about excusing herself. When the opportunity didn't arise, she settled back into her chair.

Once the group began sharing, Abbie was glad she'd stayed. As each of the ladies shared their prayer requests and talked briefly about problems and praises, Abbie felt her relationship with them shift from stranger to friend. She loved their openness and began wishing she could share as well.

But what would she pray for? That she'd never have to face Nate's family again? Should she confess that she had kidnapped her own child and been in hiding for two years and wanted to stay hidden?

Dawn set her cup on the coffee table. "I think we need to pray for the intruder from yesterday and the situation at the B&B. Let's pray that God keeps us safe from any danger and gives us peace of mind."

"Abbie in particular," Jeanette added.

"Is there anything else we can pray about for you, Abbie?" Isabelle asked.

Abbie hesitated and was tempted to offer her apologies and leave. But prayer sounded like a good idea. "Yes. I'd like prayer for clear direction with regards to buying Cold Creek. I keep going back and forth. I told Jake I was ready to sign the papers this morning, now I'm not so sure."

With the requests made, each woman prayed as she was led. Abbie prayed silently and at the end joined the others with an amen.

The women indulged in more coffee, tea and dessert before heading home, and after they left, Abbie and Dawn began gathering up dishes and taking them to the kitchen.

"Thank you for including me in the group," Abbie said.

"No problem. It gave you an opportunity to meet your neighbors—that is if you decide to buy the place."

"I appreciate that." Abbie sighed. "They seem like wonderful people. I like them all. Even Elsie."

"Don't pay Elsie any mind. She'll adjust."

"You don't think she or her husband wrote that note, do you?"

"If they did, you wouldn't have anything to worry about." Dawn lifted the coffeepot. Besides, they'd tell you straight up, not mess around with a cryptic message. Would you like more coffee or tea?"

"Thank you, but no. I don't mean to keep you away from your family." Abbie hadn't seen Keith or Cassie since she'd come back, and she assumed they were in their living quarters.

Dawn poured the remainder of the coffee into the sink. "No problem. I suspect you're a little nervous about going to your room alone."

Abbie smiled at her new friend's intuitive comment. "You're exactly right. I was even thinking of curling up on the couch in the living room."

Dawn laughed. "No need for that. Come on. I'll walk you to your room and we can check it out together."

"I feel silly asking."

"No need. If I were you, I would be scared silly."

Dawn opened the door and stepped into the room first. After a look around and a quick check of the patio door, she turned back to Abbie. "I don't see anyone."

"It looks safe enough. Thank you."

"You're welcome." She paused at the doorway. "Let me know if you need anything."

"Thanks."

When Dawn left, Abbie locked the door and turned toward the patio. The drapes stood open and she jumped when she saw her reflection. She hurried over to pull the drapes and checked the lock again. Abbie heard a door close and a creaking sound.

Probably just Dawn going to her quarters, she told herself. *Nothing to worry about.*

The closet. Abbie closed her eyes, wishing away her fears. Still, she knew she'd never be able to sleep until she had checked it out. She braced herself and pulled the closet door open. her efforts were rewarded with nothing but a few hangers and the three items of clothing she'd hung there herself after unpacking the day before. She began to breathe more easily.

Abbie had one more place to check before she could relax, and that was the area under her double bed. she lowered herself onto the floor and lifted the dust ruffle.

She heard a low growl just before a black streak came rushing toward her. A muffled scream burst between her fingers as she covered her mouth and jerked out of the way. After several heart-pounding moments, Abbie realized it was only the fat black-and-white cat she'd seen roaming about when she'd checked in.

The cat now rested next to the door, licking a paw, oblivious to the panic she'd just caused. "How did you get in here?" Abbie placed a hand over her heart as if to slow it down.

Abbie rationalized that the cat must have sneaked in earlier in the day—possibly when Dawn had come in to clean the room. She opened the door to the hallway and the cat scampered out.

Feeling considerably safer, Abbie undressed, put on her flannel pajamas, and entered the continental bathroom that she would have shared with another guest. Up until now, the door to the other bedroom had been closed.

Now it stood open, revealing the vast darkened space of the room next door. Abbie reached for the doorknob and pulled the door shut. As far as she knew, no one was staying in the adjoining room.

"Abbie? Is that you?" A hesitant voice came out of the darkness.

Abbie froze, her hand still on the knob. She knew the voice but couldn't believe her ears.

"Abbie, it's me. Open the door."

Abbie did so. "What on earth are you doing here?"

The room was lighter now, aglow from the Tiffany lamp on the bedside stand. Skye, pale and thin, stood in the doorway. With her blond wispy hair highlighted from the light behind her, she looked far too much like an apparition. "I needed to see you—to tell you good-bye."

Chapter Twenty

After dropping Abbie off at the B&B in Cold Creek, Jake headed back to Oceanside and to the dreaded meeting with Douglas Perkins. Jake wasn't looking forward to meeting with the man. He'd met people like him before, rude and obnoxious and determined to have what they wanted, regardless of the folks they had to shove out of the way to get it. He parked in the lot of the upscale restaurant, mentally shrugging into his coat of armor. He could be just as tough as Perkins—maybe more so.

Perkins had insisted they meet, despite the phone call in which Jake had assured him that the Grants had put their offer in on Cold Creek ahead of him. Barbara should have been the one confronting this guy. She was the one who talked to Perkins initially. Maybe it had been a fatal mistake.

Perkins was waiting at a window table, peering at the menu. The restaurant, Captain's Cove, was a favorite in Oceanside, with its all-windowed front offering a magnificent view of the ocean. It sat atop a bluff and patrons could watch waves pummel the shore and spray seawater high in the air.

Jake greeted the hostess and made his way across the crowded room.

"Mr. Perkins." Jack pulled the chair back. "I hope I haven't kept you waiting."

"Not at all." Perkins stood and reached out a hand. He smiled and added, "Glad you could join me. And please, call me Doug."

Jake nodded, shook the man's hand, returning strong grip for strong grip. Taking the menu from the hostess, he settled into the chair opposite the man.

"How's your day been?" Doug wanted to know.

"Great. Couldn't be better." Jake set the menu down without reading it.

"I heard about Barbara Nichols' death. Must have been a shock, huh?"

"That's putting it mildly. How did you find out about her?"

"The police questioned me." He shrugged. "I couldn't tell them much. I put in my offer for the property and didn't hear from her again." Doug looked at the selection of entrées again. "This is my first time here. What do you recommend?"

"The salmon is always good, as is the sturgeon." Jake stopped the waitress, who happened to be his niece, before she could pour the coffee. "Thanks, Tess, I'll just have water."

"Sure." Tess was Brent and Peggy's oldest, and working as a waitress here was her first job. "Are you ready to order?" She set the coffeepot on the table and withdrew a pad from her apron pocket.

"Since I've already eaten, I'll just have coffee," Jake said. He'd have to bring Abbie here. He wished she were here right now instead of Perkins.

"I'll have the sturgeon," Doug said.

Once they'd ordered, Doug leaned forward, elbows on the table. "This is a beautiful area."

"We like it." Jake took a sip of water. "What did you want to talk to me about?"

"Cold Creek. I understand that the Grants put down earnest money."

"That's right."

"I also understand that it's Abbie Campbell, not Grant, who is looking to buy the place." Doug's implications raised the hair on Jake's neck. "Abbie is Grant's daughter. They're buying it together."

"What would it take to get them to change their minds?"

"What are you suggesting?" Jake knew full well what the man was suggesting, and it was all he could do to keep his anger under wraps.

"Nothing illegal." He smiled. "Maybe they'd be willing to drop their offer for a few thousand."

"I seriously doubt that any offer of money would change their minds, Mr. Perkins."

"In that case, how about you, Jake? I'd be willing to pay you a bonus to tell them that you made a mistake and that after looking into the matter you realized my offer came in ahead of theirs."

"I'm not for hire." Jake would have punched the guy in the mouth and walked out if it weren't for his sense of propriety. He didn't want to embarrass his niece, nor did he wish to make a scene in a place where so many people knew him.

"I guess I'll have to keep trying. One way or another, I plan to have that property."

"There are other sites." Jake wondered if Perkins had made a similar offer to Barbara. Had she refused and ended up dead as a result?

"Yeah," Doug said, "but not with a lake and a creek running through it."

Jake focused on maintaining his civility. Maybe he could lure the guy away from the Cold Creek property onto something else. Jake wouldn't put it past the man to carry out his threat in a violent way. Doug's methods reminded him of the way the mafia got things done in the big cities. "Actually, I do have a listing not far from here. fifty acres, with about half a mile of shoreline. Prime property for a hotel or condominiums. It's on a hillside, so your place could offer ocean-view rooms."

"I saw it. Too steep in parts. But I suppose I could consider it if the owner came down more—I'd have to build retaining walls."

"But you wouldn't have to tear down buildings."

"True."

When his meal came, Doug seemed to back down. He asked about other properties up and down the coast. At the end of the meal, Perkins picked up the tab over Jake's protests. Jake didn't want to owe the guy any favors, even if it was only coffee.

As they left the restaurant and headed for their cars, Doug waved at him. "I'll think about some of the alternatives you came up with, but you let me know if the Campbell woman changes her mind."

Jake nodded, wishing he'd never met the man. They didn't need people like him in their community. But there it was. If Abbie and her parents chose not to buy, he would have no option but to sell Cold Creek to Perkins.

Chapter Twenty-one

Abbie drew her sister into her room. "What do you mean, you're saying good-bye?"

"Just that." Skye pulled her arm away. She was wearing jeans and a gray sweatshirt that washed out whatever color she had in her cheeks. "I can't stay with Mom and Dad. They both make me feel guilty every time I have a cigarette or go outside. Mom watches me—criticizes me. She doesn't say anything, but I hear her anyway. She sees me as a loser, and she feels sorry for me."

"She loves you."

"Right. And now Tim is home and it's even worse. He's all goody-two-shoes and I'm..."

"Don't." Abbie raised her hand. She understood those looks. Understood the kind of guilt Skye must be feeling. "Leaving might seem like the answer, but it isn't."

"You left."

"That's entirely different. I'm here for business reasons."

"And here I thought it was to get away from me. I can see the pity in your eyes too."

"I won't deny it. I do feel sad for you. I'm sorry you made the choices you did. I don't want to lose you."

"Too late."

"Where will you go?" Abbie took another tack, knowing she couldn't do anything to stop Skye—at least not at this point.

She shrugged. "Back to Portland. I have friends there."

"Street friends? Drug dealers? Pimps?" Abbie sighed and shook her head. "Please, Skye. Running away from your family isn't the answer. Don't do this. don't throw your life away."

"I'm not going back home."

"Then stay with me." The words slipped out, and Abbie's brain scrambled to piece together what they might mean for her as well as for her sister.

"Here?" Skye asked. Was that relief Abbie read in her eyes? Abbie nodded as the pieces began to fall into place. The direction she'd sought prayer for became clear and absolute. She needed to stay in Cold Creek. This town would be her new home and Emma and Skye's.

"I told Jake to get the papers ready for me to sign earlier today." Even as she spoke, her excitement grew. Grasping Skye's hand, she said, "Please say yes. I'll need someone to help me with Emma. To help me with details."

"You'd trust me to take care of her?"

"You love her, don't you? You'd want to keep her safe?"

"Of course." Skye's drawn face managed a smile.

Abbie sank onto the bed. relief and worry washed over her at the same time. Her resolve of a few moments ago began to unravel. She grasped the ends and tucked them in. She had to stay strong. She had to keep Skye from running back to her old life. "What did Mom say about your leaving?"

"She doesn't know. I left a note on the counter after she and Dad went to bed." Skye bit into her lower lip.

Thinking about the scare Skye had given her, Abbie asked, "How did you get in, and how in the world did you know where to find me?"

"I hitched a ride. While everybody was in the living room, I checked the guest register and walked in."

"But what were you doing in the other room?"

"I heard you and Dawn in the hall and decided I'd better hide. The bathroom door was unlocked, so I ducked in there. I wanted to be sure Dawn was gone before I came out. I'm sorry I scared you."

"I'll survive." Abbie sighed. "You might as well stay in the adjoining room tonight. I'll settle up with Dawn in the morning."

Skye frowned. "I was wondering... do you think, um... Remember when we were kids and you used to let me sleep with you sometimes?"

Abbie chuckled. "I'd like that."

* * * * *

In the morning, Abbie awoke with a start. It was still dark. The sheets beside her were cold. Skye wasn't there. Abbie checked the adjoining room. No sign of her sister or her backpack. Her stomach churned as she realized that the gun Jake had gotten for her, the keys to her car, and the hundred plus dollars she'd had in her handbag were gone as well.

Abbie pulled on a pair of jeans and a sweatshirt and stuffed her feet into her tennis shoes. It wasn't until she reached the driveway that she let the truth settle in. Skye had used her. The night before had seemed like old times. They'd talked and giggled over memories and childhood adventures. Abbie wasn't certain what made her heart ache the most, Skye's deception or losing her sister to the streets.

Using the B&B's phone, Abbie called her parents. Sadly, her mother wasn't surprised at the way Skye had manipulated Abbie, nor was she surprised that Skye had run away. "I think she took your car because she didn't think you'd turn her in. She knew we would. Besides, with Tim here, she wouldn't want to risk our finding out until she was long gone. I know it's hard, but you need to turn her in."

"And have her arrested? I can't do that."

"Honey, she'd be safer in jail than on the streets." Her mom hesitated then added, "Tim wants to talk to you."

After a terse greeting, Tim asked, "When did she leave there?"

"I don't know. She was gone when I woke up."

"I've already alerted the police in Portland. I'll give them a description of the car. Hopefully we can track her down before…"

"Tim." Abbie's voice wavered. "We can't let her go to jail."

"I'll do what I can, Abs, but like Mom says, jail is better than the streets."

Abbie told him about the conversation she'd had with Skye. "I still can't believe she lied to me. She seemed happy about my suggestion that she stay with me."

After a moment's silence he said, "I don't know what to say. Maybe she thought about the responsibility and got scared. Maybe having me here cramps her style. Who knows? Getting off drugs is hard, staying off is practically impossible. At any rate, she's in trouble."

"You're right. I'll press charges if you think it will help. Just find her, okay?"

"We will."

"And Tim, you need to know—she has my gun."

Tim swore. "Then we'd better pray she doesn't use it on someone— or on herself."

Chapter Twenty-two

Abbie hung up the phone, tears blurring her vision. "Oh, Lord, what do I do now?" She'd known with certainly last night that she should stay in Cold Creek. Having Skye here with her and Emma had seemed like a perfect solution.

Abbie did the only thing she could. She prayed. She was sitting at the kitchen counter, head in her hands, when Dawn came in from outside.

"Abbie, I thought you'd gone out." She hung up the keys on one of the hooks on the wall and nodded toward the back door. "Your car was gone when I went out. What's wrong?"

While Abbie explained what had happened, Dawn heated a kettle of water and placed a canister of tea bags on the counter. "I can brew a fresh pot of coffee if you'd rather. All that's left of what I made this morning is grounds."

"Tea is fine."

"I'm so sorry, Abbie." Dawn poured hot water into their cups. "I can imagine how disappointed you must feel."

"I'll pay for her staying here last night." Abbie warmed her hands on the mug.

"No, you won't. There's no need."

Abbie didn't argue. She'd compensate in other ways. Dawn turned on the oven and brought out the mixer. "I hope you don't mind if I cook while we talk."

"Not at all. I'm glad you're here." Abbie dunked her tea bag into the hot water as she gathered her thoughts. "I can't believe my sister would use me like this."

"Sometimes people do things they really don't want to do," Dawn said. "I've read that most addicts want to quit but they can't help themselves."

Abbie nodded. "I've read things like that too, I just never thought I'd have to deal with it personally."

They talked for several more minutes while Dawn mixed batter for a cake. Once it was in the oven, she excused herself to get started on her daily tasks. "I'll be praying for Skye," she said. "I hope the police find her. It seems cruel, but it's for the best."

"Thanks, Dawn. I appreciate your being willing to listen."

"Hey, what are friends for?"

Abbie carried her cup and saucer to the sink and rinsed them. She felt better for having talked. Now for the rest of the day.

She'd learned during her lengthy period of grief that it did no good to sit around and sulk. Better to stay busy.

She decided to walk to the library. If she planned to restore Cold Creek, she needed a layout of the town and the history of each of the buildings. Once again, she walked past the stately Victorian that seemed to call to her. She paused in front of it to examine it more closely.

There was something regal about the house. As if it had been built for someone important. The paint had peeled off long ago, and the wood had turned a weathered gray. She could see that it had once been white with maroon and green trim.

Abbie swung the gate open and started up the walk. An odd sensation moved through her. Not fear, she decided, though she lifted her gaze to the window on the third floor where she thought she'd seen the curtains move the day before.

There was no movement now and Abbie attributed yesterday's incident to the breeze. Still, she felt as though she were being drawn forward. The hair stood up on the back of her neck, giving her a chill. Abbie shook the feeling off and turned back. She would explore the house soon enough and not alone.

Moments later, she stepped into the library and greeted Samantha, who was putting away a stack of books.

"Hi, Abbie." Sam grinned down at her from her perch on the rolling ladder. "Did you come to chat or are you looking for something in particular?"

"Both, I guess." Abbie told her what had happened with Skye. "I need to stay busy. I could also use your help in finding out about the history of Cold Creek. Talking with you and Isabelle really piqued my interest."

"I have exactly what you're looking for," Samantha said as she stepped off the ladder. While she pulled some books from the shelves, Abbie pulled out a chair from the long table and sat, then took a notepad out of her bag.

"You might want to start with these." Sam placed the books on the table.

Abbie noticed that two of the books bore Isabelle's name. "Did your grandmother write these?"

"She did. When I moved in with her after my divorce, she told me she wanted to write her memoirs. Part of my room and board for staying with her was to organize and edit her stories. The memoir is still in progress, but we ended up writing an entire series of the history of Cold Creek. We also have a collection of old journals."

She hesitated for a moment then invited Abbie to come into a side room. "I don't usually let people see these, but since you're looking at possibly restoring the buildings, you should have a look."

There were several glass cases with books and photos displayed along two walls. A small desk sat in a corner near a window. Samantha withdrew a set of keys from her pocket and opened one of the glass cases. From it, she lifted out one of the leather-bound books. "For me, the most interesting one is from Jebediah Johansson, Granny's uncle. Jebediah worked as a lumberjack felling trees until he lost a leg in a freak accident.

"He was only forty at the time and didn't let the disability stop him. He decided the town needed a combination hotel, saloon, and gambling hall. His brother never did approve—Gunnar, my great-grandfather, was a devout Christian and felt a saloon would bring nothing but trouble." Samantha closed the case and began walking back to the main room. "Jebediah was a wealthy man and spared no expense in building the place. He ordered stained glass and tile and marble from Italy and hired local craftsmen to do the interior woodwork. The building was a work of art and was featured in the newspaper. For a while it became the place to visit, but the novelty eventually wore off.

"Cold Creek never has been a destination spot. As it turned out, the hotel had very few overnight guests." She paused. "Most people thought he should have built it in Oceanside. We never did get a lot of tourists out here."

"Was that when the hotel closed down?"

"Not at all. Fortunately, the saloon and gambling hall did very well." She gave Abbie a wistful smile. "I'd love to see the building restored. The hotel rooms upstairs would make great apartments and maybe someday we'll be able to fulfill Uncle Jebediah's dream."

Abbie frowned. "We're talking about the boarded-up building across the street, right?"

Samantha laughed. "I know it doesn't look like much on the outside, but the inside is beautiful. I'll show it to you later. Gunnar closed it down after Jebediah died. I don't think he ever tried to sell it, but by then the town had begun to disintegrate. People moved away to find jobs in the city after the lumber mill closed. There was nothing here to hold them.

"Jebediah died a rich man, however, and since he never married and had no children, the money went to his brother. Gunnar refused to touch a dime of it—not that he needed to. He was a wealthy man by then. When he and Grandma Marie died, Isabelle inherited the lot—including uncle Jebediah's fortune."

She tipped her head to one side. "There's a bit of a mystery involved with the money, though. None of Uncle Jeb's money was ever accounted for. Rumor has it that Gunnar buried it somewhere in town."

"How exciting. A buried treasure."

Samantha laughed. "A lost treasure. Over the years, people have tried. My father did. He was obsessive about it. He must have turned over every piece of dirt in Cold Creek. In the end, he drank himself to death. He was a greedy, self-centered man who ended up bitter and disappointed and broken."

"I'm sorry."

"Not as sorry as I am. He had a family and a future but tossed it all away following a dream that may not even exist." She shrugged and smiled. "I don't mean to sound bitter. In a way it was good for me. I realized early on that I didn't want to be like that. I spent a lot of time with Granny. And I don't care at all about the lost money. For me, the treasure is the stories and the building itself."

"I'm excited to see the place," Abbie said, "but I'd like to look at more of the history first. So far, it sounds fascinating."

"Uncle Jeb's journal is a perfect place to start." Sam set the leather book on the table. "Just handle it with care."

"This is amazing." Abbie paged through the entries, and as she did so, the history of Cold Creek came to life. Two brothers, Gunnar and Jebediah Johansson, established the community in 1889 around a logging camp.

The lumber industry at the time was going great guns. Trees were toppled and sent down the mountain via wood flumes to the river and into Oceanside where they awaited transport. Eventually they built a sawmill a ways out of town so the lumber could be processed before being sent out by truck. Gunnar married Marie in 1901 and had only one daughter, Isabelle, in 1903. As the money came in, they began building the general store, the millinery, a café, the post office, a church, and a library. The brothers built the mansion on the hill shortly after Gunnar and Marie married. He and his brother had a row over the saloon and Gunnar moved out of the mansion and into the hotel. He turned it into a showplace and Abbie couldn't wait to see it.

Old brown-tone photos of the hotel and the other buildings had all been placed into the handwritten journal. As she paged through the book, she paused at a page that featured the lovely Victorian she liked so much.

Tobias Carlson, the town physician, had lived there with his young wife, Sofia. Tobias, sixty-five at the time, had the house built while he waited for Sofia to come from the east Coast with several other mail-order brides. *She was a young thing,* Jebediah had written, *much too young for old Doc Carlson.*

"How's it going?" Samantha set a couple more books on the table.

"Great. I'm reading about Sofia."

"Ah, the disappearing bride."

"She disappeared?"

"It's quite a story. She was terribly disappointed when she discovered that the man she'd come to marry was old enough to be her grandfather. She threatened to go back home, but of course, there was no way she could do that. She'd signed a binding agreement and had no money.

Eventually, she went ahead and married Dr. Carlson. After all, he had paid her way and had built a lovely house for her. She was an unhappy soul, my grandmother used to say, except for those times she slipped away in the evenings after doc went to bed for the night.

"She'd head over to the hotel, where she would entertain the saloon customers with singing and dancing. Nothing more. Jebediah made that clear. Grannie thought she did it to earn money so she could return home.

"According to Jebediah's journal, Doc came into the saloon to fetch his wandering bride more than once. You had to feel sorry for Doc Carlson in a way. He thought he was getting a wife and ended up with nothing but trouble.

"It isn't written in the journal, but grandma thinks Jebediah and Sofia were in love. Sofia became pregnant after a while and stopped coming to the saloon. She left town shortly after that. Doc was grief stricken and so was Uncle Jebediah."

"That's so sad."

"It is. Doc was never the same after that. He moved out of the house after she left and went back into the room behind his office, where he stayed until he died twenty years later—hung himself in that old house. It's been empty ever since."

"Poor man." Abbie took a moment to absorb the story. "What a fascinating history. Maybe I'm getting ahead of myself, but I'm thinking we should publish a book about Cold Creek's history. I have a hunch we could sell tons of them once we get tourists up here."

Samantha's eyes widened in agreement. "I love the idea. I'll ask Granny what she thinks." Abbie's thoughts returned to the Carlson house. "Is the house part of the property that's up for sale?"

"It is. Doc stopped making payments and it went back to Jebediah and Gunnar."

"Good." Abbie grinned. "I'd like to see the inside. I'm thinking it would make a charming home for Emma and me." She'd almost included Skye but checked herself and offered up a silent prayer for her sister's safety.

"I'd offer to take you, but I have students coming in soon. You could go through it and the hotel if you want. I can give you the keys."

"I'll do that, thanks."

Abbie realized then she hadn't seen the inside of most of the buildings yet. She supposed she should do that before signing the papers, but it didn't really matter. Based on her father's figures, the asking price was primarily for the property.

To a developer, the buildings would probably be a liability, since many of them would have to be torn down. But not for

Abbie. Jake had given her a list of the buildings he considered acceptable for remodeling. The hotel and the Victorian were on the list.

Slipping the key into the lock on the hotel door, she hesitated. She'd promised Jake she wouldn't explore on her own, but...

It's daylight, she reminded herself. *Sam is right across the street.* There was no one around that she could see.

"You'll be fine," Abbie mumbled aloud. Curiosity overrode her fears. She pushed open the door and began her personal tour. Stepping inside was like going back in history. Sam had been right; the building was full of treasures.

Even though Samantha had told her about the stained glass and marble from Italy, Abbie wasn't prepared for what she found. The ceiling in the saloon as well as the hotel lobby featured carved tin tiles. Behind the marble-topped bar was a wall-sized mirror bordered with stained glass flowers and leaves. A stained-glass partition separated the saloon from what looked like a dining room or maybe the card room. In the far corner was a stage. Ragged red velvet curtains draped down each side.

Abbie couldn't have been more thrilled. This would be the perfect place for poets to read and musicians to play and actors to perform. No wonder her parents had fallen in love with the place. She could almost see them up on the stage, singing and playing and having a fun time of it.

The bar would serve as a fountain providing drinks and desserts— like Jeanette's brownies.

A wide oak staircase wound up to the second and third floors. a peek into several rooms on both floors gave her an eerie sense of stepping into the past. Each room had a decorative lamp built into a wooden stand and a double bed frame. Either someone had taken the mattresses out or they'd never been put in. There were two bathrooms on each floor. The rooms were large with tall ceilings. They were in decent shape for having stood empty for so many years. she could see signs of mouse droppings and peeling wallpaper, cracks in the plaster, but that was all cosmetic. The floors seemed solid—of course she wouldn't know for sure until she brought a contractor in.

After locking up the hotel, she headed over to the Victorian she'd taken such a liking to. The doctor seemed to have spared no expense in the décor. The wood-framed fireplace and built-in bookshelves, the ornately carved woodwork spoke of moderate elegance.

It wasn't as glorious as the hotel, but Abbie loved it. The entry opened to a large living room and grand staircase. She walked from the living room to the kitchen and the bathroom. She loved the spacious kitchen. A walkthrough pantry separated the kitchen from a formal dining room.

The pantry, she noticed, seemed a bit narrow—too narrow. The wall should have lined up with the kitchen. she shrugged it off as an optical illusion and went on exploring. The bedrooms were apparently upstairs. Climbing the stairs, Abbie paused as a shiver passed through her. When she reached the landing at the top of the stairs, she thought again of the curtain moving in the window. "Don't be silly. No one is here except you." *And maybe a mouse or two.*

She took a deep breath and wished she hadn't. Dust, mold, smells reminiscent of decay and lack of use welled up in her nostrils, reminding her of what a huge job renovating these buildings would be. She'd have to talk with Jake about hiring a contractor.

While the work would be tedious, she couldn't imagine anyone destroying these wonderful historic places. Abbie was eager now to move ahead. She thought again about the threatening note but determined not to allow one person's opposition to derail her.

Chapter Twenty-three

Jake found Abbie in the library shortly after noon. The smile that lit up her eyes when she saw him quickened his heart. He'd brought the paperwork for her to sign and hoped she'd be open to an invitation to go into town for lunch.

"Let's take care of the paperwork first," she told him. "Then we can eat. I went through several places this morning, and I'm even more convinced that this place is perfect for our artists' retreat."

"I can't tell you how happy I am that you'll be staying, but are you sure about Cold Creek?"

"Yes." Abbie took a deep breath and let it out slowly.

"But..." Jake held his breath as her determination seemed to fade.

"I'm scared, but I can't let my lifelong dream slip away because one person opposes my being here. Or because I'm afraid I won't be able to pull it off."

"One person?"

"Well, more than one, but someone felt strongly enough to threaten me. Last night Elsie Hunter basically told me to pack my bags. Though she relented a little when Isabelle told her what our plans were."

Jake couldn't help but smile. "If that's who wrote the note, you don't have anything to worry about. Elsie and Floyd and a few of the other older residents who own the property around here have been worried. Rightfully so." He hesitated, not sure if he should tell her of his suspicions.

"Abbie." Jake placed his hand over hers. "About that note. I think it might have been from the developer."

"Right. Dawn mentioned him. The guy who thought his offer came before my parents put down earnest money?"

Jake nodded. "He hired a survey crew to determine the actual boundaries. He also raised his offer on the place."

Abbie's hand formed a fist as she withdrew it from his. "If he thinks I'll fold. I won't."

With her jaw set and fire lighting her gray-green eyes she added, "Let's do this, Jake. There's no way I'm backing down. I'm not going to let that man ruin this town and its beautiful buildings."

Watching her determination, Jake felt as though his heart had expanded to twice its size. He wanted to pull her into his arms and kiss her, but he wouldn't. He wanted Abbie to stay, and part of him felt like cheering. At the same time, he wanted her safe and worried that she might be stepping into dangerous territory.

Jake withdrew the papers from his briefcase, all the while praying that he was doing the right thing. His mind went back as it so often did to Barbara Nichols. There was no evidence to connect Perkins to Barbara's death, but that meant nothing. The man was a bully and seemed determined to win. Jake vowed to protect Abbie.

When she asked about a contractor, he had just the man in mind. Brent would not only do an exemplary job; he'd be around to see that she didn't get hurt.

"Brent O'Brien," Jake said. "He's my brother-in-law. Brent built all the houses in the development where your parents and I live. I'll talk to him."

"Thanks." Abbie raised an eyebrow. "Brother-in-law?"

"He's married to my sister, Peggy. They live just outside of Oceanside on a farm—five kids. I'll have to take you out to meet them sometime."

"I'd like that." for the next few minutes, they focused on the paperwork. Jake had already gotten signatures from her parents and Isabelle, so hers would finalize the deal. He watched her, fascinated by her expressions as she concentrated on the documents. Occasionally, she asked questions about the wording and Jake translated the legal jargon into plain English.

Once she'd signed the last page, she set the pen down. Looking into his eyes, she gave him a Mona Lisa smile and he almost melted. "It's done." She leaned over and brushed a kiss against his cheek. "Thank you."

"For?"

"Bringing me home. Being patient." She sighed. "I've never owned property before, and here I've gone and bought an entire town."

"I'd say that calls for a celebration." Jake gathered the papers and placed them into a folder and into his briefcase. "Are you ready for lunch?"

"I am, but let's pick Emma up on the way. You can't believe how much I've missed her."

He chuckled. "I have too." The little girl had secured a place in his heart the moment she'd asked Abbie if he could be her daddy. "Have you thought about where you and Emma will live until your house is remodeled?"

Abbie frowned. "With my parents, I suppose, though I'd like to be closer to Cold Creek so I can keep an eye on things. I'll stay at the B&B for the time being." On the way back to Oceanside, Abbie asked Jake about the murder investigation.

"There's been no news." Jake glanced at her. "I have some ideas of my own, but…"

"Perkins?"

Jake began to tell Abbie about the talk he had with the man. "He offered to pay me big bucks to change my mind about who paid the earnest money first. I can't help but think he might have tried to bribe Barbara too. He's the type of guy who doesn't take no for an answer. Did she refuse? Maybe she threatened to call the police. I don't know."

"And he's still around." Abbie tried to put the threat from the other night out of her mind but couldn't. "It's too late now, right? Maybe he'll leave or look into another property."

"He seemed open to finding something else when I talked to him." Jake planned to see Perkins later that day. With any luck, he'd have gone back to Portland.

Abbie shuddered. "I hope he doesn't make any trouble for us."

"I've dealt with guys like him before. They're mostly bluff." Jake reached across the seat to touch Abbie's shoulder. "Just to be on the safe side, I asked Jeff to check him out." He smiled as he turned down the side street into the subdivision. "What do you say we table this discussion for the time being and concentrate on having a good lunch with Emma? I'm thinking we could take her to play on the beach for a while. Does she have a kite?"

Abbie shook her head. "She doesn't, but we can pick one up in town." Her smile was his undoing. Jake stopped the car in the driveway and reached for her. *One kiss*, he thought. A quick peck before they went inside. Her gaze met his as he leaned forward. She moved at the same time, and the connection set off sparks the likes of which he'd never felt before. She pressed her hands against his chest and leaned back.

"Jake, I..." She seemed as breathless as he felt.

I love you. The words remained unspoken as he mumbled an apology and clumsily grabbed for the door handle.

Chapter Twenty-Four

The kiss left Abbie shaken. It wasn't until she started up the porch steps and Emma came racing out that she managed to collect herself.

She braced herself as Emma threw herself into her arms. Abbie picked her up and held her close. "Oh, sweetie, I missed you so much."

"I missed you too." Emma hugged her neck hard then leaned toward Jake.

He seemed entirely too pleased with Emma's show of affection as he carried the child inside. Abbie almost tripped on the small suitcase and stuffed animals that sat in the middle of the entry. "What's this?" She bent to examine the case.

Emma twisted in Jake's arms and he put her down. "Nana helped me pack my bag. She said I could ask you if I can stay with you at the B&B. I got my jammies and some socks. And I want to take my Barbie and teddy. Can I come with you?"

"Of course." Abbie couldn't say no. Not that she wanted to.

"Can you stay with Mommy and me too?" Emma grinned up at Jake.

Jake picked up the small suitcase and winked at Abbie. "No, I have to stay at my house."

Carlene chose that moment to appear. Abbie told her about signing the papers and hoping to move into the Victorian. "I've decided to stay at the B&B in Cold Creek for the time being."

"I suppose that's more convenient, but I'm disappointed. Can you stay for a while now?" Carlene asked.

She kissed her mother's cheek. "I'll come back later. Jake is taking Emma and me out to lunch and then we thought we'd celebrate by buying a kite and flying it on the beach."

"No need to buy one. I have one I bought especially for Emma." Carlene rummaged around on the top shelf of the entry closet and brought out a long, thin package. "Here we go."

Carlene knelt in front of Emma. "You be a good girl. I'll miss you."

"Don't cry, Nana." Emma's arms went around her grandmother's neck. "You can come and visit us."

Carlene hugged her close and stood to embrace Abbie as well. "We'll be here anytime you need us. I'm thrilled you've decided to buy Cold Creek with us, but I was hoping you'd live here—for a while at least."

"I know." Abbie squeezed her hand. "But we're close."

Carlene hugged her again. "And thank the Lord for that."

* * * * *

After a delicious lunch of fish and chips and clam chowder, the trio spent an hour on the beach teaching Emma the elements of getting a kite aloft and keeping it there.

Before heading back to Cold Creek, Jake stopped at his office to make a quick call. Within minutes they were on the highway heading south to his sister's house. He had the bright idea that Emma might enjoy playing with his nieces and nephews while Abbie got to know Peggy and Brent.

He'd been right. The O'Brien clan took her and Emma into their fold the minute they exited the car. Tess, the oldest, was at school. The girls, six-year-old Patti and five-year-old Jennie began telling Emma about their playhouse in the backyard. The twin boys, Andy and Aaron, who were three, followed the girls.

Peggy ushered Abbie into the house after giving her a welcoming hug. Jake's sister looked nothing like her brother. While his eyes were a cobalt blue, hers were lighter—more grayish green. She wore jeans and an untucked blue chambray shirt and no shoes. Her hair was more chestnut than brown, and she wore it up in an untamed ponytail. Curls of shorter hair framed her tanned, freckled face.

"I've heard so much about you," Peggy said. "I bet your parents are thrilled to have you back home."

"They are." Abbie was surprised at her comment. "You know my parents?"

"Quite well. It's a long story. We'll get to that later—over coffee." She turned to embrace Jake and followed the hug with a punch to the arm. "And you. Do you have any idea how long it's been since you've been out here?"

Jake lifted his hands in surrender. "Too long, I know. I'm sorry, but things have been crazy since I got back."

Her teasing stopped as she nodded. "I know. Any news about the murder investigation?"

Jake shook his head. "Afraid not."

"Well, hopefully there'll be a break in the case soon. In the meantime, let's go inside. I made a coffee cake this morning. Must have known you were coming."

Within short order, Peggy, Jake, and Abbie were sitting at the door-sized table with mismatched chairs in a large alcove looking over the backyard. The yard was enclosed and beyond it was a set of stairs that led to the sea below. On the long winding driveway Abbie hadn't seen any other houses. On one side of the road, she'd seen a herd of cows in a large pasture dotted with a few deciduous trees and cedars and a barn. On the other was a field of hay and closer to the house, a garden.

The house was modern and had hat messy, lived in look that homes with small children have. Cozy. The kitchen had been built a step up from the dining area, and Peggy, who'd already served them coffee, turned to nab a platter of her cake squares. "Enjoy. I'll be back in a few minutes—after I get a snack for the kids." She picked up another platter of cookies and set it on a tray with a pitcher of red juice and five plastic cups.

"Can I help?" Abbie asked.

"I've got it, but if I can get my brother to slide open the door, we'll be all set."

Jake complied and Peggy took the snacks to a picnic table just off an aggregate patio and called the kids. Abbie laughed as they tumbled out of the playhouse and raced each other to the table. Emma waved at her mother as she sat on the bench between the girls.

A lump lodged itself in Abbie's throat. The scene, reminiscent of their time in Grand Forks, tugged at her heart. She missed Margie and her little boy. It had been over a week since she and Emma had driven off into the unknown with Jake Conners. She'd promised to call when she arrived at her parents', which she had. Perhaps it was time to call again. After pouring drinks for the kids, Peggy came back inside, leaving the sliding door open and closing the screen. She sat next to Abbie and lifted her cup to her lips. "I've discovered that the best way to take a break is to give the kids one."

"Very smart." Abbie watched Emma interact with the children. They looked as though they'd been friends for years. "Emma seems right at home here."

Peggy laughed. "She's adorable. My girls are already mothering her."

After a moment, Abbie asked, "You said you knew my parents."

"Hmm." Peggy set down her cup. "Brent built their house. Didn't Jake tell you?"

"Oh. I guess he did. I just didn't put two and two together. You've known them for quite a while then."

Peggy grinned. "We have. We sort of adopted them as grandparents since both Brent's and my parents are gone."

Abbie felt a stab of jealousy, but it passed as she considered how her parents, the kids, and Brent and Peggy must have benefited from the connection. "That's wonderful. Every child needs a grandparent."

"I agree," Peggy went on. "I guess that makes us related."

Jake chuckled. "My sister thinks we're all related in some way."

"Maybe she's right. You don't necessarily need to be blood relatives to have a close connection." Abbie already felt that connection, to the people here as well as to the Cold Creek property.

"Of course, I'm right." Peggy assured. "We're linked to one another and to the land—to all of nature."

"If you haven't already figured it out," Jake said, "My sister is an environmentalist. She's the farmer in the family."

"And proud of it. When our parents died and Jake and I had to split things up, I took the farm and he got the money. I love being self-sufficient."

"Hey, bro." A sturdy-looking man with Sandy-blond hair and a deep tan walked in and patted Jake's shoulder then went around the table to plant a kiss on Peggy's lips. "Sorry I'm late, hon. I got tied up with the powers that be at city hall. Man, those people must take lessons on how to make our lives miserable."

Jake chuckled. "It's taken you this long to figure that out?" He leaned back and gestured toward Abbie. "This is Abbie Campbell, the new owner of Cold Creek. Abbie, you've already probably guessed, this is Brent." Abbie reached over to shake Brent's hand. "Hi, Brent. nice to meet you."

"Back atcha." His wide grin lit up dark brown eyes.

Honest eyes, Abbie decided.

"Jake says you bought Cold Creek and want some remodeling done." Unlike Jake, who wore slacks and a dress shirt—he'd discarded his tie earlier—Brent had on a navy rugby-style shirt and khaki shorts.

"Stop right there." Peggy stood and slipped an arm around her husband's waist. "No shop-talk until after dinner. I want a chance to get to know Abbie before you steal her away with business stuff." To Abbie she said, "Once these guys get started on building projects, it's impossible to get them away."

* * * * *

Abbie, Emma, and Jake ended up spending the rest of the evening with Brent and Peggy. Abbie loved the easy camaraderie between them and especially liked the way they included her. She let herself wonder what it would be like to be part of the family unit as Jake's wife.

She quickly discarded the idea each time it tried to take root. As much as she liked Jake, she couldn't let herself get involved romantically. Abbie watched him now as he and Brent played ride-the-horsey with the twins. Her heart swelled with love, completely disagreeing with her mind.

She recalled the night they met when he'd asked her to dance and how she'd momentarily mistaken him for her childhood idol. Abbie could easily imagine herself falling in love with Jake.

But she couldn't allow herself that luxury. She'd only been a widow for two years. and even though Jake had told her there was no warrant against her, she had kidnapped her child from the woman who had legal custody. Now she'd come out of hiding. She'd plunged into a dream but feared it might end up a nightmare.

Panic spread a tangle of vines through her mind. Her throat seemed to close. She felt the urge to take Emma and run. This was a mistake. What if Leah found out where she was?

"Abbie?" Peggy's voice filtered in through the jumble of thoughts. A touch on her shoulder made her jump.

"Oh, you startled me."

165

"I'm sorry." Peggy grinned. "You seemed far away, are you okay?"

Abbie nodded. "Just thinking."

"And feeling overwhelmed, I'll bet."

"A little." Abbie laughed. "A lot. I'm having trouble believing that we actually bought a town."

"I can only imagine." Peggy touched her arm. "I have just the solution to bring you back to earth. How about helping me bathe the kids and get them into bed? Emma too, if you'd like. She can spend the night or just sleep until you and Jake are ready to go."

"I'd love that."

At nine, having tucked in the children, Peggy and Abbie descended the stairs. Jake and Brent sat at one end of the large oak dining room table and waved the women over. Abbie grabbed her bag from beside the couch and took the chair beside Jake. Looking over the papers scattered on the table, she said, "Did you start without me?"

"Not really. We were talking about Perkins."

"Coffee, anyone?" Peggy went into the kitchen. "Cookies?"

They all waved an assent. "I can't believe this is really happening." Abbie opened her notebook and took out a pen.

"I have to tell you, Abbie," Brent said, "I already like your ideas. Just tell me where to start."

"I think it might be best to begin with the Victorian on Spring Lane. Samantha told me that a doctor used to live there. I'm hoping you can get the original blueprints. I could be wrong, but I think the pantry is off—narrower than you'd think by looking at the kitchen. Sometimes older places have cubbies or hidden rooms."

Jake looked impressed. "I'm surprised you'd spot something like that. I've only been in it a couple of times—never noticed."

Abbie smiled. "Artists are trained in perspectives. I've always had a good eye for that sort of thing."

"Could be it was assembled wrong." Brent wrote something on the pad he'd taken out. "I'll look into it. The house was built around 1923. It's one of those Sears and Roebuck houses you could order from their catalog." He chuckled. "I love those old places. They were surprisingly well built, as long as the builder knew what he was doing."

"I'd like the hotel done as soon as possible too. I'll need places for artists to stay, and in some cases to live. I noticed that some of the hotel rooms are fairly large, and I'm thinking they can be converted into studio apartments."

"I suggest we work on both the Victorian and the hotel at the same time." Brent rubbed his chin. "I'll get a cleaning crew into them first so we can better assess what needs fixing and rebuilding."

Abbie nodded. "And then there's the retreat center I'd like built on the lake where Travis's trailer is. Maybe we could move the trailer and he could stay in it while the retreat center is being built."

"That's doable. Travis and I work together quite a bit. In fact, Keith might be able to help out too." Brent tapped his pen on the legal pad. "It'll take me some time to draw up the plans. Since you're an artist, maybe you could sketch out what you want."

Abbie's enthusiasm ratcheted up several notches as she described what she'd been imagining. There would be large studio apartments on the second floor of the retreat center. On the lower level, she wanted four meeting rooms or classrooms, each with a view. There would be a library and offices and a reception area and restaurant with a well-appointed kitchen and a fireplace. "I also want a caretaker's cottage off to one side that has a view of the lake."

"By the way, Abbie." Jake grinned at her. "I told Travis what you said about his artwork and about him possibly staying on as caretaker. He loves the idea. Said he'd be happy to teach woodcarving, if that's what you have in mind."

Abbie clasped her hands together. "Perfect." She squeezed Jake's hand. "It's going to work, isn't it?"

The percolator perked, announcing the coffee was ready. Abbie helped herself to a chocolate chip cookie and felt as if her world had finally become a friendly place.

* * * * *

When Abbie arrived at the B&B that evening, it seemed as though everyone had retired for the night. She used her key to get in and locked the door behind her. She'd fully expected to have Emma stay at the B&B with her but hadn't had the heart to wake her. Peggy promised she'd bring Emma out to the B&B first thing in the morning when she took Patti and Tess to school.

As Abbie stepped from the entry to the living room, a light near one of the chairs caught her eye. A portly man sat in the chair, his head tucked down and resting on his chest. Apparently, he'd fallen asleep. She hesitated, wondering if she should wake him. Sleeping in that position would be uncomfortable.

At that moment, he snorted and woke himself up. His eyes opened and he shifted in his chair, picked up the book from his lap, and began to read. He hadn't seen her, and she didn't especially want to be seen.

Abbie continued down the hall to her room. she was curious about the man, but not enough to disturb him. When she reached for the door handle, she was surprised and startled to find it unlocked. Had she forgotten to lock her room? Had dawn forgotten to lock it after cleaning it that morning?

Had Skye come back? That thought spurred her forward. Abbie pushed open the door. The room was dark except for the dim light from the patio door and windows. she snapped on the light and stepped inside. after closing the curtains and checking things out as she had done the night before, Abbie let herself breathe. As far as she could tell, everything was as she had left it.

168

She checked the locks once more before changing into her pajamas and climbing into bed. She was exhausted, but her mind churned with random thoughts—excitement, fear, concern, questions. Had she made the right decision?

Should she stay at the B&B or go home to her parents? Where was Skye? Was she safe?

Who was the man sitting in the living room? A guest, no doubt. Despite the rambling trails her brain took, Abbie managed to fall asleep just after midnight.

Chapter Twenty-five

Jake sat outside the B&B for over an hour that night. The dark blue sedan parked in the lot unnerved him. He'd seen the vehicle or one like it before—or thought he had. At any rate, its presence troubled him. Undoubtedly, the car belonged to a guest, and normally the idea of a new guest at the B&B wouldn't be a problem or cause for alarm.

Normally, he reminded himself, there wouldn't have been a murderer on the loose either.

Jake stepped out of the car and walked around the grounds. finding nothing out of the ordinary, he got back in the car and headed back to Oceanside and home.

* * * * *

Abbie awoke feeling refreshed and ready to start the day. At ten she would meet with Brent to go through the buildings and discuss remodeling plans. First, however, she wanted to talk with Dawn and bring her up-to-date. As expected, she found the busy caretaker in the kitchen making breakfast. Dawn greeted her with a cheery "Good morning" as she placed a cup on the counter. "Coffee or tea?"

"Tea—Earl Grey if you have it." She'd had more than enough coffee at the O-Brian's place yesterday.

Dawn poured hot water from the kettle and handed Abbie a tea bag. "I'm surprised to see you up and about so early."

"I'm too excited to sleep in." Abbie told her about signing the papers and of her plan to live in the doctor's house.

"You really did it?" Dawn pinched her lips together.

"What's wrong? I thought you'd be happy."

Dawn gave her a crooked smile. "I am, I suppose. The artists' retreat will be great for business and for Cold Creek. It's just that the note and Barbara's death…. I've been worried for you."

"Thank you." Abbie dunked the teabag into the hot water several times. "It's meant to be, Dawn. It really is. Things are coming together already. Brent is going to be the contractor."

Dawn nodded. "You might have him hire Keith. The job in Lincoln City is ending, and it would be a good idea to have someone here in Cold Creek to keep an eye on things during the remodeling." Frowning, she added, "You said you were planning to remodel and live in old Doc Carlson's house?"

"Yes." Abbie set the teabag on her saucer. "I know it might seem silly, but there's something about the place that draws me to it. It'll be awhile though, since it's going to need a fair amount of work."

"It's spooky." Dawn took a sip of her coffee and checked whatever she had in the oven. The scent of fresh bread spilled out of the oven and filled the room. "The rumor is that Doc's ghost is still there. He hung himself in there, you know."

"Sam told me. I read the story about his mail-order bride."

"Yeah, I heard about that," Dawn said. "Sad. He died penniless and brokenhearted. Some say his ghost wanders through the place, looking for his wife."

Abbie smiled. "I guess I'll have to see if Brent can evict him."

"Suit yourself, but that's the last place I'd choose." Dawn pulled a skillet out of a lower cupboard.

"I won't let myself be scared away by the person who left me that note, and I doubt I'll let a ghost story stop me either."

Abbie took a sip of the still hot tea. "It'll be awhile before I can move in though. In the meantime, I'll need to find a more permanent place to stay."

"You could stay here. You and your little girl. Skye too, if she decides to come back."

"Are you sure there's room?" Abbie had counted six rooms in her wing but wasn't certain all of them were for guests.

"Of course." She laughed. "It's a B&B, remember? I'll work up a monthly rate for you."

"That's so kind, but what about other guests?"

"What guests?" Dawn shrugged. "This is Cold Creek. even with Skye, I'd have four extra rooms. It's not like people are beating down the door to stay here." Abbie noted the melancholy in her voice and suspected a bit of cynicism as well.

"I hope that will change soon. I see the day coming when you'll have a waiting list."

Dawn grinned. "I wish I had your optimism."

"What about the man I saw here last night?"

Dawn leaned toward Abbie and lowered her voice. "Him I could do without. He's rude and ungracious. But he paid in advance for a week, so I shouldn't complain."

The phone rang and Dawn hurried to pick it up.

Abbie laughed. "That's probably another guest calling for a reservation." Dawn shook her head and smiled as she answered with her professional greeting, "Cold Creek Bed & Breakfast."

Abbie left the room to give Dawn privacy and to freshen up before breakfast. When she came back, Peggy had arrived with Emma. Emma flew into Abbie's arms. Peggy greeted her and Dawn.

Peggy set Emma's bag just inside the door. "She was upset this morning when she woke up and saw that you were gone. The girls managed to cheer her up though."

Abbie kissed her cheek. "I'm sorry, honey. I thought you liked the idea of staying overnight at Peggy's."

"I did, but I missed you."

Abbie hugged her closer. To Peggy she said, "Thanks for bringing her."

"No problem." She chuckled. "She's already had breakfast."

"Would you like to stay for coffee?" Dawn asked. "I have a fresh pot."

"Thanks, another time. I need to get the girls to school."

"Peggy…" Dawn raised an arm to stop her. "I'm running late this morning; would you mind dropping Cassie off as well?"

"Be happy to." Dawn opened the door to their private quarters and called up the stairs. "Cassie, are you ready to go?"

"Coming." Shoes clattered on the steps and a moment later, Cassie, dressed in a navy and white school uniform, burst into the room.

"Peggy's taking you this morning."

"Yah!" Cassie kissed her mother good-bye then stopped in her tracks when she saw Emma. Looking from Abbie to Emma she asked, "Is she yours?" Abbie introduced them. Cassie came closer and took hold of Emma's hand. "Do you like to play dolls?"

Emma nodded; her eyes wide with wonder.

"We can play when I get home from school. okay?"

"Okay."

"See you later." Cassie waved and hurried out the door.

Emma waved back and turned to her mother. "Can she be my new friend?"

Abbie chuckled as she kissed her daughter's cheek again before lowering her to the floor. "I think she already is."

"Breakfast is almost ready," Dawn announced.

"Wonderful. I'll put Emma's suitcase away and be right back."

A few minutes later Abbie came back to the dining room. The man she'd seen from the night before was sitting at the head of the table. He stood when she entered. "You must be Abbie Campbell." He reached a hand toward her.

Abbie let him shake her hand, but when he seemed intent on holding on to it a bit longer than appropriate, she pulled her hand back.

"Abbie," Dawn said as she set a platter of scrambled eggs on the table, "This is Douglas Perkins."

Chapter Twenty-six

Morning brought clarity and an answer to the question of where Jake had seen the sedan that had been parked at the B&B the night before. He kicked off the covers and hurriedly showered and dressed. He needed to go out to the B&B to warn Abbie. Of course, he could have simply called, but he wanted to go in person.

Once he'd gotten into his car and begun the drive to Cold Creek, he realized it was too late to warn her. They were probably eating breakfast together at that very moment. He lifted his foot off the gas pedal a bit, slowing the car to within the legal speed limit.

Before leaving the house, he'd called Jeff to let him know about Perkins staying at the B&B. Jeff hadn't been impressed. Jake supposed he was right. It was a free country, and if Perkins wanted to check into the B&B, there was nothing Jake could do to stop him. Still, the man's actions vexed him. He had no business being there.

Jake pulled into the parking lot at the B&B, but before getting out of the car he took several deep breaths and offered up a couple of prayers to get his emotions under control.

Abbie stiffened but managed to maintain her composure. "Mr. Perkins." She focused on helping Emma onto the chair.

"I feel as if I already know you," Perkins said.

"Oh?" What was he doing here? Had he come to make good on his threat? If so, why check into the B&B? She perused his face as he helped himself to a generous portion of eggs and sausage. He didn't seem threatening, and after dishing up servings for herself and a small portion for Emma, Abbie decided she was in no immediate danger.

"I understand you and your parents are the new owners of Cold Creek." His tone was pleasant enough, but did she detect a sliver of aggravation?

"Yes." Abbie pasted on a smile. "And I understand you were hoping to buy it."

"I was, but apparently there was some misunderstanding."

"These things happen." Abbie nodded. "I'm sure you'll be able to find another property suitable for your plans."

"I'll be looking at a number of them today."

The door opened and closed. Perkins looked up, surprise registering in his eyes. "Jake. I didn't expect to see you out here. I'd planned to meet you at your office in town. Didn't you get my message?"

Jake seemed taken aback by his comment. "No, I didn't." Not waiting for an invitation, he seated himself at the table between Abbie and Perkins. He shot her a questioning look.

"Hello, Jake." Dawn set a steaming stack of blueberry pancakes on the table. "Would you like some breakfast?"

"I would, if you don't mind." He turned toward Perkins. "You wanted to look at some property?"

"Yes. around one o'clock if that's all right with you."

"Sure." Jake nodded and helped himself to the eggs. Abbie allowed herself to relax and began to help Emma with a pancake. For someone who'd already eaten Emma was making a good-sized dent in her breakfast.

Her edginess at Perkins being at the B&B settled into curiosity. Jake was here and later would be taking Douglas Perkins to look at property. She still wondered why the man had chosen to stay at the B&B when Cold Creek was no longer available to him.

When Perkins had finished his meal, he excused himself and went to his room.

He'd no sooner gone than the phone rang. Dawn answered it. "Sure, Jeff. Hold on a second. I'll get her."

Jeff? "Maybe he has some news about Skye." She hurried to the phone.

"Hello, Abbie." The tone in his voice gave Abbie the impression that the news wasn't going to be good.

"Did you find her?"

"They found your car. Unfortunately, Skye wasn't in it. She apparently abandoned it, out of gas, in downtown Portland. Tim is on his way to Cold Creek with the car as we speak.

"I don't understand. Why would she leave it? She had money. She could have bought gas."

Jeff hesitated before putting into words something she already suspected. "Do you really think she'd spend the money on gas?"

Anger flared and died as quickly as a match. As much as she wanted to deny Jeff's suspicions, she couldn't. "You're probably right. I'd like to believe otherwise, but I need to face facts. She's an addict. Denial on my part isn't going to change that."

"I'm sorry, Abbie. As soon as we hear anything more, I'll let you know."

Abbie thanked him and hung up. She turned to find Jake standing beside her. She gave him the condensed version of Jeff's report.

Jake drew her into his arms. "I'm sorry."

Abbie leaned against him, soaking up the comfort he offered. Jake kissed her forehead and stepped back, his hands resting on her shoulders. "We can still pray and hope she turns around."

"Thank you, Jake." Part of her wanted to stay right there beside him. But she'd promised herself that she wouldn't rely on him. Needing to keep her distance, Abbie went back to the dining room where Emma was drinking the last of her milk.

After excusing herself, Abbie took Emma to their room where she could wash the syrup off her hands and face. She gave Emma her dolls and settled her in the living room. Jake was still there.

"What are your plans for the day?" he asked.

"I'll wait for Tim. If he gets here with my car early enough, I thought I'd run into Oceanside to pick up the rest of our clothes. Brent will be here after lunch to go through the buildings with me."

"Looks like I'll have a full day as well." He frowned. "I need to get back to the office. Truth is, I drove out this morning as soon as I realized that Perkins was here. Wish I'd realized last night it was his car."

"No harm done. I don't think he's a threat to me, Jake. He seems to be okay with my buying Cold Creek, though I don't know why he'd stay here."

"Maybe he likes the setting. Just be careful. I'll talk to Brent about him. In the meantime, I need to get to the office—see what other calls I've missed."

"Jake, I feel like a broken record by asking so often, but is there any news about Barbara?" He shook his head. "Nothing. Jeff says they may have lost their window of opportunity. The first few days of an investigation are the most important. They have no crime scene and no evidence connecting anyone to the murder."

Abbie thought about the old newspaper article she'd seen in Travis's kitchen drawer. Should she say something about it? Truth is, she should have shown it to Jeff or the sheriff right away, but she'd been afraid to call attention to herself for fear they'd discover her crime.

She still couldn't believe that Leah hadn't called the police. Maybe she had and then not followed through by pressing charges.

"Jake." She reached out to him as he turned to go. "There's something I need to tell you." After explaining what she'd found in Travis' kitchen drawer, Jake stared out the window.

"I don't know what to say, Abbie."

"I know he's your friend, but Travis told us he didn't know about her connection to the robbery. At the time, I thought he was telling the truth."

"I'm sure he was."

"Then how do you explain the article being there?"

"The real killer could have planted it. Travis would have no reason to hide something like that. I don't think he knew it was there." His eyes clouded with questions and disbelief. "Do me a favor and don't say anything to the authorities yet. I'd like a chance to talk to him. If it's still there, I'll tell him to take it to Jeff."

"You mean confront him? Are you sure that's wise?"

Jake nodded. "He's my friend, and regardless of how it looks, I trust him."

Jake left, saying he intended to visit with Travis right away. Abbie gathered her wits and took Emma for a walk to the library, where Sam showed them the children's books.

* * * * *

Travis welcomed Jake and within a few minutes the two old friends were sitting on the deck overlooking the lake. The article Abbie had told Jake about lay in a plastic bag on the table between them. Travis had opened the drawer and begun to lift it out when Jake stopped him. If his friend hadn't known about it, his prints wouldn't be on it, but someone else's might.

"You need to show it to Jeff," Jake said.

179

Travis frowned and ran a hand through his unruly hair. "I know you're right, but what do I say? It's already looking bad for me. The less they find evidence-wise to implicate someone else, the more the sheriff points toward me. Jeff's the only reason I'm not sitting behind bars already. If I show this to Jeff now, he'll have to show it to the sheriff. Jeff will probably think I'm guilty too."

"Not Jeff. He'll believe you, but I see your point. He'll be forced to show it to the sheriff." Jake stroked his stubbly chin. He'd forgotten to shave. "But remember, your prints aren't on it."

"Maybe not, but that's not going to make a difference." Travis fingered the corner of the bag. "Too bad Abbie found it. I could have tossed the thing in the fire."

Jake shook his head. "You don't want to do that. I'm thinking that whoever planted it is looking to blame you. Since you dated Barbara, you're an easy target. He might find another way to point the finger at you, and it might be a lot worse than an article."

"An article that apparently catches me in a lie."

"You know what you need to do, Trav. It'll go easier on you if you talk to Jeff. Tell him you had no idea it was in the drawer until Abbie mentioned it to me and I told you. Even if the sheriff doesn't believe you, the evidence is circumstantial at best. We'll get a lawyer if we need to."

Travis sighed and shook his head. "I still can't believe Barbara is gone. I wish now I had been a little more aggressive in trying to find out what she was doing and who she might have been with."

"Don't blame yourself. I could say the same thing. According to Jeff and detective Meyers, she may have been looking for that bank robber. This article might hold the key to her death. Maybe she found the guy."

Travis stared out at the lake. "Guess I don't really have another option. I'll run this into Jeff this morning."

"Or have him come out here," Jake said. "Maybe he can lift some prints from the counter or the drawer."

Travis shook his head. "If there were prints, they aren't there now. I'd have wiped everything clean."

Jake left after a few minutes and, in his rearview mirror, noticed Travis backing his motorcycle out of the carport. Seconds later, Travis sped by. The road from Cold Creek to the lake stopped at Travis's place. Jake wondered if Abbie would extend it. He hoped not. He liked the wilderness of the coastal range.

When he drove past the B&B, he noticed that Abbie's car hadn't been returned—either that or Tim had brought it and she'd gone into town. Perkins' dark blue sedan was gone as well.

He caught sight of Travis several times as they maneuvered the curvy road into Oceanside. Jake hoped he had given Travis the right advice regarding the article. Jake worried about the outcome. Even without the article, Sheriff Moore had been ready to blame Travis. Maybe he should have advised his friend to burn the article after all.

Chapter Twenty-seven

Abbie reached her parents' home just as her mother was coming out to work in her garden. Dressed in jeans and a loose cotton-print top, she greeted them with a wave. "Hi, you two. You're just in time to help me pull weeds and gather some vegetables for lunch." After hugging them both, she proceeded into the small shed attached to the garage.

"I know how to pull weeds. Margie showed me." Emma took her grandmother's hand.

Abbie hesitated. "That sounds like fun, but I just came by to get the rest of our clothes. We'll be staying at the B&B after all." Abbie had hoped to spend more time with her mother, but with Brent coming after lunch, she needed to step up her plans.

"I figured as much." Her mother plucked a straw hat from a peg on the wall and disappeared inside for a moment. When she emerged, she had a basket of gardening tools. Abbie could tell the news disappointed her but also knew she wouldn't admit to that disappointment. Show business did that to people. Not that she wanted her mother to object.

"Can I help, Nana?" This from Emma, who'd poked her head into the shed to watch.

"Only if Mommy says you can."

Emma bounced and grinned. "Goodie. Mommy say yes. Please." Abbie sighed as expectant gazes locked with hers. She'd wanted the trip to be short but felt herself waver, then realized that having Emma stay with her mother would work out well. "Tell you what. If Nana doesn't mind, I'll let you stay here and help her while I go back to Cold Creek to meet with Brent. Then I'll come back and get you."

"And you'll stay for dinner?" Carlene asked.

Abbie chuckled. "Absolutely."

As Abbie pulled out of the driveway, she noticed a rusted red pickup parked a few houses away. As she drove past, the driver ducked out of sight. All she could see was the green plaid of a shirt or jacket. At first, she wondered if someone had been following her, but as she made her way toward Cold Creek, Abbie tossed the idea aside.

More than likely, the driver was reaching for something on the floor or in the glove box. she wished she could stop being so paranoid. still, as Jake had told her, she needed to be on her guard.

*****

For the next two weeks life settled into a routine of sorts for Abbie. still, she continued to feel unsettled. They had heard nothing from Skye, and Douglas Perkins was still using the B&B as his temporary home. His being there had unnerved Abbie at first, but she'd become accustomed to having him around. Almost.

Most afternoons he looked at property with Jake. There was certainly nothing illegal about his being there, but his methods seemed odd to Abbie. He apparently wanted something in the area and hadn't found it yet.

As for Barbara, the police hadn't been able to crack the case. According to Jake, Travis had turned the newspaper clipping over to the authorities. There'd been some flurry over it, with the sheriff wanting to make an immediate arrest. However, Travis's prints hadn't been on it and the article wasn't enough to make a case against him, so the matter hung there, suspended over them all like some dark and mysterious cloud.

She didn't want to think about Barbara but couldn't help it. She had gone to the library to learn more about the bank robbery Barbara had been so obsessed about.

According to the newspaper records, the gunman had been masked. In the struggle to take one of the women as a hostage, his mask had come off. With the bank employees' help, a police sketch artist had put together a likeness.

Abbie studied the grainy drawing. Had Barbara seen someone in the Cold Creek area who resembled this man? If so, why not go to the police?

Perhaps she thought they wouldn't listen. Had Barbara called them so often with false leads that they no longer considered her information viable? If that were the case, she might have wanted to give the police proof.

Travis had told them that she'd cancelled their date just before she disappeared; that she'd had a meeting. Had that meeting been with the bank robber?

Frustrated, she'd made a few notes and gone back to the B&B. There were too many questions—too many missing pieces. Now, as she contemplated Barbara's death again, she wondered if she might be able to find more information. Tim could dig into the case for police details that hadn't appeared in the papers. But would he? Probably. No, she wouldn't ask that of him. Maybe she could talk to Jeff again. On the other hand, why not talk to Barbara's family in Portland? Maybe they could fill in some of the missing pieces. True, the police had talked with them, but they may have missed something.

Dawn had vacated the kitchen by the time Abbie decided to give Jake a call. Judging by the sound of the vacuum cleaner upstairs, Dawn was busy. Abbie would call her mother to see if she'd take Emma for the day. Then she'd let Jake know of her plans and hope he could join her. They hadn't spent much time together lately and she missed him.

Abbie didn't know why she felt so determined to investigate Barbara's murder. Perhaps the driving force came from the fact that she had found Barbara's scarf, which led to finding her body. Or, perhaps she feared that Barbara's death was somehow connected to the note she'd received before purchasing Cold Creek.

None of that mattered really. All she knew was that she felt obligated to Barbara in some strange way.

Besides, going to Portland would give her a chance to look for Skye. She had no idea where to start, but she had to try.

Abbie made her phone calls, took Emma to her mother's, and stopped at Jake's office.

Though he'd initially tried to talk her out of going to see Barbara's parents, he relented. and Abbie didn't think it was only to accompany her. They'd talked often of his colleague's death and Abbie knew the going-nowhere investigation played on his mind as much or even more than it did hers.

When she arrived at Jake's office, Jeff was sitting in the chair in front of Jake's desk with his feet propped on the top. He lowered his legs when Abbie came in. "Hi, Abbie."

"Hi, Jeff. Good to see you again." Her greeting came with a smile, but at the same time, she gave Jake a questioning look.

Jake cleared his throat. "I called Jeff to get Barbara's parents' phone number."

Jeff sighed. "I have it, but I'm not sure I should give it to you."

"We could get it easily enough. There aren't that many Nichols in the phone book."

Jeff nodded. "That's true. What do you hope to learn by going there? We've already questioned them, and they weren't able to give us any new information."

Abbie sighed and shrugged. "I can't stop thinking about Barbara. There are so many unanswered questions, like what did she do after the robbery? Why after five years would an article end up in Travis's kitchen drawer? What happened to the woman who was taken hostage? Why did Barbara come here to Cold Creek?"

"That's what we keep asking ourselves, Abbie, and we keep coming up empty. I can't stop you guys from going to see her folks, but I'm not sure it's a good idea."

"I understand your concern, but I feel such a strong connection with Barbara. It can't hurt to talk to them. since I'm now the owner of Cold Creek, and I found her scarf, I'm involved. Maybe I can learn something." She licked her lips. "I don't know, really. The idea of talking to them came to me, and I'd like to follow through."

Jeff rose. "I can't keep you from going. If you do learn anything that might be helpful to the case, I'd appreciate you letting me know."

"Of course." Abbie breathed a little easier. She was stepping into the unknown, but it felt like the right thing to do.

Jeff handed Jake a piece of paper. "Here's the number." Turning to Abbie he said, "I imagine you also plan to check on your sister." She nodded, feeling like she was being cross-examined and warned at the same time.

"I'm giving you the name of the officer I talked to on the narcotics squad. He has orders to bring her in if he locates her."

"Thank you."

"Talk to him. and don't go looking for her on your own."

* * * * *

Jake had agreed to go with Abbie for one reason only—okay, make that two. He wanted to protect her and didn't want her carrying out any harebrained schemes alone. He had no doubt that she'd ignore Jeff's warnings and try to locate Skye on her own.

Plus, he wanted to be with her as much as possible. Of course, he'd been elated to be able to cancel his plans to meet with Perkins. Jake suspected the man had no intention of buying anything, yet still hadn't been able to figure out why he kept looking. While he hadn't been exhibiting any threats, Jake felt certain he was up to something.

"Thanks for coming with me." Abbie shifted in her seat, turning to face him.

Jake met her eyes for a moment and thought about stopping the car and kissing every concern and thought from her mind except for him. He reached over to take her hand. "My pleasure." He cleared his throat and added, "I'm still not sure why we're doing this. It's been five years since the robbery. We don't know for certain if it has anything to do with Barbara's death. What do you think we'll find that the police haven't?"

"I don't know. I want to know what happened to her and maybe her parents can help."

Jake had called from his office to set up an appointment with Barbara's parents. He'd met them when he'd gone into Portland for the funeral and they were open to seeing him and Abbie. Jeff hadn't been too happy with the plan but, as he said, it was a free country. "How is the renovation coming?" he asked.

"Good. Those three guys are perfect." She grinned. "The remodels are going slower than I expected, but they're thorough. Both the saloon and the house are shored up. They had to replace some rotting beams in the basement of both places. Brent said he was surprised at what good shape the buildings were in. Keith has been cleaning and tearing out wallpaper and preparing to paint. Travis is repairing and refinishing the woodwork." She laughed. "All that to say I'm thrilled with the way things are coming together."

"Good." Jake eyed the rearview mirror, startled to see a dark sedan behind him.

"What's wrong?" Abbie slipped her hand out of his. "Probably nothing. The car back there looks like Perkins'." Abbie twisted around to look then turned back. "It does, but why would he be following us?"

Jake shook his head. "He probably isn't." Jake shared his suspicions about Perkins with her. "I wish I knew why he was hanging around. I don't trust the guy."

"Neither do I. He makes me nervous." Abbie clasped her hands and sighed. "I wish he'd go back to California."

"Me too, but there's not much we can do about him. Maybe he's hanging around hoping you'll change your mind about Cold Creek."

"That's not going to happen. Maybe we should just come out and ask him what his plans are."

"I have," Jake admitted."

"What did he say?"

"Not much. He told me he'd know the right property when he found it."

The dark sedan pulled to within a few feet of Jake's Cadillac. Much too close. Catching sight of the driver, Jake gasped. "It's definitely Perkins."

Jake gripped the steering wheel and pressed his foot to the accelerator as he took in the terrain around them. They were driving through the coastal range along a curved road with steep drop-offs to the right. He managed to create sufficient space between the two cars, but Perkins closed the gap.

"Hold on. I think he's going to hit us from behind."

Chapter Twenty-eight

Abbie ducked and closed her eyes, braced her feet against the floor and her hands against the dash, waiting for the impact. Jake's arm pressed her against the seat. A jumble of thoughts raced through her head. Thank the Lord Emma wasn't with them. She didn't want to die, and yet death seemed inevitable the way they were racing through these mountains. Had God given her so much only to take it away?

When nothing happened except for hearing a honking horn and the roar of an engine. Jake's arm no longer secured her. Abbie looked up.

"He passed us." Jake lifted his foot from the gas pedal. A look of fury flashed across his face. "I don't get it. I could have sworn he meant to force us off the road. I'm sorry for the scare."

"It's okay. Why did you think he was going to hit us?"

"He came up too fast for one thing and was following way too close. I guess my imagination went into overdrive. I've been building him up as a bad guy."

"Maybe he only meant to frighten us."

"Or intimidate." Jake hauled in a deep breath and released it.

"He succeeded. On the other hand," Abbie added, "maybe he's just a terrible driver."

"Humph. One way or the other, the guy is trouble." He glanced over at her. "Are you all right? Sorry about the restraint—it's an automatic reaction."

Abbie reached over and placed her hand on Jake's arm. "I'm fine. I do the same thing with Emma." She let her arm drop and looked away. Even in their brief exchange, she saw too much in those blue eyes. He stretched his arm across the seat, and she knew he wanted to put his arm around her. It would be so easy to lean on him. So easy to fall under his spell. But no. She couldn't let herself become attached to Jake. She couldn't give in to the desire she saw in his eyes. She couldn't let herself fall in love.

It's too late for that, Abbie Campbell. Love came the moment your eyes met his and you danced to "Strangers in the Night." Doing the exact opposite of what she intended, Abbie scooted across the bench seat and rested her head on his shoulder. He kissed her cheek as his arm went around her, and for one precious moment, Abbie felt that her heart had found a home.

"Abbie."

"Hmm?" she turned her head, admiring his profile and luxuriating in the warmth of his embrace.

"I…" He pressed his lips against her forehead. He was going to tell her he loved her. The realization stopped her cold. She wasn't ready to hear those words if it meant having to return them. She couldn't do that. Not yet.

She pressed her fingers against his lips to silence him.

Jake seemed to understand. He turned his attention back to the road, seemingly content to have her sitting beside him.

*****

They arrived in Portland shortly after noon, and Jake stopped at a hamburger place so they could, as he put it, refuel. When they returned to the car, Abbie stayed on her half of the bench

190

seat. Lunch had given her perspective and turned her thoughts from romantic feelings to the gritty hard-core job she'd fashioned for herself— that of finding out more about Barbara and hopefully uncovering something that might help the police find her killer.

Barbara's parents lived in the Rosemont district. The two-story house, a white Cape Cod with dormers, had a wraparound porch and looked welcoming. Two large maples grew on each side of a concrete walkway. Since they had arrived fifteen minutes early for their one-thirty appointment, they waited in the car while Abbie rehearsed in her mind what to say to these grieving parents. Had she made a mistake in coming?

A few minutes later, a woman stepped out onto the porch and waved them in.

Abbie started up the walkway, feeling anxious as a child asked to read aloud in class. She wasn't ready.

"You must be Abbie and Jake." The woman smiled as she held open the door and motioned for them to enter. She'd wound her graying hair in a twisted knot at the top of her head. A white apron circled her full figure, and she wore a blue and pink floral-print housedress that reached the middle of her calves. Though she was about the same age as Abbie's mother, Mrs. Nichols looked much older and reminded Abbie of Leah.

"Yes." Abbie hesitated. "Mrs. Nichols, thank you so much for agreeing to talk with us."

"Call me Rosalie. and you're welcome." Her smile faded "Come in and meet my husband."

Once inside, she introduced them to George, who rose from his easy chair to shake their hands. "You came to talk about Barbara?" His gruff voice and sagging jowls gave him the look of the bulldog that lay unperturbed beside the chair. The dog raised a sleepy eye to peer at them before snorting and subtly changing positions.

"That's Oscar," Rosalie said. "he's not much of a watchdog, but we love him."

"Please, have a seat." She motioned to a sage-green couch. "Can I get you anything—coffee, tea? I made some peanut butter cookies this morning."

Abbie started to decline but caught herself. Rosalie had gone out of her way to welcome them. The last thing she wanted to do was hurt her feelings. "Coffee would be great, and I love peanut butter cookies."

"I second that," Jake said as he sank onto the couch. She left the room and Abbie took a seat next to Jake, leaving the padded rocking chair for Rosalie.

In the ensuing silence, Abbie's gaze skimmed over the fireplace mantel that held a vase of fresh flowers and a photo of a young woman.

"That was Barbara's graduation picture," George said.

A lump formed in Abbie's throat. She hadn't seen a photo of Barbara before, and this one was slightly out of focus. She had a beautiful smile and sky-blue eyes. The photo next to it showed two young women with the seashore as a background.

"Who's this?" Abbie asked.

"A friend." George frowned. "I forget her name."

Abbie wondered if she was the woman who'd been abducted. Abbie slid her gaze to the fireplace and used a knuckle to wipe the gathering moisture from her eyes. Seeing the photos brought the tragedy into stark reality. someone had murdered this girl—Rosalie and George's daughter.

"Don't know what we can tell you that we haven't already told the police," George said.

His out-of-the-blue comment startled her.

"I don't know either," She said, "but I felt as though I needed to see you—talk with you about her."

"As I told your wife on the phone," Jake said, "Barbara worked with me in my real estate office. We miss her."

"She never talked much about her job." George reached down beside him to rub Oscar's head.

Rosalie set a large silver serving tray on the coffee table in front of the sofa. "Probably because she didn't care much about it. All she could think about was that bank robbery. She was obsessed with it. Her best friend, the one in that picture you were looking at, was the one that got kidnapped."

"Barbara must have been devastated." Abbie stirred cream and sugar into the brew.

Rosalie nodded. "Went to pieces. I kept thinking she'd get over it, but the more time that went by, the worse she got. She quit her job at the bank and at one point she even tried to kill herself." Rosalie stared into her cup. "Pills."

"I'm so sorry." Abbie knew only too well what Barbara must have felt during that time. In her own grief, Emma was the only thing that had kept her from taking her life after she lost Nate and little Ashley.

"We found her and got her to the hospital in time. After a while, she seemed to pull herself together. Barbara never said much about the robbery after that. We thought she'd moved on. She studied and got her real estate license, and then one day decided to move to Oceanside." Rosalie nodded toward Jake. "That's when she went to work with you."

Jake nodded.

"Said she needed to get out of Portland." George leaned forward, resting his elbows on his legs. "All this time we thought she'd come to terms with the robbery and losing...."

"Valerie, Rosalie supplied. "That was her friend's name."

"But she hadn't come to terms." Abbie lifted a cookie from the plate. The last thing she wanted right then was food.

"Not at all." Rosalie bit her lip. "We know now that she had collected everything she could find related to the case. She kept boxes full of information—newspaper articles, journals, pictures. Broke my heart."

Abbie's pulse quickened. "You have those boxes? Here?"

Rosalie nodded. "We found them in her bedroom after..." She stopped and tipped back her head as if doing so could stop the pain. Rosalie pulled a tissue from the box beside the rocking chair and apologized. "After the funeral, I went to her room to be close to her. She'd stored the boxes on the shelf in her closet along with her school mementos. I had only meant to look at the school albums, but…" Rosalie bunched her apron in her hands.

When she didn't go on, Jake asked, "Did you see anything that might explain why she went to Oceanside?"

"I don't know." Rosalie set her cup down on the small round table beside her chair. "She wrote things down. I could show them to you."

"Please," Abbie said.

Minutes later Rosalie out three large shoeboxes and set them on the dining room table. Abbie and Jake moved to join her. For over an hour, they sorted through the boxes. One contained articles like the one she'd seen in Travis's kitchen drawer and in her research at the library.

What provided the best insight were Barbara's journal entries. She didn't write every day and, as far as they knew, hadn't started until a year or two after the bank robbery. The entries clearly showed her frustration with the police as well as her grief over the loss of a friend. She had written down several names along with where she had seen them that compiled a suspect list. she'd also listed area bank robberies—three of them occurring on the Oregon coast.

These robberies, Barbara wrote, were connected to the bank robbery in Portland. The police agreed, but the cases remained unsolved. Her last entry in the journal talked about doing whatever she had to do to find the man who'd abducted and probably killed Valerie.

"When did she move to Oceanside?" Abbie closed the journal and set it aside.

"Two years ago. she'd been selling real estate here and said she needed a change of scenery." Rosalie closed her eyes for a moment. "I knew it must have had something to do with the robbery. She'd stopped talking about it by then, but I can see now that she rarely thought of anything else."

Jake leaned back. "Have the police seen these?"

Rosalie shook her head. "No. Do you think they'll want to."

"There could be some valuable information here," Abbie said. "If it's all right with you, we can take them with us. We can get them to authorities in Oceanside."

"Will we get them back?"

"Eventually," Jake answered. "The police will want to hold onto them for a while at least."

As they repacked Barbara's boxes, Abbie stared at the five-by-seven artist's sketch of the bank robber. The larger picture made his features easier to see. He looked vaguely familiar. A chill shuddered through her as she thought about the people she'd met in Oceanside and Cold Creek. Could the man in the police sketch be one of them? Several of the men, including Travis and Jake, seemed to fit the description. She frowned. The drawing was simply too generic.

Upon leaving the Nichols' home, Jake headed toward downtown Portland, where they stopped at the police station. When they announced who they were and what they wanted, the officer at the desk asked them to take a seat. Minutes later, another officer led them back through a secured door and into an office.

It took less than a minute for the detective to arrive. He was tall and gangly and dressed in a suit, with his tie hanging loosely around his neck.

"Abbie, Jake," He said as if he knew them. Extending a hand to Jake and then Abbie, he introduced himself as Detective Ellsworth. "I just got off the phone with officer Stuart in Oceanside. He said you'd be coming in." The detective placed a file on the table and gave Abbie an assessing look.

"I understand that you're Skye Grant's sister."

Abbie nodded. "Have you found her? Is she…?" She pressed her lips together.

"We may have."

Abbie gripped Jake's hand, preparing herself for the worst. "Please tell me she's okay."

"We got a call last night from the hospital, saying they had a Jane Doe. We started looking at our missing person file. She fits your sister's description, but her face is badly beat up, so it's hard to tell. She didn't have any ID on her."

"Can I see her?"

Detective Ellsworth nodded. "I'll take you there myself."

Chapter Twenty-nine

Twenty minutes later, Jake and Abbie followed the detective into the hospital parking lot where he was waiting for them.

Detective Ellsworth led them to the elevator and took them to the medical surgical ward. Abbie could hardly breathe. she hoped the woman they'd found was someone else and at the same time prayed it would be Skye.

Abbie had to lean on Jake for support as she walked into the room. A nurse, who stood on the opposite side of the bed, adjusting an IV, looked up.

"Any change?" the detective asked.

"I'm afraid not. She still hasn't spoken."

"This is Abbie Campbell. I'm hoping she can identify our Jane Doe."

The patient shifted and made a sharp mewing sound.

Abbie stared at the small figure lying in the center of the bed. She looked more like a child than an adult.

The detective had told them that their Jane Doe had been beaten, but nothing could have prepared Abbie for the sight that greeted her. Her heart seemed to implode, sending shock waves through her entire body. Her knees buckled, and she tightened her hold on Jake's arm.

"It's Skye. It's my sister." Her baby sister's face was puffy and misshapen, like some grotesque mask. Bandages covered one side of her head. What Abbie could see of her hair was tangled and matted with dry blood. Her eyes were closed and swollen.

"Skye." Abbie lunged forward, releasing Jake's arm and gripping the bedrail. Skye groaned in an awkward attempt to lick her dry, cracked lips. Abbie closed her eyes for a moment. She was the eldest, the strong one. Falling apart was not the answer. Skye needed her now more than ever.

Abbie leaned over to take her sister's frail hand. "I'm here, sweetheart. Everything's going to be all right."

"A—" Skye struggled to raise her head.

"Shh." Abbie stroked Skye's arm. "Don't try to talk. Just rest. I'm here and I'll stay until we can take you home."

Skye seemed to settle down then. Tears slipped from her eye and trailed into her matted hair. Maybe it was the pain medication, or just relief, but Skye's breathing worked itself into a rhythm of sleep.

Jake came up behind Abbie and placed his hands on her shoulders. She leaned back against him. "Thank you for coming with me, Jake," she whispered.

"You don't have to thank me." Jake moved back to capture a beige plastic chair for her. She released Skye's hand and dropped into it.

The detective stepped over to the end of the bed. "Abbie, I'm going to need to talk with you and ask some questions."

She nodded.

The nurse, who had apparently stepped out of the room, came in with a clipboard and wanted a medical history. The next hour flew by as Abbie telephoned her parents and answered questions. Carlene insisted on coming to the hospital, but Abbie persuaded them to wait until Abbie could talk with the doctor.

"Maybe we can transfer her to the hospital in Oceanside," Abbie told them. "I'll call as soon as I hear anything."

By midafternoon things had quieted down. Abbie rested her head on the bed, still unable to believe what had happened. A woman in a white lab coat came in around six and introduced herself as Dr. Amanda Parish. "Your sister is a very lucky woman."

"So, I hear." Abbie watched as Dr. Parish woke Skye and began her examination.

After a few minutes, she took the earpieces of the stethoscope from her ears and hung the instrument around her neck. "The nurse said that you're hoping to transfer Skye to the hospital in Oceanside."

"Is that possible?"

"It is, but it won't be necessary. Skye's injuries look a lot worse than they are. She has no broken bones. Lots of bruises, yes. We had to stitch up some cuts on her face and along the side of her head. The worst was along her left jaw. It'll likely leave a scar, but it'll fade with time."

"Are you saying I can take her home?"

"If she's able to take fluids. I'm ordering a liquid diet for now. I think she should spend the night, and if all goes well, I'll release her tomorrow." She hesitated. "As for you taking her home, that will depend on the police."

"They wouldn't arrest her now, would they?" Abbie tried to wrap her mind around the impossible.

"The good news is that her lab work shows no sign of drug use."

Relief flooded Abbie. "Thank you."

When the doctor left, Abbie called Tim to let him know what had happened, but he'd already heard and was on his way.

Between Tim, Abbie, Jake, and the detective, they managed to get Skye released from police custody. Skye had not broken any laws in Portland that the police were aware of. The warrant for her arrest had come out of Lincoln County, and Tim would be able to transport her there as soon as she was released. Abbie, of course, dropped the charges, and the rest of the paperwork could be taken care of once they reached Oceanside.

By morning, Skye was able to take fluids well enough to discontinue the IV. The first words she said to Abbie came as an apology.

"I'm sorry I took your car and the money. I needed a fix so bad. I couldn't think straight."

"I wish you had come to me."

"I do too. When I got to Portland I hooked up with a couple of friends, but when I saw them, I couldn't believe how pathetic they were. I used to be just like them and here I was, planning to go back. I don't want to live like that, Abs." She reached for her water and took a sip.

Abbie held the glass for her. "Oh, Skye. I don't understand. If you walked away, how did you end up like this?"

"Jamal must have overheard us talking. I started to go but he blocked my way." She cringed and Abbie took hold of her hand. "It's all right now, Skye, he can't hurt you now."

"Can you give us a last name?" Detective Ellsworth asked.

"No. The only thing anyone called him was Jamal or Cobra."

"How about a description?"

"He's a big guy. Shaves his head. He has a tattoo of a Cobra on his—his right arm. It's scary. He told me I'd better stay put or he'd kill me. He made me stay with him. I managed to sneak away and…"

"Thank goodness someone found you," Abbie gripped her sister's hand.

"I know the guy you're talking about," the detective said. "We'll get him. A couple of our narc guys have been working undercover. In fact, you have one of them to thank for getting you here."

"Tell him I said thank you."

The detective nodded. "I'll do that." He glanced down at his notes. "One more question. I understand you took your sister's handgun."

"What?" Skye shook her head. "No. I didn't." Tears welled up in her eyes as she reached for Abbie's hand. "I took the money—but no gun. I didn't even know you had one."

The detective looked to Abbie for confirmation.

"I–it's still missing."

"I didn't." Panic edged Skye's voice.

"Shh. I believe you." Abbie held her close. If Skye hadn't taken the gun, someone else had. But who and why?

Hauling in a deep breath, Abbie set the worry aside. Right now, she needed to focus on her severely damaged sister.

The doctor discharged Skye after lunch. Abbie tucked Skye into the backseat and the two of them rode with Jake, while Tim took his car. They drove in tandem back to the coast.

*　*　*　*　*

They had no sooner settled Skye into her room at the Grant home than Jeff showed up with shocking news.

"It's Brent," Jeff said. "Someone ran him off the road as he was heading home from Cold Creek last night."

Chapter Thirty

"Is he all right?" Abbie and Jake asked together.

"He's alive. We only found him a little over an hour ago," Jeff said. "Peggy called us last night around midnight. Brent worked into the night sometimes, but never that late. We started looking for him. Finally found his truck down an embankment in the river. He'd managed to climb out through the window and make it to shore."

Abbie could hardly take it in. She immediately thought about Perkins and the scare he'd given her and Jake on their drive into Portland. "Do you know who did it?"

"Brent said it was someone driving a rusty red pickup. We found it alongside the road about a mile from Cold Creek."

"Sounds like Floyd Hunter's old rig," Jake said.

Abbie's thoughts jumped back to that day a couple of weeks earlier when she'd left Emma with her parents and driven to Cold Creek to talk with Brent. The pickup had been sitting off to the side of the road.

"It is Floyd's," Jeff said. "I talked to him this morning. He told me he hadn't driven it for a while and seemed surprised when he opened the shed and it was gone. I think he's telling the truth. seems strange, though, that someone would go to the trouble of taking Floyd's old truck."

"Maybe he's lying," Abbie said. "I don't know if it means anything, but when I first came to Cold Creek, his wife made it clear that they didn't want the town sold. I got the feeling they'd stop me from buying it if they could." Abbie also told the men about the pickup being parked near her parents' home.

Jeff made a notation in his small black notebook. "I'll keep that in mind, Abbie, but I really doubt that Floyd and Elsie would do much more than complain."

Abbie wasn't so certain of their innocence, but she let it go.

"This is crazy." Jake ran a hand through his hair. "Who'd want to hurt Brent?"

"Perkins?" Abbie heard herself say. The two men looked at her, apparently expecting her to go on. "Everything points to him. He was dealing with Barbara before she went missing. He's staying in Cold Creek, even though it's no longer on the market. He still wants the property, and maybe he thinks he can muscle his way in."

"Abbie's right. Perkins is up to something." Jake told Jeff about the incident they'd had coming into town. "It's like he's putting on the pressure and hoping Abbie will give up."

"That would be hard to prove, and I can't make an arrest because you suspect someone."

"You could question him," Abbie said.

"And I will."

Jeff and Jake left together. Jake promised to come back that evening. "We need to talk," Jake whispered in her ear as his lips brushed her cheek.

She didn't have much time to think about his comment or about all the bizarre happenings in Cold Creek. Emma, having awakened from her nap, had climbed into Abbie's lap to snuggle. The blanket she held was a favorite that Leah had made when Emma was born. The fraying worsened with every wash, but Abbie didn't have the heart to throw it away.

While she held and rocked her little one, Abbie let her mind wander back to Iowa and the farm and Nate, Daniel, Leah, and Murray. Though Nate's death and Leah's hostile takeover had spurred her to leave, there were good memories as well. No one could have been a more loving and doting grandmother than Leah. Having Emma was the one thing Abbie had done right.

Abbie was different now. She had come through the pain of losing Nate and Ashley. And Leah hadn't pressed charges. There had been no warrant for Abbie's arrest. She had taken good care of Emma and shown herself to be a worthy mother. Abbie considered calling Leah. The least she could do was to let her know that she and Emma were safe. Abbie erased the thought. She couldn't take the chance. On paper, Leah still had custody.

Abbie couldn't bear the thought of losing her Emma—not even for a moment. Maybe once her attorney was able to reverse the guardianship issue, maybe then. They all deserved an apology, especially Daniel.

Once Emma had fully awakened, Abbie gathered their things and bid her siblings and parents good-bye, promising to come back the following day. "My offer still stands," she told Skye. "When you feel up to it, come out to the B&B and help me take care of Emma."

"I'll think about it." Skye apologized again.

Abbie kissed her forehead. "You're forgiven. Just don't go back to that life again."

"Don't worry. I won't." She seemed sincere, but Abbie was fully aware of the addictive cycle.

After hugs, Abbie headed back to the B&B via Oceanside hospital, where she picked up a floral arrangement and card to take to Brent. Peggy greeted her and Emma as they came into the room. "Abbie, I'm glad you came by. Hi Emma. Good to see you again."

"Where your kids?" Emma asked.

"The girls are at school and the twins are home with my neighbor."

"I brought flowers." Abbie said. "I feel terrible. If Brent hadn't been working on my project, this wouldn't have happened."

Brent frowned. "You have nothing to feel bad about, Abbie. I've suspected things weren't right for a while now, but never thought anything like this would happen."

"What do you mean?"

He shrugged. "I thought maybe some kids were just fooling around in the hotel at night. or maybe a transient needed a place to sleep. Things were out of place, but nothing was taken or damaged that I could see. I locked up every night, but whoever it is must have a key or found another way in."

"How odd." Abbie settled into a chair, Emma on her lap. "You're sure nothing's been taken?"

"Not that I could see." Brent winced as he shifted in bed. His casted leg rested on a stack of pillows. "I mentioned it to Jeff and the sheriff. They didn't think the incidents were connected to being run off the road. I tend to agree. The sheriff thinks old Floyd had a few too many and didn't even know what happened."

Abbie didn't know what to think. She visited with her new friends for a few minutes more and then said her good-byes and drove out to Cold Creek.

So many things had happened, and Abbie felt they were all tied together somehow. With Emma tucked into the seat next to her, she mentally ran through the recent series of events, beginning with Barbara's death.

Perkins had claimed to be the first to put down earnest money, but Jake insisted her parents' offer had come in first. Then, there was the note telling her to leave while she still could.

She'd gone ahead with the purchase and Perkins decided to stay at the B&B. Why? Then, on the way to Portland, Perkins practically forced them off the road. Had he wanted to frighten them? Of course, it was possible that he was just a careless driver.

She couldn't forget the article in Travis's kitchen drawer or the possible connection with the bank robbery. and now, Brent, her contractor, had been run off the road and injured. Add to these events Brent's suspicions that someone had been in the saloon at night. She came up with nothing.

What did it all mean? And what could she do about it? Abbie sighed and turned her attention to Emma, who was chatting with her baby doll. The events were disconcerting at best, but at least she and Emma were still safe.

* * * * *

An older model Desoto was parked in the space Perkins had used. Had another guest checked in?

"Here you go, sweetheart." She helped Emma out of the car and handed her the doll. "Go on inside. I'll be right there." Abbie grabbed their jackets and the doll suitcase before heading in.

As she pushed open the entry door, she heard her daughter speaking to someone. She heard another voice as well. One she hadn't heard in two years but recognized immediately. She dropped everything and stared, openmouthed, at the man hunkered down in front of Emma.

"Daniel."

He straightened and held out his arms. Abbie, tears already sliding down her cheeks, ran into them. "I'm sorry, Daniel. I'm so sorry I used you. I didn't know what else to do."

"Shh. It's all right." His arms tightened around her. In the next moment, he lowered his head and kissed her.

Chapter Thirty-one

Abbie pushed away from him. "What—what was that?"

Daniel dropped his gaze to the floor. "I'm sorry. I wasn't thinking."

She apparently hadn't been thinking either. What confused Abbie was not that he had kissed her, but that for one heartfelt moment she had kissed him back.

Any joy she might have felt at seeing him shattered when her senses returned. "How did you... Why are you here?"

He looked down again, reminding Abbie of how quiet and shy he'd always been. She didn't need an answer. Somehow, he'd found her and if he was here, Leah couldn't be far behind.

"You know why I'm here, Abbie. I came to take Emma back home." He spoke so softly Abbie had to strain to hear him.

"I can't let you do that, Daniel."

A pained expression crossed on his face. "I'm afraid you don't have a choice. I have a court order." He reached into his shirt pocket and produced a letter.

She glanced at the legal document, stomach roiling. It had been signed by the same judge who'd given custody to Leah.

"I was supposed to bring a police officer with me." Daniel folded the letter and placed it back in his pocket. "But I couldn't do that. I wanted to talk to you first."

"Talk to me?" She drew Emma to her side and the child wrapped her arms around Abbie's leg as if she knew and felt Abbie's alarm. "About what?"

"I don't want you and Emma to be separated." Daniel folded his muscular arms across his chest. He reminded her so much of Nate. He had the same build—sinewy and all muscle. His brown eyes seemed to plead with her.

"It's not going to happen. I have an attorney."

"I know. That's how we learned you'd come here. Your attorney was asking questions about the case. A friend of Mom's at the courthouse got wind of it and—"

"I can't believe this." Abbie ran a hand through her hair. So much for discreetness and confidentiality.

"Look, Abbie, if it's any consolation, I don't want..." He glanced down at Emma. "Please hear me out. What I have to say could be best for all of us."

Daniel had been more than a brother-in-law during her years on the farm. He'd so often been her confidant, easing away her frustrations and anger with Leah and even at times with Nate. Even though he was Nate's younger brother, he'd always seemed wiser.

She would listen to what he had to say. He deserved that after the way she'd used him to escape.

"This isn't a good time." Abbie lifted Emma into her arms. Suddenly shy, Emma buried her face in her mother's neck.

"No hurry. I'm spending the night here. We can talk later."

She nodded. "You look good."

"You do too." He hadn't changed much except for a few crinkles around his eyes.

"Emma sure has grown up." He smiled and the tension between them seemed to melt away. "Don't suppose she remembers me."

Abbie swallowed back her remorse that wove itself around her heart. "She was only two." She'd taken Emma from this kind, gentle uncle who adored her. "Emma, this is your uncle Daniel." Emma raised her head. "Can you say hi?"

She shook her head and hid her face again, but this time she was smiling. Abbie tickled her. "You silly goose."

Before long, Daniel and Emma had become buddies and Abbie couldn't help but wonder if, on some deep level, Emma remembered him. Abbie had relaxed some too, and at dinner that night she marveled at how this soft-spoken Iowa farmer had refit himself into their lives. He seemed to harbor no ill feelings toward her, and for that, she was grateful. At dinner with Keith, Dawn and Cassie, he seemed comfortable as they talked about his trip and about how long he planned to stay. They didn't know why he was there, and Abbie didn't plan on telling them.

"If you want a job," Keith said, "We could use a hand with the remodeling Abbie has us doing." He began telling Daniel about Brent's unfortunate incident. "I'm taking over the house, but I'm sure Travis could use some help over at the hotel."

It was the most Keith had spoken since Abbie had met him. In fact, she hadn't seen him that much, with the family taking most of their meals in their private quarters. As he spoke, a strange sense of déjà vu came over her. Her mind went back to the newspaper articles and bits and pieces of information she'd pored over at Barbara's parents' home and to the sketch of the bank robber.

Keith caught her looking at him and winked, dispelling her thoughts. "Oops. I'm overstepping my bounds here. Abbie's the boss."

Abbie pushed aside her suspicions. For half a second she thought Keith resembled the sketch of the bank robber. But then, so did hundreds of other men including Jake and Travis. Pushing the idea from her mind she said, "No problem, Keith. Daniel could work with you and Travis if he wants, but he's probably not going to be here for long."

"I appreciate the offer. Might take you up on it." He glanced at Abbie. "I'll be here for a few days and there's nothing I hate worse than having nothing to do."

Keith nodded. "I'll show you around tomorrow."

Keith and Cassie went into their private quarters shortly after dinner so Cassie could finish her homework. Abbie helped Dawn with the dishes, after which she assisted Emma with her bath and tucked her into bed.

As she did so, Abbie found herself looking forward to visiting with her brother-in-law. After Nate's death, he'd been her rock and her best friend.

She remembered all too clearly those days after the funerals.

Leah blamed her for losing the baby, and Abbie had willingly absorbed the guilt. If she'd taken better care of herself, eaten better, maybe she wouldn't have miscarried. But Nate's death had left such an enormous hole in her heart she nearly ceased to exist. The doctor had told her that she was not in any way to blame. Her baby girl had had a heart defect and even if Abbie had carried her to term, little Ashley would have died soon after her birth.

Daniel had told her repeatedly not to take his mother's words to heart. "It's her way of grieving," he'd say. "She'll get past it."

But she didn't. Leah's disapproval grew more evident each day, and Abbie found herself spending more and more time thinking about going home to her parents. "I'd like to settle down there. Buy a house," she'd told Leah one day.

"Leave the farm? What about Emma? She needs us." Leah rolled her eyes and shook her head. "That is by far the most ridiculous idea I've ever heard. You and Emma belong here."

"Now Leah," Murray had said, "The girl wants to be close to her family. You can't blame her. What I want to know is where you plan on getting the money, Abbie. I hear that houses out west don't come cheap. I know you got money from Nate's insurance. That might be enough for a down payment, but what'll you live on?"

"I have money. My parents set up a trust fund for me and my sister and brother years ago. If I need to, I'll eventually get a job. I'm thinking I could paint and sell my work."

"Humph. how much money are you talking about?"

"Enough. around two million."

Murray whistled. "That's quite a chunk. I didn't know show people got paid so much."

"They can if they're famous. My parents recorded a number of records that still earn royalties."

"Why haven't we seen any of this money?" Leah asked, her eyes narrowing. "Lord knows we could have used some extra cash last year. Did you know we had to mortgage the farm to come up with enough money to ride out the winter?"

Abbie wished Nathan hadn't kept her financial situation a secret from his parents. "I told Nate I'd help out, but he didn't want me to. He wanted me to keep it for our own place and now…" she hesitated.

Daniel came to her aid, as he often did. "She's telling the truth, Mom. Nate didn't want her to use her money on the farm."

Leah picked up her crocheting. "You shouldn't be thinking about moving. It's too soon. Emma needs a stable environment."

"Emma will be fine."

"Will she?"

Abbie couldn't answer. Most days she was barely able to function. But she was Emma's mother. She could pull things together. Finally, Abbie said, "Yes. She needs to know her other grandparents too." Abbie stood. "I'm going to bed. see you in the morning." She caught Daniel's eye. He didn't want her to leave the farm either, but she knew he'd stand by her decision.

Abbie didn't go to bed that night. At around ten, she slipped down the stairs and let herself out the back door and down the long driveway. Her walk took her along the fields that now lay barren. The air smelled musty and slightly sour from the rotting vegetation that, once decayed, would be absorbed as nutrients into the already rich soil. Come spring the cycle would start all over again.

Was Leah right that the only stable environment was Leah's home? Would taking Emma away so soon after her daddy's death be too traumatic?

"What should I do, Nate? What's best for Emma?" Instead of her husband's reassuring voice, she heard nothing and felt only the chilling wind seep into the fibers of her cotton jacket.

Abbie knew she could no longer stay on the farm. Her soul felt as decayed as the dead plants littering the field. At the main road, she turned left and headed toward town. She wouldn't go far, just far enough to clear her head.

While she walked, Abbie weighed the pros and cons of staying in Iowa against moving to Oceanside. If her heart had any say at all, Oceanside would win. Every time she thought about living near her family, she felt ten pounds lighter, as if a heavy burden had been lifted off her shoulders. But she needed to think about Emma too.

Lost in thought, questions still unanswered, she turned into the road that led to the cemetery. A light in the churchyard glowed around her, lighting up her watch and letting her know it was a quarter past midnight. She hadn't planned to walk this far. Or maybe she had. Her legs ached from the three-mile trek as she padded through the grass to Nathan's grave.

She hadn't been here since the funeral.

Leah came every Sunday with a fresh bouquet of flowers, mostly brilliant blooms of dahlias from her garden. Every Sunday Leah asked Abbie to come with her. Every Sunday she declined as more guilt and anger washed over her. Abbie hadn't been ready to visit the grave, but Leah couldn't understand that.

Now she was here. she dropped to her knees and felt the dew from the grass seep into her jeans. "I shouldn't be mad at you, Nathan Campbell, but I am. I'm more angry than sad." She closed her eyes and sat back on her heels. "Why did you have to die? Oh, Nate, what am I going to do without you?"

Live. she could almost see him sitting there next to her. *Be happy.*

"I'm trying." Abbie saw headlights approach and swing into the church road. She shielded her eyes as the lights swung past her then went out. Daniel jumped out of the truck and started toward her, not speaking until he reached the spot where she was still kneeling.

"What are you doing out so late?" she asked.

"Worrying about you." His tone bore a hint of anger, but she heard compassion as well. He reached down, offering her a hand up. Abbie took it, and he pulled her to her feet.

"I'm okay. Just needed some air."

"Emma isn't," he said. "She had a bad dream and was looking for you. She told me you weren't in your room."

"I'm sorry." Abbie turned and headed toward the truck.

"She's all right now. I tucked her into your bed and told her I'd bring you home. She's probably sleeping by now."

Abbie stepped up into the pickup when Daniel opened the passenger side door and then waited for him to get in. "Thank you for taking care of her."

"Glad to do it. You should let one of us know if you're going somewhere."

"I had only planned on a short walk." She looked over at him. "Daniel, why does your mother hate me so much?"

"Hate you? Abbie, she doesn't hate you. She's afraid you'll leave us. So am I, when it comes down to it. We've just lost Nate, and now you're talking about leaving and taking Emma with you."

"It's not like you'll never see us again. We'll visit. And when she's older, Emma can come and stay for a week or two in the summer." Daniel picked up speed once he reached the main road. "When are you leaving?"

"Next Sunday."

"How are you getting to the train station?"

"I was hoping you'd take me."

He nodded. "You're sure that's what you want?"

"Yes." The affirmation sounded like a lie. "I have to do this, Daniel. I have to."

Daniel seemed to understand but warned her that his mother wouldn't let Emma go without a fight. In the end, Leah had won.

And now they had found them in their Oceanside retreat. She knew deep down that she couldn't escape their radar forever. Abbie seriously thought about packing a suitcase and slipping away after Daniel had gone to bed. She could go back to Grand Forks. Margie would welcome her with open arms. But no, she had told Jake that she'd stop running. She belonged here and Emma belonged here with her.

She wasn't the same woman now as the frightened, grief-stricken widow who had kidnapped her baby and run away. She was a mature woman who would face the dragon and win.

Abbie ducked her head and uttered a quick apology to God for thinking of her mother-in-law that way. She would hear Daniel out and, in the morning, she'd call Jake and the attorney. She wished Jake had come for dinner as he had developed a habit of doing, but with Brent in the hospital, he was probably helping Peggy and offering his support. While she missed him, she admired his devotion.

In her room, she closed the curtains and made sure the patio door was locked before going into the main room to talk with Daniel.

Daniel was waiting for her in the living room. He'd been talking to Perkins and when he saw her, he stood.

She glared at Perkins, her temper rising. "You. After that stunt you pulled yesterday, I can't believe you'd show your face here again."

"Huh?" Perkins looked as though he had no idea what she was talking about.

"You nearly ran Jake and me off the road."

A grin lit up his face. "You thought that? I was just speeding up to pass you."

Abbie shook her head. "What you did was irresponsible and dangerous."

"Sorry. Didn't mean any harm."

I'll just bet you didn't. "Let's go outside, Daniel," Abbie said. "I could use some fresh air."

Chapter Thirty-two

The air was crisp and cool, and Abbie felt a slight chill through her sweater. Daniel walked beside her in silence as she headed for the main part of Cold Creek.

Daniel stuffed his hands into his pockets. "I can't believe how beautiful and green it is out west."

Abbie nodded. "Of all the places we lived when I was a kid, the Northwest is my favorite. I love being near the ocean and in the mountains at the same time."

"Perkins was telling me that you and your parents bought this place."

"Yep." She told him about the artists' colony and shared her ideas. Eventually, the talk ran out and they walked in silence.

"You said you wanted to talk with me about something," She finally said.

He stopped and turned to face her. "First off, I want you to know that I disagree with my mother. Dad and I have been trying to talk sense into her from the beginning."

"Thank you for that."

"That said, taking Emma like you did broke her heart. She pushed you too hard and her plan backfired. After you left, she wanted to go to the police, but dad and I talked her out of it. In a way, I'm glad you resurfaced." He sighed. "And, in a way, I wish you hadn't. It's all started again. She's threatening to call the authorities this time. I told her to wait and let me talk to you first."

"Why? To persuade me to move back to Iowa?" Abbie started walking again. "There's no way that's going to happen."

"Abbie, please, just hear me out. She has the law on her side. Do you really think the court will grant you custody? You're living in a bed & breakfast. Your sister is a drug addict and you're planning to have her help you take care of Emma."

"How do you know all this?" Abbie's confidence seeped out like air in an inflatable mattress. Jake had been so sure of the attorney's ability to clear her.

"I had a long talk with Dawn."

"I thought you were on my side."

"I am. I haven't told my mother about Skye living with you. She already knows Skye's history." He pressed his lips together. "Do you know how bad this looks? Mom will follow through this time, Abbie. You broke the law when you took Emma. She could have you put in jail. You're planning to live in a commune with your sister, who is a known addict. Are you really willing to put Emma in that kind of danger?"

"Commune? Since when is my artists' colony a commune? And come to think of it, what exactly is wrong with a commune?"

"From what I've heard, you'll have all kinds of artists living out here. How do you know you can trust them?"

"Where is all of this coming from, Daniel?"

"I'm just saying that you need to look at the facts. If you were a judge, who would you grant custody to? A woman like my mother, who's lived on a farm all her life, who is active in her church and is well-established, or a single woman, an artist with plans to build an artists' colony, who has a drug-addicted sister for a babysitter? Do you even go to church, Abbie? Do your parents? How stable are they? They raised you on the road."

"My parents did an excellent job. Sure, they were entertainers, but they are good people."

"That doesn't matter. What matters is how things look."

Fear nipped at her nerves. What he was saying made sense. If a judge were to choose the suitable guardian for Emma, he'd choose Leah. What had she been thinking?

"I don't want you to lose Emma." Daniel wrapped his hands around her upper arms. "I've been thinking a lot about this and I know how we can work things out."

"How?"

"Marry me."

"Excuse me?"

"I've always cared for you, Abbie. You can keep Emma with you and Mom will have her grandchild back. Come back to Iowa, live on the farm. I'll build you that house you always wanted. I'll even add an art studio with lots of light."

Abbie stared at him. "How could you suggest something like this? You know how I felt living there. We talked about it often enough. and we're not...I don't... Your mother hates me."

"No, she doesn't. When you left, she missed you as much as she missed Emma. She hates what you did. But I know she'll forgive you. Just like I have."

"I can't..."

He silenced her with fingers pressed against her lips. "Pray about it, Abbie. My mother and father love Emma. She deserves to have her granddaughter close."

"So do my parents, Daniel. What about them?"

"They have money. They can come and visit. And they can stay in our spare room. I'll build the house big enough."

Abbie had no words to give him.

"I know you don't love me—not like a wife should love a husband, but we could make a good team. And maybe we could even learn to love each other that way." Abbie turned and walked away, leaving his insane suggestion hanging in the air.

It wasn't until she'd gotten ready for bed and reached for the light on the bedside stand that she saw it. A note had been neatly folded and propped up against the lamp with her name on it.

Not again. Her hand shook as she unfolded it.

Hi Abbie, Jake called. I told him you were out, and he said he'd see you in the morning. Sleep well. Dawn.

Relief settled her racing heart back into its parameters. She was far too edgy.

Abbie slept very little as Daniel's comments echoed through her head. Maybe his suggestion wasn't as crazy as she'd first thought. What if he was right? Could her plans and her lifestyle cause a judge to rule against her? Could she end up losing Emma after all?

She'd always gotten along with Daniel. Living with him wouldn't be so bad, especially if she could be in her own home. If she had to, she could do this for Emma.

Much had changed since she'd plotted her escape two years ago. She'd matured and moved beyond her grief. There had been times she had even missed the farm.

Maybe it wouldn't be so bad. She could almost envision herself painting again and possibly collaborating with local artists much as she had in Grand Forks.

What about Jake? She turned to her side and punched her pillow. Abbie had come to love him, but if walking away from him meant she could stay with Emma, then she had no choice. Abbie prayed herself to sleep, asking for strength and courage and wisdom.

Morning broke with far too many uncertainties and far too much confusion. Emma was still asleep, so Abbie slipped on her robe and made her way down the hall following the scent of fresh coffee.

Dawn must have heard her, because a steaming cup sat on the counter along with an envelope bearing her name. Dawn gestured toward it. "I found this tacked to the front door this morning." Abbie examined the smudged white envelope, noting the pinprick in its center. Her name had been written in block letters. Alarm bells went off in her head again. "I'm almost afraid to open it."

"You think it might be another threat?" Holding her mug in both hands, Dawn rested her elbows on the counter across from Abbie.

Abbie hauled in a long breath. "I feel silly. I went through this last night when I saw your note about Jake."

"I'm sorry. You were with Daniel and I didn't want to disturb you."

Abbie nodded.

"Would you like me to open it for you?"

Grinning at her, Abbie said, "Thanks, but I think I can manage." She slipped her finger under the flap and ripped it open. Inside was a folded piece of notebook paper. She hesitated for a moment before unfolding it. When she did, a lock of golden hair fell to the counter. "What in the...?" On the note, written in red ink, were the words:

It's time for you to go. Your life is not the only one in danger.

The hair was the exact color and texture of Emma's.

Chapter Thirty-three

Adrenaline soaring, Abbie raced back to her room. Emma still lay sleeping, safe and alive, but on the pillow lay several strands of hair. someone had come in during the night—possibly while she'd been with Daniel—and cut off a lock of her baby's hair. She gripped the railing on the youth bed, willing her insides to quiet.

Dawn had followed her in and now placed a gentle hand on her shoulder. "Thank the Lord she's okay. We need to call the sheriff."

Abbie nodded. "Could you? Please. I need to stay here with her."

"Of course." Dawn hurried out and Abbie reached down to pick Emma up.

Threatening her was one thing, but this—this blatant violation of her baby. She could hardly take it in. Who would do this?

Emma stirred and Abbie held her close. "There, there, sweetheart. Mommy's got you. Everything's going to be all right."

But was it? she lowered herself into the easy chair and stroked Emma's head and back. When she heard a knock, she lifted her gaze to see Daniel filling the doorway.

"Can I come in?"

"Please."

"Dawn told me what happened." He strode to the chair and kneeled beside her, cupping Emma's head.

A lump caught in Abbie's throat as she took in his gentleness and read the love in his eyes. She blinked away the sudden tears. "Someone doesn't want me here." Anger began to replace her fear. She didn't want to give in, yet what choice did she have? She felt cornered and bewildered.

"I know. Dawn told me about the first threat too." He shifted his gaze from Emma to Abbie. "Come home with me. Let me take care of you. Both of you."

She read compassion and concern in his eyes. Part of her wanted to say yes. "After the first note, I decided not to allow fear to dictate my life. Giving in to this maniac isn't the right answer. I can't let him win."

"You can't take the chance that he'll hurt Emma," he answered. "You'll be safe on the farm."

"Would we? Nathan wasn't." He looked away, but not before she saw the pain she'd inflicted. Nate's death had affected Daniel as much as it had her.

"That was an accident. Nate didn't deliberately set out to get himself killed."

"No, but he stepped in front of a raging bull."

"He was trying to save a guy's life."

"I know." Abbie placed a hand on his sun-browned arm. "I'm sorry."

He stood. "I'm going home tomorrow. I'd like to take you and Emma with me. If you decide not to come, I'll need to take Emma. There's no way I'm leaving her here, Abbie. I have a court order and if I have to, I'll use it."

He bent to kiss Emma's forehead. Then he cupped Abbie's chin and looked directly into her eyes. "Please, Abbie. Do the right thing." He brushed his lips against her forehead. His kiss went through her like a gentle rain. She could do nothing but stare after him.

Emma opened her eyes, cuddled for a few moments, and then wanted to know why she wasn't in her bed. "I wanted you to wake up, sweetheart. Uncle Jake will be here soon and we're going to spend some time with Nana and Papa." A plan formed as she uttered the words. Perhaps the safest place for Emma right now was at her parents' home. With four or five adults present, Emma wouldn't be alone for a minute, and Tim would be there to provide police protection.

Jake and sheriff Moore arrived just as Abbie finished dressing herself and Emma and packing their bags. Dawn showed the note to the sheriff.

"Abbie." Jake drew her forward and settled an arm around her shoulder. "I'm sorry. I thought we were in the clear."

Sheriff Moore set the note on the counter and shook his head. "There's nothing I can do here." Annoyance tinged his gravelly voice. "We have no idea who wrote it and unless it's acted on, there's nothing I can do." He lifted his belt with both hands, but it quickly settled below his stomach again. "For all we know, you could have written the notes yourself."

Abbie gaped at him, too angry for words. how could he be so unconcerned?

"That's the most ridiculous thing I've ever heard." Jake's nostrils flared as he balled his hands into fists.

Sheriff Moore shrugged. "Her parents are in show business. These people will do anything for attention."

"Thank you for enlightening us, Sheriff." Jake opened the door and stepped aside. "Sorry we bothered you. We'll let you get back to work."

When the sheriff stepped out, Jake slammed the door behind him.

"Can you believe that guy?" Dawn asked.

"He's an idiot." Jake stepped over to the phone. "I'm calling Jeff."

"What's the point?" Abbie asked. "The best we can do is to make certain Emma is safe." She told Jake about her plan to go back to her parents' place in Oceanside.

"I agree," Dawn said as she headed back to the kitchen and set out plates for breakfast. "Keith and Travis can keep an eye on things out here until Brent comes back."

Jake agreed and made his call to Jeff, asking him to meet them at the Grant's home.

Perkins joined them for breakfast and seemed taken aback about the note. His concern surprised Abbie, especially since he topped her suspect list. He was her only suspect other than Floyd and Elsie. And maybe Travis, but somehow, she couldn't see him as a person who would threaten a child.

As soon as they'd finished breakfast, Abbie called her parents, who were more than happy for them to stay. Abbie didn't tell them about Daniel. Time enough to do that when they got there.

He'd threatened to take Emma with him when he returned home to Iowa tomorrow, but she could probably persuade him to give her more time. She worried though that this new threat might make him more insistent.

* * * * *

After breakfast, Abbie drove into town with Emma in her car. Jake followed. She tried to get her mind around this latest threat. The writer hadn't followed through on the first warning. Several weeks had passed. She had not only purchased Cold Creek; she had begun the renovation. Why wait this long to surface again?

Once more she thought about Barbara and wondered if there might be a connection. And Brent—had the same person run him off the road? The questions circled around in her head and mingled with Daniel's ultimatum. Should she forget this craziness and go with him?

If she did go back to Iowa, it would be a permanent move. She wouldn't run away this time. And if Daniel didn't build the house he'd promised, she would do it herself. After all, she still owned Nate's part of the farm.

"How can you even think about going back?"

"Who's going back, Mommy? Back where?"

Abbie didn't realize she'd spoken aloud until she heard Emma's question.

She smiled and reached to take her daughter's hand. "Nowhere, honey. I was just thinking out loud."

"Oh." She didn't seem convinced. "Can Nana and me go to the 'musement park again?"

"Nana and I," Abbie corrected.

"You want to come too?"

Abbie chuckled. "Maybe."

"Can Unca Daniel come too? I like him."

"He's very nice."

"And Unca Jake too?"

"Hmm." Abbie made the noncommittal sound, wishing she and Emma had driven with Jake as he'd wanted, but she thought she might need her car. Somehow being with Jake gave her strength and made her feel safe. She sure could use some of that strength about now.

* * * * *

After seeing Abbie safely to her parents' place and waiting there to talk with Jeff and Tim, Jake had gone to work. Perkins had made yet another appointment, and he had plans to meet three other potential buyers as well. "I'll be back after dinner." He kissed Abbie good-bye. She hugged him, wishing he would stay and shelter her against the tide of confusion that threatened to wear her down.

"Are you going to be all right?" he asked. "I could cancel…"

Please stay. I need you here. Aloud she said, "You don't need to do that. I'm shaken up, but I'll survive."

225

"I'll see you as soon as I can get away." He kissed her again and as he drove off, Abbie ached with the realization that she might have to say good-bye forever.

That afternoon, after Abbie had put Emma down for a nap, she made iced tea and joined Skye on the porch swing. Most of the swelling had gone down on Skye's face, but the bruises had grown darker, more purple, blue, and green. "You look better."

"Liar." Skye's mouth slanted in a lopsided grin.

Abbie sipped at her tea, glad her sister was there and safe. At least for now.

"What are you going to do?" Skye asked after a long silence.

"About the note?" Skye nodded and pressed the chilled glass against her jaw.

"I don't know." Should she tell her about Daniel? "I need to do whatever I can to keep Emma safe."

"Are you going to run away again?"

Abbie shook her head. "Not this time. But…there is a chance I'll need to go away for a while."

"Like where?"

"Iowa." Abbie told Skye about Daniel and the court order.

When Abbie finished, Skye leaned her head against Abbie's shoulder. "You can't go, Abs. It's not fair. Leah can't do that to you— to us. And what about Jake? He's crazy about you."

Abbie sighed. "I haven't had a chance to tell him." The swing stopped and Abbie set it to rocking again.

"Jake won't let you go."

"He won't have a choice."

"Daniel's a jerk."

"He's doing what he thinks is best for Emma."

"Humph. he's following mommy dearest's orders. And to think I used to have a crush on him."

"Really? I didn't know that."

"You were too starry-eyed over Nathan. Daniel danced with me at the wedding." Skye sat up. "He was so cute. I wrote to him for a while—before I went south."

"South?"

"That's how dad refers to my…indiscretions."

"Hmm."

"I really messed up, didn't I?"

"Yes."

"Don't go with him, Abs. Stay here and fight." She frowned. "Hey, I just thought of something. Don't you think it's strange that you get this note threatening to hurt Emma the same time Daniel shows up to take her away?"

"Are you suggesting that Daniel wrote that note?"

She shrugged. "Do the math."

* * * * *

Abbie was just about to retire for the night when Jake showed up. He was wearing his tennis shoes and casual slacks and had a sweater over his shoulder. "Ready for that walk?"

"I am. I got your telepathic message just as you pulled into the driveway."

"I'm sorry I'm late. One of the couples I showed houses to today decided to buy."

"And Perkins?"

"Perkins is still looking for the perfect place."

"Maybe he'll get his wish. Maybe if I sell Cold Creek to him the threats will stop."

"Are you serious?" Jake took her hand as they descended the stairs and headed for the beach.

"Daniel is here."

"I know. Dawn told me last night when I called. I wanted to come out, but I was over at Brent and Peggy's taking care of the kids."

He pulled her closer. "How did they find you?" Abbie told him.

"Great. so much for confidentiality."

"None of that really matters, does it? He has a court order to take Emma." By the time she finished telling him about Daniel's offer, she was in his arms sobbing.

"What am I going to do, Jake? I can't lose Emma and I need her to be safe. Right now, going with Daniel seems like my only option."

Jake gathered her in his arms and held her until the sobbing stopped. "You can fight this. We'll fight it together. We'll talk to Leo in the morning. Just remember, no one is better able to take care of Emma than you are. You've provided a loving home for her. Your parents and your sister don't factor into the equation." "

You make it sound as though I have a chance."

"That's exactly what I'm saying."

"What about the note? Skye thinks Daniel might have left it for me to convince me to leave."

"Would he do that?"

"No. Daniel adores Emma." She sighed. "But I do feel as though I'm being manipulated."

"Maybe you are. Who else knows that Daniel is here?"

"Dawn, of course, and Keith. Keith asked him if he wanted to work. He said he'd talked to Travis about having Daniel help. They don't know why he's here though." She frowned. "Perkins. He was at dinner last night."

"That's strange—Keith asking Daniel to work with them. Did Daniel give any indication that he planned to stay more than a day or two?"

"At first he said a few days. Now he says he's leaving tomorrow—I have to decide by then."

"I don't want to lose you," his voice cracked.

"Jake."

His head lowered until his lips met hers. She melted into him, matching him need for need. When they finally drew apart, Abbie thought her heart would break. How could she ever consider leaving him?

"Abbie, I love you."

"I love you too."

He kissed her again as though to seal the bond that had grown so strong between them. She did love Jake, but love might not be enough. She should walk away now. But as she had ignored the warnings all those weeks ago in that dimly lit ballroom when he'd asked her to dance, she also ignored the voices telling her to run now.

Abbie closed her eyes and her mind to what lay ahead and immersed herself in the here and now. Tomorrow would be soon enough to worry about tomorrow.

* * * * *

For Abbie the day of worries came too quickly. She awoke in a panic. Jake had gone home at midnight with the promise to call her attorney first thing in the morning. There had to be something they could do to stop the court order and keep Daniel from leaving with Emma.

Abbie prayed it would be so but didn't hold out much hope. "Have faith," Jake had told her.

She was trying.

Her father had the coffee percolating when she ventured downstairs. She'd told her parents everything the day before.

"Jake called." Pop's pulled a cup out of the cupboard for her.

"Already? It's only seven."

"He wants you to meet him at the lawyer's office in an hour."

"I'd better get dressed."

"Sit. Have a cup of coffee with your old man." Abbie settled into a chair at the table. "All right, but just for a minute."

"I've been thinking about your situation here."

"And?" He placed two cups of coffee on the table. "Your mother and I feel badly about what's happened. We had no idea buying Cold Creek would cause so much trouble for you."

"You couldn't have known. And turning Cold Creek into an artists' colony is a brilliant idea. Unfortunately, someone doesn't think so."

229

"And then there's this crazy custody thing." He rubbed the lines in his forehead. "That woman has a few screws loose."

"Dad."

"I know. I shouldn't be badmouthing her, but she's got no business taking Emma away from you."

"She thinks she does, and she may be right. We've inadvertently gotten ourselves into a dangerous mess. If we can't keep Emma here, I'll have to go with Daniel."

"You and I both know that's not the answer."

Abbie sipped at the coffee. "What would you suggest?"

"Maybe going back to Grand Forks for a few weeks until this thing blows over."

"It's tempting but running away isn't an option anymore. Jake is right. I'll talk to the attorney this morning and hopefully send Daniel on his way without Emma. If I have no choice in the matter, I'll go to Iowa with Daniel and fight Leah from there."

"Hmph. I doubt it would be a fair fight.

"I need to get dressed." She drained her cup and took it to the sink.

Before leaving the house, Abbie went back to Emma's room to check on her.

Emma, looking like a princess, lay in a cloud of pink sheets and ruffled comforter. Abbie kissed her forehead and brushed back her silky hair. Her stomach recoiled at the thought of someone cutting her baby's hair. Who would be so evil, so desperate to threaten a child?

"God, please keep her safe. Please don't let Leah take her away from me." Abbie tiptoed out of the bedroom and made her way out of the house and to the car. Jake had written the directions to the attorney's office on one of his business cards the night before. A few minutes later, she pulled in front of an older building on the wharf that looked as though it had been recently remodeled. The building housed a bookstore, a boutique, a café, and several offices.

Jake must have seen her park, because he stepped out to escort her into the attorney's office. He introduced her to Leo, and after a few brief pleasantries, they sat down.

"I have some great news for you, Abbie," Leo said. "I pulled in a couple of favors. We've secured a date for a custody hearing for two months down the road. It will give Child Protective services here in Lincoln County a chance to assess your situation and determine whether or not you should maintain custody. The injunction from Iowa has been lifted."

If Abbie hadn't been sitting, she might have collapsed in a puddle on his floor. "How did you… I mean, thank you."

"I've been working on your case since Jake first told me about it," Leo said. "I'm sorry about stirring up the waters in Iowa and giving away your whereabouts, but we eventually would have had to contact Mrs. Campbell anyway."

With the necessary paperwork in hand, Jake and Abbie left Leo's office and headed to Cold Creek to give Daniel the news.

He was working with Travis on the hotel when they caught up with them. Hands gray with dust, he took the form from Jake and began to read.

A smile worked its way into his lips as his eyes met hers. "You may not believe me, Abbie, but I'm glad for you."

Abbie stretched up to kiss his cheek. "I know."

"Mom will fight this, you know."

"I'm sure she will. I know how much she must miss Emma. Why don't you tell them to come here to see us? We can have a nice visit."

"I'll tell her, but I doubt she'll come." He frowned. "What about that threat? It seems to me you'd want to get as far away from here as possible. My offer still stands."

Jake stirred. "There's no way I'd let…"

Abbie shushed him. "Hopefully the police can figure out what's going on. I've decided to keep moving forward with my plans for Cold Creek. Emma and I should be safe staying with my parents." She told Daniel about Tim being with the state police.

Daniel grinned and seemed to have lost some of the moodiness he'd exhibited before. "I'd like to see him and the others. In fact, maybe I could stay here awhile longer. I want Emma to know me better. I could help out around here."

"I'd love to see you stay. In fact, why don't you plan on coming to dinner at the house tonight?"

"Does that mean you're not mad at me?"

"I knew from the beginning you didn't want me to lose Emma. You didn't have to offer to take me with you. I have no animosity toward you. You are and always will be my brother."

He hugged her and accepted the dinner invitation. "I guess I'd better call Mom. let her know I won't be bringing Emma home."

"Daniel." Abbie touched his arm. "Emma *is* home."

* * * * *

After a week, Daniel had become part of the family. He seemed happy and in no hurry to leave. He worked with Travis on remodeling the hotel and spent a fair amount of time at the Grant home playing with Emma and talking with Tim and Skye.

There had been no further threats, but Abbie wasn't about to let down her guard. Perkins was still staying at the B&B and Abbie had yet to understand why.

Brent had been released from the hospital and with the help of crutches went back to work on the Victorian. It was later that day they made a startling discovery at the old house. While he'd been in the hospital, Brent had looked over the floor plans again and determined that Abbie's suspicions were correct. There seemed to be a secret panel behind the cupboards in the pantry that had been built between the kitchen and living room. Abbie insisted on being there when they tore down the wall.

Samantha speculated that the secret wall space might be where Gunnar had buried the missing money.

Dismantling the cupboards to get to the inside space proved quite a task. Travis had taken over the job for Brent and began

232

knocking out the plaster and brick of the façade. When the opening was large enough, he poked in a flashlight and began to examine the inside. "It's narrow, only about a foot wide." He moved the flashlight beam around the walls and down. "Uh-oh."

"What?" Abbie moved forward, but he stopped her.

"Trust me, Abbie. you don't want to see this." He backed away. "There's a skeleton in there. We need to call the police."

What started out to be a curious adventure ended in a grisly discovery.

Chapter Thirty-four

By the end of the day, they had uncovered a critical and gruesome part of Cold Creek's past. When removing the bones of an adult female, they discovered the skeleton of a fetus along with a rusted knife. The remains were old and thought to be those of Doc Carlson's missing wife and unborn child.

Samantha shared the journal and other writings with the police. They concluded that the doctor had killed his lovely wife. He'd put up a fake wall to hide her remains and told everyone she'd run off. Perhaps he'd thought her unfaithful, or perhaps she'd tried to leave. No one could say for sure.

Isabelle suggested that there might have been something going on between her Uncle Jebediah and Doc's wife.

No wonder the doctor had moved out of the house. What they didn't know and might never know was why the doc had gone back to the house to hang himself. It was a find that brought forth stories of ghost sightings and eerie sounds.

Abbie shared the story with Dawn when she arrived just before dinner.

Dawn shuddered when she heard the news. I'm glad the mystery is solved, but how could you possibly want to live there now.

"It's a sad story but most older places have some sort of secret. I'm not going to change my mind. I still love the house. Even more now that the mystery has been solved. The history adds to the mystique."

One morning a few days later, when the flurry of activity over finding the bones dissipated, Abbie went back to the house to see how the men were progressing.

She examined the lovely staircase Travis had restored. The house still needed electrical updating, but Brent thought Abbie would be able to move in within a month.

* * * * *

As evening settled in around Cold Creek the next Saturday, the townspeople got together for their weekly campfire near the B&B. They gathered at the edge of the lake where a fire pit had been established a century or more ago. Rustic wooden benches circled the stone pit. Though she'd heard about it and thought it was a wonderful way to bring the community together, Abbie hadn't yet been able to experience the event and was pleased when Jake suggested they go.

She had struggled with the option of bringing Emma with her and in the end decided to do so. Her parents had come along with Skye. Emma was standing between her nana and pupa, talking with Cassie.

Keith and Travis started the fire.

For a brief time, Abbie almost forgot about Barbara and the mystery that still hung over them. Watching the men brought back the questions and concerns.

Abbie had gotten to know both men and couldn't imagine either of them participating in any criminal activity. Yet they both sort of fit the description of the man in the bank robbery article. They were both around five-ten and slender. Travis had dark hair and eyes. Keith's hair was lighter, and he had brown eyes as well. They were around the same age. Abbie shook off the idea. she was beginning to see the robber in everyone she saw.

And yet, Barbara had come to this area for a reason, and her mother believed it was because she thought the man who had robbed the bank and taken her friend hostage had escaped Portland and settled here.

Suppose Barbara had suspected Travis? Why would she take the chance of dating him? To get close to him? To search his home? Again, she thought about the article she'd found in his kitchen. Had it been there the entire time, or had someone placed it there? If so, who? Barbara had taken a terrible chance even looking for the man.

With a start Abbie realized that if Barbara recognized the robber, he might have recognized her as well. In her journal Barbara had written about going to the police several times, thinking she'd found the robber. Her leads had never panned out. Eventually, after over a dozen false tips, the authorities had stopped listening.

What or whom had Barbara discovered here, and had that discovery gotten her killed?

Jake nudged her, bringing her back to reality. "Ready for a roasted marshmallow?"

"What?" Abbie veered from the crazy path her thoughts had taken. "Oh, sure."

"What were you thinking about?" Jake grinned at her and lifted a perfectly browned marshmallow from the coals.

"Nothing important." She pulled the soft gooey treat from the end of the stick. "Thank you," she said before popping it into her mouth.

She really needed to stop speculating about Barbara's murder. There was no reason to think the robbery related to the notes she'd received. And why she kept slipping Travis into the bad guy role, she had no idea. She savored the warm, sweet taste of the marshmallow and then had another—this time with chocolate and a graham cracker.

"You were pretty deep in thought."

She sighed. "I can't stop thinking about Barbara."

"Hmm. I think about her too, but there really isn't much point, is there?"

"I suppose not." For her own sanity, Abbie needed to stop obsessing over possible suspects.

* * * * *

For the next few days Abbie worked on plans for the artists' colony. Having been through all the buildings, she worked with Brent to determine which of them needed the least amount of work. She hoped to be able to bring artists in by October and put on the first artist show by the first of December, in time for Christmas.

She visited art galleries up and down the coast and placed ads in newspapers in Oregon and Washington to let artists know what she planned to offer. Travis had provided a few names as well. By the week's end, she had ten artists willing to participate, two of whom volunteered to serve as board members.

She had also spent some time sprucing up her wardrobe. She found a great shop in Oceanside where she bought a variety of outfits to wear when she interviewed the artists. Today she wore a long tan skirt and vest with a cream ruffled blouse and a loosely woven shawl of orange, red, cream, and tan yarns.

Pulling the community together had filled her days and her mind, but her thoughts were never far from Barbara, the murder and the threatening notes aimed at her and Emma.

After breakfast, she headed to the Victorian to see how the remodel was progressing and spotted Travis examining something under the porch steps.

He jumped back when she called his name. "Whoa. You shouldn't sneak up on people like that."

237

"Sorry. What were you looking at?"

He stepped away from the porch. "Nothing. I thought I saw something is all. Probably just a rabbit."

"Hey, Abbie." Keith came out of the house. "I thought I heard you out here."

"I just came over to see how things are going. I'm anxious to get moved in." She let her gaze wander over both men. Once again, the grainy depiction of the fugitive drifted into her mind.

Could Travis be the bank robber and/or Barbara's killer? Or Keith? No, no, no.

She had to stop this nonsense. Both men had been working for her for weeks and she had no reason to believe they had anything to do with Barbara's death. They were nice guys who happened to live in Cold Creek and who knew Barbara.

"Shouldn't be too long now," Keith said. "We'll need to shore up the porch and repair some of the rotting wood. Brent wanted us to finish up the interior before we tackled the outside."

Abbie nodded. "I really appreciate all the work you've been doing."

Travis grinned. "It's been fun restoring this place. feels like a page out of history. I really hope this idea of yours takes off."

"Thanks, Travis. I do too." She again chided herself for considering him a suspect.

"That reminds me," Travis said. "I have a couple of friends who show at Newman's art gallery in town. Genna is a potter and Margaret a watercolorist. They're both exceptional, and when I told them about the artists' colony, they said they'd be interested in teaching as well as showing their work. I thought of my friend Eric too. He's a potter, but he specializes in raku."

"Raku." Abbie said the word almost meditatively. "I love that technique."

Keith frowned. "What's raku?"

"Raku is a special kind of firing where the artist takes a red-hot piece from the kiln, places it into a barrel of combustibles. A lid immediately goes on it," Abbie offered. "The combustibles catch fire and leave brilliant coppery colors and indentations on the pottery piece. The results are spectacular."

Keith nodded. "Sounds nice." He walked off, scratching his head.

"Anyways," Travis said, "I thought I'd invite them out to my place for dinner in the next day or two so you could meet them."

"I'd love that." Travis had been even more helpful than Jake had when it came to meeting the artists in the community. Of course, being an artist himself, he knew many of them.

"Good. Let's plan on Saturday. Bring Jake. I'll do one of my famous barbeques."

"Perfect. let me know if I can bring anything."

"Just yourselves."

Abbie waved good-bye as she headed for the hotel, where she found Brent sitting on a stool, his casted leg stretched out in front of him, sanding the front of the bar. A large work light formed a cone around him. Though the boards had been taken off the windows, the daylight coming in wasn't enough to provide the light he needed.

He looked up when she came in. "Abbie, what a pleasant surprise."

"Hey, Brent. How goes it?"

"Great. I gotta tell you, the more I work on this place, the more I'm loving it."

"Me too. How's the leg?"

"A pain in the you-know-what, but the cast'll be off soon. Fortunately, there's plenty I can do that doesn't require walking or standing." He hesitated. "Did you need something?"

"I just stopped to see how you're progressing."

He gestured toward the bar. "Sanding is almost done on the bar. This is one amazing place." He chuckled. "I'll have to show you what I did yesterday." He picked up his crutches and hobbled around to the back of the bar. "I cleaned the glass, replaced the mirror, updated the wiring, and replaced the old burned-out bulbs with the new fluorescent type. Come here and

I'll let you do the honors." She walked around beside him. He pointed to a light switch that had yet to be mounted.

"Go ahead and turn it on."

She did. The light flickered for a moment and then lit up the stained glass that framed the large mirror. She gasped. "It's beautiful. I knew it would be but look how bright the colors are." Her gaze took in the intricate designs—the red hues of the roses, the greens of the leaves.

"Yeah." Brent grinned. "Amazing what cleaning off years of dust will do. Just think, a hundred years ago customers sat here at this bar, looking at this—this masterpiece." Abbie walked around the room, her gaze never leaving the glass. "I didn't expect it to be so elegant. It makes me feel like I paid too little for the place."

Brent chuckled. "Trust me, Abbie. You may have gotten a good deal, but the remodel isn't going to come cheap. We're extremely lucky the glass was in such decent shape. As it was, I had to hire a stained-glass artist to secure some of the lead."

"I didn't realize that." She asked for the artist's name and added it to her collection.

After saying goodbye to Brent, Abbie wandered around the town for a while, making notes. At noon she decided to head back to Oceanside for lunch and a nap with Emma.

As she approached the Victorian, she realized that she'd forgotten to talk with Travis about finding someone to run the program with her. Perhaps one of the artists he had mentioned, although she planned to offer Travis the position first.

Neither Keith nor Travis was inside, and Abbie suspected they'd gone somewhere to eat. She stopped by the B&B and found Dawn and Keith standing out by his truck, talking.

"Don't worry about it, okay?" Keith was saying. "I'll take care of it."

"When?" Dawn sounded none too happy. "You should have moved it before...."

Keith must have seen Abbie, because he stopped his wife before she could say more. "We'll talk about it later. Abbie's here."

"I'm sorry." Abbie took a step closer. "I didn't mean to interrupt. I was looking for Travis."

"No problem." Dawn's annoyance disappeared behind a smile.

"I imagine he's at home."

"Thanks. I'll see if I can catch him there."

Abbie walked back to the Victorian where she had parked her car, and a few minutes later she pulled into Travis's driveway beside his pickup. She was halfway to the house when she heard a gunshot. The bullet zinged into a nearby tree, ripping the bark. She froze for a moment before adrenaline took charge and propelled her forward and into the woods behind the house.

Early on, Jake had mentioned hunters, but Abbie feared that the bullet had been meant for her. She expected Travis to come out to see what was going on, but there was no sign of him.

Staying under cover of the woods and scrub brush at the perimeter of Travis's yard, Abbie made her way around to the side of the house and near the lake. If she could make it to his porch, she could crawl under it and hopefully find protection there. She straightened and looked around, thinking to make a run for it. Someone opened the patio door.

Most likely Travis. He must have heard the shot and come out to investigate. Her relief lasted about two seconds. Someone wearing a ski mask and sunglasses stepped onto the porch and scanned the tree line alongside the lake through the rifle's scope. He stopped then, and pointed the rifle directly at her. This was no hunter.

She dove into the water just as the rifle exploded. A dozen or more thoughts scrambled through her head. Pain seared through her right leg. She'd been hit.

Chapter Thirty-five

Fearing the shooter would try again, Abbie ducked behind a large downed tree that floated near the lake's edge. The shooter, apparently satisfied that he'd hit her, jumped off the deck and ran into the woods heading toward Cold Creek.

Abbie forced herself to breathe. The icy water had saturated her clothes, weighing her down. She managed to crawl out of the lake. Sitting on the bank, she lifted her skirt to reveal a cut on her thigh. Blood mixed with water ran down her leg and into her skirt. She was going to be sick.

"Focus, Abbie," she told herself. "You have to stop the bleeding." Shaking more from terror than the cold, she twisted excess water out of her shawl and wrapped her wounded leg as tightly as she could then knotted it to keep it secure. She fell back against the grassy bank, her mind whirling. She had to get up. Find help. If she could just make it to Travis's house, she could call Jake. But no. What if the shooter had been Travis? He'd come out of the house, hadn't he?

She had to get out of there. Abbie forced herself into a sitting position and turned over to get up on her knees. She sucked in a deep breath and then, staying low and once again under cover of the woods, made her way to her car. She must have fallen a dozen times. Abbie saw no sign now of the shooter as she emerged from the woods.

As she opened the car door, a motorcycle pulled into the driveway. The driver took off his helmet as he strode toward her. Travis.

"Abbie?" He stood there, apparently in shock, as his gaze roamed over her wet hair and clothes. "What in the world happened? What are you doing here?"

She started shaking uncontrollably. "I-I came out to see you and s-someone started shooting at me." His gaze took in the bloodstains on her skirt. "You're bleeding." She looked down at the darkening patch of blood on her thigh where the blood had soaked through the shawl. Her knees buckled.

"It's okay. I've got you." Travis caught her, lifted her into his arms, carried her into the house, and set her on the sofa. He lifted her sopped skirt and took off the shawl to examine the wound. It was still seeping but not as badly. Going to the kitchen, he pulled a towel out of a drawer and returned to wipe the area around the wound dry.

The bullet had sliced through her thigh leaving a gash two inches long. "Looks like it just grazed the skin," he said. "That's good, but you need stitches."

"It doesn't feel so good." Abbie looked away.

She winced when he pressed the cloth to the wound. "Hold this and put some pressure on it while I get my first-aid kit."

She heard a couple of doors slam, and when he came back, he was carrying a large white box. While he bandaged up the wound, Abbie explained what had happened.

"Are you sure the guy came out of my house?" Travis finished by wrapping an elastic bandage around the leg.

"Trust me. I would never in my wildest dreams make up something like this."

"I believe you. What I can't fathom is why someone would fire at you. The only thing I can think of that makes sense is that it was a hunter who mistook you for a deer."

"I suppose that's possible. I mean—who would want to kill me—except maybe the guy who's been leaving me those notes." Her teeth chattered as she spoke.

"You have a point." Travis stood. "We need to get you out of those wet clothes before you end up with pneumonia." He disappeared into the bedroom and came back with a sweatshirt, boxer shorts, and a pair of khaki shorts. "I don't have any women's clothes so these will have to do. Take off your wet things and I'll warm up an electric blanket for you to wrap up in." He helped her walk into the bathroom. "I'd better call Jeff and Jake. You should have Jake take you to a doctor."

She nodded. "Thank you."

Jake was coming. Abbie couldn't stop shaking. She rubbed the wetness from her skin with a dry towel and pulled on the red sweatshirt. The clothing, though baggy, had already begun to warm her. When she emerged from the bathroom, she was still shivering and couldn't wait to get under the electric blanket.

Emerging from the bathroom, she heard voices coming from the living room. Travis was with detective Meyers. As before, the detective wore a brown suit, and under his jacket Abbie could see a holster.

"Hello again." His concerned gaze met hers.

Puzzled, Abbie shook his proffered hand and sank into the chair where Travis had placed the warm blanket. She wrapped it around herself and eyed Travis. "I thought you called Jeff."

"I did. Detective Meyers is here about something else, but he wants to hear your story."

"I understand someone shot you." Meyers settled back into his chair and lifted a small notebook out of his pocket. "Want to tell me about it?"

Abbie shared her story again and glanced at Travis before going on. "In all honesty, Travis, I thought it was you, especially when the guy came out of your house."

"Definitely not me." Travis raised his hands. "I'm sorry this happened. It could have been anyone. I usually don't bother locking my doors."

"I don't suppose you can ID the guy." Meyers tapped his pen against the notebook.

"No." Abbie frowned, trying to remember. "He was wearing a mask—black, and a greenish plaid shirt. Jeans, I think. I was too busy trying to stay out of sight."

"Not a lot to go on. Did you see a vehicle?"

"No, just the pickup that's out there now."

"Which would be mine." Travis poured them each a cup of coffee. "I was riding my bike. I didn't pass anyone on the road when I came in. The only other way out of here is the trail through the woods, which means the shooter was on foot."

A car door slammed, and Travis got up to look outside. "It's Sheriff Moore." Travis and Meyers went out to meet him.

Abbie expected them to come inside, but the men stood in the open doorway while Travis told the sheriff about the shooting.

"I'll get right on it," She heard the sheriff say. "It could be too late, but we might be able to catch him." To Meyers and Travis, he said, "Why don't you two follow the trail into town and we'll come in from the other side? I'll set up a roadblock at the entrance to Cold Creek."

"That is, if he took the normal path," Travis said. "He could have cut through the woods to one of the old logging roads."

"Then we'll have to broaden our search."

"What about Abbie?" Travis asked. "Someone needs to stay with her—at least until Jake gets here."

"I'll have one of my deputies stay here and guard the house." The sheriff radioed for assistance as the men came back inside.

"At least this time the sheriff is taking me seriously," Abbie mumbled as she tugged the blanket closer around her. She was finally warming up, but the reality of what had happened sank in with the force of a blizzard.

"I'll get my gear and meet you outside," Detective Meyers paused in the doorway and headed back outside to his vehicle

"You'll need to stay here, Abbie. Make yourself at home." Travis pulled on a pair of boots. "The detective and I are going to look around here and take the trail into town."

Abbie nodded. "I heard."

"Jake will be here any minute. Lock the doors and stay put." Travis lifted a rifle from its mounting inside the entry closet and grabbed a handful of shells then stepped outside to where Meyers stood beside his unmarked car. The detective had taken off his suit jacket and now wore a navy-blue nylon windbreaker and boots, which he apparently kept in the trunk.

As soon as the deputy pulled into the driveway, the men jogged down the road a short distance then headed into the woods. Abbie, feeling too warm now, tossed off the blanket and reached around the chair to unplug it. Beside the chair was a basket containing books and magazines. She noted a couple of art magazines she might look at later.

For now, however, Abbie checked the locks on the patio door, the door at the back of the kitchen, and the front door. Then she checked them again. Checking the locks brought the realization that the shooter could still be close by and waiting for another opportunity.

Even with the deputy watching the house, the idea unnerved her. Abbie shook the thoughts aside. At least she'd be safe inside the house. Satisfied that the house was locked up, she snagged her wet clothing from the hook behind the bathroom door and tossed everything in the washing machine in a closet in the hallway. Her leg hurt. It might have been just a flesh wound, but it had begun to throb incessantly.

Opening the medicine cabinet in the bathroom, Abbie found a bottle of aspirin. She shook two into her hand and hobbled to the kitchen for water. She would see a doctor later.

Abbie had no idea how long the search for the shooter would take, but she had to keep busy lest she think too much about the surreal incident. Unfortunately, there were no dishes to do and nothing looked as if it needed cleaning. Travis kept his house relatively clean and picked up.

She was about to resort to looking through the magazines when she heard a noise at the front door. Fear reinserted itself, and she instinctively spun around and ducked.

Someone knocked. "Abbie?"

The breath she'd been holding swooshed out. "Jake."

Abbie hurried to the door and flung it open. She reached for Jake and pulled him in before slamming the door behind him and locking it again.

"What's going on? Jeff told me you'd been shot."

Without answering, she threw her arms around his neck and held on. Jake's closeness and the tender way he drew her to him loosened her resolve and the tears came. "I'll tell you in a minute. Just hold me."

*****

Jake was more than happy to comply. He'd come unglued when Travis told him Abbie had been shot. He told his clients he had an emergency and took off, leaving them in the office to find their own way out. When he reached the outskirts of Cold Creek, he was stopped by a roadblock. After checking his ID, the deputy let him through.

"I'm sorry." Abbie leaned back. "I didn't mean to—"

"Shh." He pressed his fingers to her lips then lifted her into his arms and carried her to the couch.

"Thanks for coming." She tipped her head back against the cushion and closed her eyes.

Jake took in the red sweatshirt and shorts. "Why are you wearing Travis's clothes?"

She opened her eyes and reached for him again. "Mine were soaked. I dove into the water to keep from getting shot again."

He touched the bandage on her leg. "What were you doing out here?" The anger welling up inside spilled over into his voice. "With all that's been going on, you should know better than to come out here alone."

"I came out to talk to Travis about the artists we've been talking to. I saw his pickup and thought he was here. I was walking toward the house when I heard a bang and..." Abbie gripped his hand. "When I realized someone was shooting at me, I ran." She told him about the gunman firing at her from the deck.

If she hadn't been sitting there with the proof of her story on her injured leg, Jake might not have believed it. "Let's hope they catch whoever is doing this. Maybe we need to concede. Sell Cold Creek to Perkins like he wants."

"I don't think Perkins shot at me." Abbie frowned as if trying to remember. "The gunman wasn't that big."

"He could have hired someone."

"Maybe you're right." Abbie's eyes met his, and he melted a little. "The thing is, now that I've come this far, I don't want to give up my dream. I suppose we could sell this place to Perkins and find another spot. Nothing is worth endangering our lives."

Jake nodded. "I'll talk to Perkins. In the meantime, what say we raid the fridge and pantry? It's after two and I haven't eaten anything all day."

* * * * *

After eating a lunch of peanut butter sandwiches and milk, Abbie curled up on the sofa next to Jake and promptly fell asleep. She wanted to go back to Oceanside, but the detective had insisted she stay at Travis's place until they returned.

Detective Meyers and Travis returned at four, having given up the search. There had been no sign of the gunman and they figured that he'd gotten away, having possibly stashed a vehicle on one of the logging trails.

Just prior to their return, Abbie had retrieved her clothes from the dryer and gotten dressed. The cotton outfit was wrinkled but dry. The skirt had a tear in it, which she'd closed with a piece of tape. She'd stitch it up later.

She wanted to leave, but Travis asked her and Jake to stay. "Remember, Abbie, I told you detective Meyers was here for something else? I called him this morning, and you need to hear what I have to say."

Meyers sat and took a couple of sips of the hot coffee Jake had made. He looked over at Travis, who lowered himself to another of the chairs in the grouping in front of the fireplace. "You said you might have some information on the bank robbery." Meyers aimed the statement toward Travis.

Travis leaned forward, elbows resting on his knees. "Jeff, Jake, and I have been trying to make sense of Barbara's murder. Someone put an article about the robbery in my kitchen drawer. I turned it over to Jeff."

"Right. I have it."

"The thing is," Travis went on, "I can't understand why someone would do that. The only thing that makes sense is that the person who killed her is connected in some way to the robbery and is trying to make it look like I killed her."

"I understand that," Meyers interrupted, "but…"

Travis held up his hand. "Just bear with me. Barbara had a connection with the property and had a buyer on the line. He lost out to Abbie and her folks. We thought that maybe Douglas Perkins was responsible for both Barbara's death and the threats.

"With that article showing up," Travis went on, "we couldn't help but wonder if Barbara had found something here in Cold Creek regarding the robbery."

"She was obsessed about that robbery," Abbie ventured. "At least according to her journals." When Meyers sent her a questioning look, she explained how she had talked with Barbara's parents and gotten the material Barbara had been saving. "Travis and I took the boxes to Jeff, but not before reading the journals."

Meyers sighed. "I worked on the case. None of the tips she gave us ever panned out. Several years went by and we didn't hear anything at all from her. Then a few weeks ago Barbara left a message saying she'd found the bank robber. "I tried to call her back, but never could reach her. Then, a couple of days later, she ends up dead. I'm thinking the guy recognized her and killed her before she could turn him in. Unfortunately, there's nothing to indicate who she was talking about."

"I may have something." Travis leaned back. "I may have found the bank robber and the missing money."

"What?" Meyers uncrossed his legs and leaned forward.

"Keith Morgan and I have been working on the old Victorian here in town." Travis hauled in a long breath. "I could be wrong, and I hope I am, but last night, I was driving back from Oceanside and saw a light on at the house and noticed someone poking around. It was Keith, and he was digging under the porch. When he saw my headlights, he threw the shovel off to the side. I parked and went over to ask what he was doing. He told me he'd dropped his cigarette lighter and had come back to retrieve it. I didn't believe him, but I helped him look anyway. A few minutes later he lifted it up to show me he'd found it.

"He headed back to the B&B and I went to my truck. I was going to go back to see what he was doing but figured it could wait till morning. Then this morning I saw that he'd dug a good-sized hole under there. I could be wrong, but you must admit the guy in the sketch does look a little like Keith, and he fits the description. He and Dawn have only lived in Cold Creek for about four years."

Meyers cleared his throat. "I hate to tell you this, Travis, but your suspicions aren't enough to arrest the guy."

"I know, but this morning he was acting strange. Antsy. I noticed he had something in the back of his truck. It was covered and…" Travis shrugged. "I lifted the canvas to have a look and saw an old dirt-covered suitcase. I think he went back after I left to dig it up."

"And you think it contains the money from the bank robbery."

"You have to admit it makes sense."

Abbie couldn't believe what she was hearing.

"Look," Travis added, "I like Keith. I didn't connect the guy or the suitcase to the bank robbery until this morning. I called you as soon as I figured it out. When I said I may have found something, I meant it. I could be wrong and in fact, I hope I am, but I thought you'd want to have a look."

"And you're right to be suspicious. Let's just hope the case still there."

They all headed for the B&B. Abbie insisted on driving herself back so she'd have her car. Since it was such a sort drive, Jake reluctantly agreed.

On the short drive she recounted what they had learned. Could Travis be right? Could Keith be the bank robber? She had thought he resembled the sketch of the man, but she'd thought the same about Travis. Another thought struck her. What if Travis had lied about the old suitcase? What if he had been the one to dig it up and then put it in Keith's truck?

If Travis was telling the truth, then Keith might have killed Barbara, fearing that she would expose him. He probably wanted Abbie out of the way as well for fear the remodeling efforts might unearth the money, or worse, the body of the woman who'd been taken hostage. Come to think of it, before Brent was hurt, he'd been working with Keith on the Victorian. Had Keith run Brent off the road to slow down the remodel and get him out of the way too?

When Abbie pulled into the parking lot at the B&B, Detective Meyers, Jeff and Travis were talking with Keith.

Abbie climbed out of her car and moved closer to the group.

Keith seemed surprised when detective Meyers asked him about the suitcase. He narrowed his eyes at Travis. "You called the cops?"

"Never mind that." The detective nodded toward the satchel. "I'd appreciate it if you'd open it. Since you found it on Abbie's property it belongs to her."

Keith shook his head. "Open it yourself."

Dawn came outside and demanded to know what was going on. "Oh, for heaven's sake, Keith. Whatever is in it belongs to

Abbie." She hoisted herself up onto the truck bed and flipped open the case. It was empty.

Keith folded his arms, indignant at being accused. The question remained. Had Keith already taken the money out of it? Or had there been anything in it in the first place? How had he known the suitcase was under the porch?

"I discovered it yesterday," Keith told them when the detective asked him that question. "I was digging out a rotten beam under the porch and hit something hard. I guess I should have told you all about it right away, but I thought there might be something in it—like that old buried treasure we've heard so much about. I thought I'd take it home and see if there was anything of value. I hadn't had a chance to look inside. I don't know anything about a bank robbery or missing money. I was just curious."

Abbie found it hard to believe that he hadn't already opened it. Maybe he had done so and stashed whatever was in it somewhere else. One thing was certain, though, he had not been the one to shoot at her. When the detective questioned him about the shooting, he admitted to hearing gunshots. "I was helping Brent over at the hotel at the time."

Brent backed his story up, saying Keith had been with him when they heard the shots.

When everyone had compared notes and gone their separate ways, Dawn took Abbie aside. "I can't believe someone actually shot at you."

"Neither can I."

"You must be terrified."

"I was. I'm still shaky."

Dawn herded Abbie toward the B&B. "Come on in and I'll make you something warm to drink."

"That sounds wonderful."

Once inside, Dawn poured a cup of coffee for each of them and handed one to Abbie. "What's worse is that whoever did it is still out there. What if he tries again?"

"I don't know. We'll have to pray that doesn't happen."

"I just want this craziness to stop. Travis just accused my husband of being a bank robber." She waved her hand. "Okay, he shouldn't have dug up the stupid suitcase without telling anyone, but he'd never kill anyone. Keith is a good man."

Abbie smiled. "I'm sure he is." But was he? He could have easily removed whatever had been in the trunk. Still, he had seemed genuinely surprised that it was empty. That thought led her back to Travis. Could he have taken the money and placed the empty case in Keith's truck? But no, that didn't work. Keith admitted to digging it up.

"I'm just glad you're okay." After finishing off her coffee she exclaimed, "Oh, I just... I should have...Do you need me to take you to a doctor?"

"No, I can manage."

"Okay. If you're sure you don't need me, I have some gardening to do."

Abbie followed her out and headed for her car. Her heart quickened. The shooter was out there somewhere. She needed to go to Oceanside to check on Emma and her parents.

She'd just reached her car when Jake came up behind her. He'd apparently been talking to the other men. "Are you going somewhere?"

"I need to make sure Emma and my parents are okay."

"I agree. Let me drive you back to Oceanside. You shouldn't be driving with that leg wound. You need to see a doctor."

Abbie thought for a moment. Her leg was painful but not bad enough that she couldn't drive. "I'll be all right. I managed to drive myself from the lake into town. Besides, you'll need your car."

"That was different. We're talking about a twenty-minute drive on the highway. I can have someone bring me back out here." Worry filled his blue eyes as he reached for her keys. "I don't feel comfortable with you driving by yourself."

"Thanks, Jake, but it makes more sense for me to drive. You can follow me all the way to the house if it makes you feel better."

He finally gave in and followed almost too close as they drove through Cold Creek and out onto the highway. She eyed the white caddy in her rearview mirror and waved at him through her open window then concentrated to the road and on getting to Oceanside safely.

Abbie used the driving time to pray and think. She felt heartsick at the thought of walking away from Cold Creek. The small town tucked into the mountain so near the coast seemed an ideal place for the artists' colony. Still, what else was she to do? Continuing with her plans was proving too dangerous. Threats were one thing, but getting shot was still another.

Why would anyone go to these lengths to keep her from fixing up this deteriorating town? Obviously, someone didn't want her there. Perkins wanted the place for himself, everyone knew that. Had the same person who shot at her killed Barbara? Was all of this connected to the bank robbery?

Abbie tried to put herself in Barbara's place for a moment. The woman had watched the gunman rob the bank where she worked. She had seen him escape with her friend. What a horrific thing to go through. Barbara's journals had been painful to read. She'd talked with the police and thought she had spotted the culprit time and again. So often that the police had stopped taking her seriously.

Apparently, that hadn't deterred Barbara. She saved everything pertaining to the case. At one point she'd written that she would never stop looking. Her writing reflected her obsession and determination.

Then she'd moved to the coast. Abbie suspected that Barbara had continued the journals, but according to Jeff, they hadn't found anything like that. Abbie doubted that Barbara would stop writing—especially since her reason for coming to the area had been to find the bank robber.

Abbie felt certain any journal she'd kept since she moved had been stolen, and Jeff agreed. Had Barbara found the man who had kidnapped her friend? And where was this friend?

She'd never surfaced, and police suspected that the bank robber had killed her. But had he?

What if he hadn't really kidnapped the woman? What if she knew the bank robber and was in on the heist? Abbie wondered if the authorities had considered this. Probably. "I should run this idea by Jeff." She said aloud.

She brushed aside the idea. "You're not a detective, Abbie Campbell," she muttered to herself. "Not even close." She needed to stop trying to solve the puzzle and focus on keeping her family safe.

She drove directly to her parents' home. Noting the time, the doctor's visit would have to wait.

* * * * *

Jake saw Abbie safely to the Grant home and stayed for dinner, after which the family, minus Skye and Emma, gathered in the living room to talk seriously about offering the property to Perkins.

They quickly agreed that while they hated giving in to intimidation, they would back out. As Abbie had said, and her parents agreed, they could buy something else. "The main thing is that we have our Abbie back home," her father said as he took hold of her hand. "We don't want to lose her."

"I say we offer it to Mr. Perkins right away," Carlene said. "The sooner the better."

Jake nodded and headed for the phone. "I'll call the B&B." a few minutes later, Jake hung up. "Perkins isn't there and Dawn says she hasn't seen him all day."

"Do you suppose he's given up?" Abbie asked.

"I don't think so. He didn't check out of the B&B and his car is still there." He turned his gaze to Abbie. "Are you sure he wasn't the shooter?"

She tried to bring an image of the gunman to mind, but it had already grown fuzzy. Abbie shook her head. "I'm not sure of anything."

Jake nodded understanding. "I should go. I need to check my messages at the office before I head home."

"I'll walk you to your car." She slipped an arm through his.

Before opening his car door, Jake pulled Abbie into his arms. His kiss was sweet and filled with longing. Abbie didn't want it to end. He pressed his forehead to hers. "I'll try to contact Perkins in the morning. I wish I knew for sure that he's behind this craziness and that it will end when he gets his way."

Abbie placed her hands on his shoulders. "But you don't think so?"

"Like you said, I don't know what to think. I've gotten to know him these past weeks. I have trouble seeing him as the killer type. Pegging him as the bad guy is too convenient."

"I know what you mean," Abbie said. "But if not him, then who?" She sighed. "On my way into town earlier I thought about Barbara. She died after going to Cold Creek to show Perkins the property. I came to Cold Creek and became the target. You sold me the property, but no one has harassed you. What do Barbara and I have in common?"

Jake kissed her forehead. "If we knew that, we'd know who's behind all the trouble."

"What are we missing, Jake?"

"I wish I knew." Their lips met again, and Abbie drifted for a moment into the safety of his arms. When they came apart, she didn't want him to leave. "I wish there was a way I could stay in Cold Creek. Giving up doesn't seem right."

"I do too."

"Isabelle won't be happy if Perkins gets his way."

"Neither will the others. Folks were getting excited about your project."

"What did Dawn say when you told her we were selling to Perkins?"

"I didn't tell her. No sense upsetting them until the deed is done."

Too soon, Jake left. Abbie watched as his taillights disappeared into the night. she turned and headed for the house.

"That was a long and sweet good night."

Abbie brought her hand to her chest. "Skye? you startled me."

"Sorry."

"What are you doing out here?"

"I wanted to talk to you."

"About?" Abbie settled into the swing beside her sister.

"Remember when you said you were staying in Cold Creek and you offered to let me live with you?"

"Of course."

"What happens now?"

"I'm not going anywhere. If I can't stay in Cold Creek, I'll find another place."

"Did you see Daniel today?" The question came out of the blue.

Abbie frowned. "No, why?"

"He's thinking about moving out here." Skye pulled her knees to her chest.

Abbie recalled Skye's admission that she'd had feelings for Daniel when they'd first met. "It sounds like you're interested in him again."

"Maybe. He's nothing like I thought."

"Really? Tell me." Abbie sensed that her sister meant the remark in a positive way.

"I think he likes me." The moon lit up the night sky enough for Abbie to see Skye's smile.

"And you like him."

"It's different now. He wanted to know why I stopped writing to him. I told him the truth."

His comments about Skye being a druggie still stung. Had he changed his mind? Was he trying to gather ammunition to prove that Emma was being exposed to the wrong sort of people? And yet, here he was talking to Skye and thinking about moving there.

Abbie told Skye what Daniel had said about her being an addict and being a bad influence on Emma.

"I know. He told me."

"He did?" That surprised her.

"He only told you that because Leah made it sound like I was trash." Skye closed her eyes and tipped her head back, tears glistening on her cheek. "That I'm incapable of taking care of Emma."

Abbie didn't know what to say. She didn't entirely trust Skye, but she'd never do anything to harm her. Yet, drugs can greatly influence a person's choices.

"I'm not, am I, Abs? I'd never do anything to hurt her."

"I know." Abbie gathered her sister close, far too aware of her bony frame. "Leah doesn't know you. Or me."

Skye leaned her head against Abbie's shoulder. "Thank you."

"As for Mom and Dad, she barely knows them. Lord knows where she got her ideas that they were bad people just because they're in show business."

"Daniel says she's always been judgmental and she's worse now than ever."

"I suppose some of that is my fault." Abbie sighed. "I know now that running away with Emma was the wrong thing to do. I should have stayed at the farm and gone through the courts."

"Maybe so, but Leah shouldn't have tried to take Emma away from you."

"She was afraid I'd move west to be closer to Mom and Dad and probably thought she wouldn't see Emma again or at least not very often."

"Did you know that Daniel knew what you were going to do?"

"What do you mean?" Abbie scrunched down a bit and tipped her head back against the cushion.

"He knew you were leaving that day."

"Really?" The news didn't come as a complete surprise. Daniel had known how she felt. That he would keep her secret all this time proved what she'd known all along—that Daniel really was on her side.

"Did he tell you that he offered to marry me?"

Skye nodded and raised her head. "He seriously thought Leah had the law on her side. He talked her into letting him come here to get Emma and bring her back. Daniel was telling the truth when he said he didn't want to take Emma away from you."

"I know. And he was willing to sacrifice his own happiness to keep me from losing her."

"He loves you—as a sister I mean."

"I know. I'm just thankful we were able to stop Leah. I suspect she'll fight it, but she won't win."

"She won't. Especially not now. Daniel told me that if he had to, he'd testify against his mother on your behalf."

"I hope it doesn't come to that." Abbie set the swing in motion. "Leah would be devastated."

"She deserves it."

Abbie hesitated. In part, maybe Leah deserved to lose Daniel's allegiance. "Leah's not a bad person."

"Maybe not, but she drove you away and she's driving Daniel away too."

"I'm sure he still loves her, Skye. He just doesn't agree with her tactics."

"It's more than that. Daniel wants to stay here and see if—if we can start over."

Abbie smiled and squeezed Skye's hand. Could Daniel be the catalyst to turn Skye around?

"I can't believe he still likes me after all this time. I mean, look at me. I'm a mess."

"You're beautiful. I'm glad Daniel can see beyond your past."

"And beyond the bruises."

They sat in silence for a few minutes longer, bathed in moonlight. Abbie had never thought in terms of Daniel and Skye as a couple. She liked the pairing. Daniel would be good for her sister. She didn't even want to consider the reaction Leah would have when she found out that Daniel was thinking of moving here, and even considering a relationship with Skye.

She'd be furious, but under all that anger would lie a broken heart, and Abbie couldn't help but hurt for her.

* * * * *

That night, Abbie dreamed about being chased. She fell and tumbled into an abyss. She heard screaming and awoke, realizing that the cries had come from her. Feeling hot and sweaty, she tossed off the covers and, after lying awake for several minutes, made her way downstairs to the kitchen.

It was just after four. Moonlight poured into the kitchen and living room. She filled a glass with water and ambled into the living room to enjoy the view. Why did life have to be so complicated?

Abbie reminded herself that things were looking up. She no longer had to worry about losing Emma. Some unknown beast had forced her to give up Cold Creek, but there would be another, perhaps more suitable, place.

When one door closes, another opens, her mother had reminded her earlier in the day. Abbie agreed. If she were meant to create this artists' retreat, it would happen.

She drained her glass and set it in the sink. It was too late to try to go back to sleep, so she turned on the lights and went upstairs to collect her art supplies.

The moon had paled a bit and Abbie was reminded of her first night back. The painting she'd started was still waiting to be finished. This was as good a time as any.

She went to work, highlighting the translucent waves as they crashed to shore. With a pen, she sketched out the craggy rocks and the outline of a couple, who in perspective were only about an inch high. She thought of Jake as she drew, her heart full of longing to be with him again.

260

By six, she'd placed the finished painting on an end table in the living room and stretched out on the couch for a nap. That was where her parents found her.

She enjoyed her morning coffee and chatting with her parents. Today, she'd be free of Cold Creek and the danger surrounding it. Though the idea brought relief, it also brought heartbreak.

* * * * *

Peggy called on Friday morning, asking Abbie about her injury.

"I'm doing fine," Abbie said. "A little pain, but nothing I can't manage."

"Are you up to going to the campfire in Cold Creek tonight? Dawn and I are planning a barbeque picnic beforehand—around six-thirty. We're bringing the kids, and I know they'd love to see Emma. Cassie will be there too, of course."

"Emma would love that." Abbie hadn't allowed Emma any playtimes since the threat they'd gotten with the tress of Emma's hair. She still felt a bit anxious about taking her out. Maybe an outing would be in order. Besides, she'd have Jake, herself, and Peggy and Brent watching her.

"We'd love to come."

"Great."

"Can I bring anything?"

"Just yourselves."

* * * * *

That evening, everyone seemed in an especially good mood. Maybe it was the food—or the company—or both. Abbie and Jake had come out around six and Emma was thrilled to be able to play with the kids. Peggy and Abbie looked after the children while Dawn, Samantha, and Jeanette busied themselves in the kitchen of the B&B preparing the food. There had to be twenty people gathered there.

After dinner things seemed to wind down as everyone crowded around the roaring campfire. Abbie kept a watchful eye on Emma as the child talked with Cassie and Peggy's girls. She looked so grown up.

When it was time for s'mores, the men—Jake, Travis, Keith, and Brent—fixed up sticks for the children to help them roast their marshmallows. for several minutes everyone focused on sandwiching the roasted marshmallows and chocolate bars between graham crackers. Laughter rose along with satisfied moans as folks enjoyed their treats. Abbie waited in anticipation while Jake built his s'more and shared a bite with her. Their eyes met in a moment of longing and love, and Abbie found it almost impossible to turn away.

He lowered his head to give her a quick kiss and offered to make her a s'more of her own.

She laughed and nodded. Her gaze shifted back to the children, who'd been sitting beside her. Emma wasn't there.

Abbie sprang to her feet, feeling as though her heart would burst.

Chapter Thirty-six

"Emma!" her gaze darted around the circle.

Jake snapped to attention and let his stick drop to the ground. "She was just here."

"Emma!" She called again as she turned and scanned the darkness outside the fire's glow. In a few moments, everyone seemed to be calling Emma's name. They found one of her dolls near the bench where she'd been sitting with the other kids, but no Emma. They questioned the children who thought Emma had been with them the entire time. No one seemed to know where she'd gone or when.

"Maybe she went inside to use the bathroom," Peggy suggested.

When they couldn't find her in the house or anywhere on the property, Jake called the police. Abbie called her parents.

The likeliest scenario, the sheriff suggested, was that Emma had wandered off. Abbie hoped that was the case but feared the worst— that someone had followed through on their threat and taken her baby.

The sheriff took charge and set up search parties, and soon most of the adults had spread out through the town and the woods. The sheriff insisted Abbie stay at the B&B, which would function as a command center. She'd argued until he reminded her that she was needed in case Emma returned, or on the off-chance Emma had been kidnapped and someone called to demand a ransom.

Her mom and dad, along with Tim, Daniel, and Skye, arrived and the sheriff assigned them to tasks almost immediately. Tim, Pops, and Daniel would join the search teams while her mother and Skye assisted at the command center. Abbie paced back and forth across the living room, going over and over in her mind who she'd seen that night who might have taken Emma.

Perkins came to mind. His car was still parked in the lot of the B&B, but he was nowhere around. She voiced her suspicions to the sheriff, who thanked her. He assured her that they would find Perkins and her little girl.

How ironic. She'd been ready to hand the property over to Perkins last night. *Please God. Don't let him hurt her.*

Weary and prompted by her mother, Abbie sat on the sofa, dazed and unable to believe that Emma was gone. Life went on around her, but she felt as though she were somewhere outside of herself. She'd felt this way only one other time in her life—when she'd lost Nate and Ashley.

You haven't lost Emma.

She managed to grasp the thought and from it took the courage to go on. *He has her. Perkins has her and the authorities will find him.*

By the next morning, Emma was still missing, and dozens of people had joined the search. With daylight came the hope that they would be better able to find her. Jake had come in earlier looking bedraggled and exhausted, promising that he'd go out again as soon as he'd eaten something. He was there when she approached the sheriff about joining the search herself and let her mother stay at the B&B.

The sheriff relented, suggesting she stay with the team that would be going through the buildings in town again. He wanted her close by in case they heard anything.

Jake offered to go with her, and though the searchers had gone through the buildings the night before, the sheriff thought they should try again in case Emma had gone into one of them during the night.

Jake and Abbie spent the morning going through one building after another.

"You need to rest, Abbie," Jake said as he waited for her to step out of the building that had once housed Cold Creek's newspaper office.

"I can't. I'm sure Perkins is behind this. His car is still here, so he can't have taken her far. Somehow, I don't see him going into the woods. He must have hidden her here somewhere." This scenario had been playing out in her head for some time now and was the driving force behind her determination.

"Abbie, think about what you're saying. Why would Perkins take Emma and stay here in Cold Creek? It doesn't make sense."

"I don't know. But if he didn't do it, who did?"

Tired to the bone, she had to keep from dissolving into a puddle of tears. She had to find Emma.

The next building to search was the hotel. Abbie pulled out a set of keys, thinking she would need to unlock the door. When the heavy door groaned as it swung open, she stepped back in surprise. "It should have been locked."

"The searchers must have forgotten to close the door after they went through here last night." She heard a thumping noise and grabbed Jake's arm. "It sounds like someone is here."

Jake stepped in front of her. "Stay here while I have a look around." Abbie waited for a moment before stepping up behind him.

"I think we should stay together," she whispered.

"Shh." Jake held up his hand. "Listen."

A distant moaning broke the silence. Relief flooded her. "Emma!" The word caught in her throat and came out in a muffled cry.

Jake held her back when she would have raced ahead. "It might not be her, and even if it is, she might not be alone."

Abbie gripped his sleeve as they went back outside. "What should we do?"

"Wait here for me while I get Jeff."

Jake was right. They should wait for the police, but the noise she'd heard sounded like a cry for help. She stepped back inside and listened. She heard it again. It wasn't Emma, she realized now. The tone was too low and masculine. It seemed to be coming from under the floor.

She moved to the center of the room. If she remembered correctly, there was an entry into the basement under the stairs. Abbie crept behind the wide stairway and noticed that the trapdoor leading to the basement was slightly elevated. She reached for it and jumped when Jake and Jeff came in with the sheriff. Abbie stepped back, allowing Jeff access. "Someone's down there."

When the groaning came again, Jeff pulled the door to the side. He drew his gun and began to descend the stairs. "What in the world?" Then a moment later he called, "Sheriff, call an ambulance."

Chapter Thirty-seven

The search for Douglas Perkins ended, but he was no longer a suspect in Emma's abduction. He'd been lying injured at the bottom of an enormous hole in the basement of the saloon for two days. Abbie stood at the edge of the yawning hole, full of questions.

Perkins, however, was in no condition to answer them. He had apparently dug the hole and somehow fallen into it. Jake, Jeff, and Tim worked with two medics to lift the large man up and out of what could have been his grave. For now, at least, the questions would have to wait.

Abbie and Jake followed the emergency technicians out of the hotel and to the waiting ambulance.

"So." A harsh female voice reached her ears before her eyes fully adjusted to the sunlight. Abbie didn't need to see the speaker to know who she was. "My granddaughter is missing, and you are out here doing God knows what."

"Leah." Abbie forced away the sudden guilt Leah heaped on her. "We were looking for Emma."

"Humph. Knowing you, Abbie, you probably took her and stashed her away yourself."

"Mom, don't." Daniel stepped up beside his mother. "You know Abbie would never...."

"What? Kidnap Emma? We both know what she's capable of."

Abbie lifted her questioning gaze to Daniel. "When did she get here?"

"Last night. We stayed in a hotel in Portland and drove down this morning."

Meeting Leah's narrowed eyes, Abbie said, "How do I know you didn't take her?"

"How dare you suggest such a thing?"

"You would do anything to take Emma away from me. How do I know you didn't take her last night?"

"That's ridiculous. I wasn't even here."

"No more ridiculous than you accusing me." Abbie felt herself softening. Leah hadn't taken Emma, and she knew it.

"You ran away. You took my Emma and you ran away." Leah's voice broke.

Abbie ran a hand through her hair. "I didn't know what else to do. I was wrong to run, but you were wrong too."

Leah turned and walked away, her head bent, her gait unsteady, a cane in her left hand. Abbie shook her head, wishing she could ease the woman's pain. But she didn't have time to deal with Leah. Emma was still missing.

After sending Abbie an apologetic look, Daniel went after his mother.

Jake stood behind her and placed a steady hand on her shoulder. She leaned back against him for a moment, then sprang forward. "We need to keep looking."

* * * * *

Jake could hardly take it all in. By the end of the day, they still hadn't located Emma. Nightfall and exhaustion ended the search. They'd head out again at daybreak. Abbie had wanted to stay out in Cold Creek but agreed that she needed to clean up and change clothes.

More than anything, Jake wanted to promise Abbie that he'd take care of everything. Instead, he guided her into the living room of her parents' home. He was surprised to find Leah and Daniel sitting in the living room with Lyle and Carlene. They all rose when Abbie and Jake entered the room, expectant looks on their faces. He was surprised to see that much of the animosity the families had had toward one another had melded into mutual concern.

"She's still missing," Jake said. "We'll head out again at first light."

Abbie dropped onto the loveseat. She hadn't wanted to stop, but Jake had reminded her repeatedly, they had to take breaks in order to keep going.

"There are leftovers in the oven," Carlene said. "I'll fix plates up for both of you."

"Nothing for me, Mom." Abbie pushed to her feet and headed for the stairs. "I'm going upstairs." She leaned heavily on the banister, obviously in pain. She had refused to go to the doctor to have the gunshot wound looked at.

Jake started to go after her, but she clearly wanted to be alone. He felt certain that Abbie blamed him for everything, and she was right. As his gaze took in each of the grandparents, he felt like a failure. He'd promised Abbie he'd take care of her and make sure she stayed safe. Now, Abbie had been shot, Emma abducted, and he was helpless to do anything about it.

Guilt tore him up as he thought about the role, he had played in bringing Abbie and Emma out west. Admittedly, he'd been thrilled when the Grants voiced an interest in purchasing Cold Creek. And when Lyle and Carlene asked him to try to find Abbie, he'd been more than happy to oblige.

He hadn't wanted to appear pushy, but he had to admit to being delighted when they finally signed the papers. If he hadn't gone to get Abbie—if he hadn't enticed her to come back with him, Abbie and Emma would still be safe in Grand Forks.

Carlene brought him a full plate on a tv tray. He had no appetite but ate anyway. The meatloaf and gravy and potatoes melded together in a glob. He choked it down as best he could and excused himself. "I appreciate the dinner, Mrs. Grant." After thanking her, he announced his plan to go home.

Jake parked in his driveway but didn't go inside. Instead, he headed for the path that led to the beach. He needed to do some heavy thinking. Around one, he ascended the steep staircase to his deck and fell into bed.

The following morning Jake received a call from Jeff. He'd been at the hospital that morning and had gotten the whole story from Perkins. "He never intended to buy Cold Creek or any other property. He isn't a developer either. The guy is one of those big-time treasure hunters. He lives in California and goes all over the world looking for buried treasure."

"In the basement of the hotel?" Jake shook his head.

"I talked to Isabelle about it," Jeff said. "She admits that awhile back—shortly after her father and uncle had died—her son claimed that Jebediah's fortune had been buried somewhere in Cold Creek because her father wanted nothing to do with tainted money."

Jake snickered. "Right. Abbie told me about that when she was researching the area. Sam's father dug up most of the town looking for it and never did find anything. But what's that got to do with Perkins?

"Samantha confirmed the story that Gunnar may have buried his brother's money, but in the end, the family decided that Jebediah had squandered his money on the hotel and had nothing left to leave to the family or to bury. End of story."

"Not quite. This is where it gets weird. Perkins' father used to live out here and apparently knew Sam's dad personally. He'd even helped him dig a couple of times.

The two had been drinking buddies. For a while, a lot of people were speculating about the missing money but then things died down. Perkins grew up hearing about the missing money, and when he heard the town was for sale, he figured it was the perfect opportunity for him to do some digging himself. At any rate, he came to Cold Creek to follow through on his father's ideas that the fortune was hidden somewhere in the saloon.

"He'd been digging in the basement at night for the past month, and then a couple of nights ago, the ground gave way underneath him."

"So, all of his plotting and scheming were for nothing."

"Looks that way."

"Serves Perkins right. But I don't really care about Perkins right now. We need to find Emma."

"Believe me, I'd like nothing better. I don't think she's in the area, Jake. We're thinking that whoever took her was driving, and that means she could be anywhere. We know Perkins had nothing to do with her abduction. We'll keep looking, but as far as evidence is concerned, we're at a dead end."

Jake didn't want to hear that. somehow, somewhere, someone knew where Emma was. They had to keep looking.

* * * * *

Abbie heard all these things from Jake that morning over breakfast but didn't care about any of them. She just wanted to find Emma. The police had no leads. No one seemed to have seen Emma leave the campfire, and police suspected she'd walked away or been lured away by someone she knew.

The FBI had been called in and since the Grants were a family of wealth, they expected a ransom call or note. But nothing came.

Abbie had been surprised to see Leah and Daniel at her parents' house the night before, but she might have known that her mother would work to patch things up. Daniel too, for that matter. Leah and Daniel were already there when she came downstairs for breakfast.

271

"I hope you were able to sleep," her mother said.

"A little." Abbie poured a cup of coffee for herself before joining the others at the table.

"I don't know how you could have slept at all," Leah said. The tone bordered on critical, but when Abbie looked up, she saw only concern in her mother-in-law's eyes. Abbie was surprised that the strong woman who had never shed a tear during all the years she'd known her was crying now. Leah buried her face in her hands.

"I'm so sorry, Abbie. This is all my fault. I see that now. I wanted you and Emma to stay on the farm. I wanted my family close." Leah used her napkin to mop up her tears. "All I did was drive you away. Now I may never see my Emma again."

"We'll find her, Mom." Daniel settled an arm across his mother's shoulder. "Don't cry."

They would find her—they had to. Abbie managed to eat a few bites of scrambled eggs and toast then rode with Tim to Cold Creek, where the search had resumed. Because Barbara's body had been found there and the notes had both been written there, it seemed the likely place to search. A state-wide alert had gone out in case someone had taken Emma and left the area.

At two in the afternoon, Dawn told the others she was heading back to the B&B to make sandwiches and snacks for the searchers. Peggy had offered to pick up Cassie from school since she was unable to join in the search.

At two-thirty, Abbie finally took Jake's advice and they returned to the B&B to get a bite to eat. She had agreed to rest for half an hour and dutifully settled on the couch.

Two hours later, Abbie woke up. she couldn't believe she'd fallen asleep let alone slept for so long. Jake was gone. He'd left a note on the counter saying he hadn't had the heart to wake her. The sense of urgency that had followed her all day came back with a vengeance. Still feeling groggy from sleep, she made her way to the kitchen for a glass of water.

The door from the kitchen to the mudroom stood open. Dawn, who'd apparently been outside, slipped off her jacket and hung it on one of the pegs where several coats and jackets were kept. Beneath the outerwear was a messy row of boots and shoes.

"Hey, sleepyhead," Dawn said as she stepped into the kitchen and turned to close the door behind her. "Want some coffee?"

Abbie nodded in response, but her gaze lingered on the door dawn had just closed.

"I'm so sorry this has happened. I can't imagine how you must feel." Abbie turned her toward Dawn, her mind whirling with what she had just seen.

"Abbie? are you all right?"

"Um… No. Yes." Reason worked its way into her mind. She had to be mistaken. Dawn had hung her jacket next to one she'd seen before. If memory served her right, it was the same one she'd seen on the shooter. Dawn set an empty mug in front of her. "Can I get you anything else?"

Abbie offered up a wan smile. "I…ah, no." She had to be mistaken. A lot of people around here wore plaid shirts, red, green, brown, blue.

"You're like me," Dawn said. "It always takes me awhile to wake up—especially after an afternoon nap. The coffee should be ready in just a minute. While it's perking, I need to wash up. Be back in a few minutes." Dawn headed for their private quarters. Abbie slipped off the stool and hurried toward the back door. She had to have another look. She couldn't be sure, but the green plaid jacket looked far too much like the one the shooter had worn. What she saw next stopped her cold. lying on the floor just behind a leather boot was a black ski mask. Had Travis been right? Was Keith the bank robber after all?

Abbie picked up the mask. Dawn would be devastated. Should she tell her what she was thinking?

Not yet. Something wasn't right. Keith had been working here in town when Abbie encountered the shooter. Or had he? Brent said Keith had been working at the house. He could easily have slipped out unseen, trailed her to Travis's house, tried to kill her, and then gone back into town where he joined in the search for the gunman. Abbie dropped the mask. The clothing meant nothing. Still, why would the ski mask even be out this time of year? There wouldn't be snow in the area for another four to five months.

"Abbie?" Dawn called.

Great. how was she going to explain why she'd gone into the mudroom? There was nothing she could do but reveal her whereabouts. "I'm right here. I was admiring your mudroom. My parents have one too."

Dawn eyed her warily. "It keeps us from tracking dirt through the rest of the house. Things get pretty muddy around here— especially in the rainy season."

Abbie stepped back into the kitchen. "Looks like the coffee is ready."

Instead of pouring coffee, Dawn stepped into the pantry and picked up the ski mask, which was now lying in front of the shoes.

She tossed the mask into a bin full of hats and fastened her gaze on Abbie.

"I—" Abbie swallowed around the lump in her throat. "I hate to say this, but I think Keith might be the one who shot at me."

"He didn't shoot at you." Dawn walked into the living room and lifted the lid on the rolltop desk. Opening one of the small drawers, she pulled out a gun. Abbie could have sworn it was the one Jake had purchased for her. The one she thought Skye had stolen.

"It was me."

"I don't understand." Abbie took a step back as Dawn advanced.

"I hoped it wouldn't come to this, Abbie," Dawn said. "I like you. I tried to warn you, but you bought the place anyway."

"You wrote those notes?" Pieces of the puzzle began to fall into place.

"I had to stop you."

"What about Barbara? Did you kill her?"

Sadness etched her face. "I had to. She recognized Keith and me."

"You…you're Valerie." Abbie couldn't believe she hadn't seen the resemblance before. Dawn looked older than the girl Abbie had seen in the photo, and she had lost weight and changed her hair color. Still, Abbie should have made the connection between Dawn and Barbara's friend. "But you were taken hostage."

"Yes and no. The abduction was all part of the plan. Now, turn around. We're going to take a walk." Dawn intended to kill her.

Abbie had to find a way to stop her. All Abbie could think to do was to keep her talking and look for a way out. "Killing me isn't going to help matters."

"I have no choice." She waved the gun. "Outside. Now." Abbie turned, Spotting the coffeepot on the stove, she lunged forward.

In the next instant, she threw the pot full of scalding coffee into Dawn's face. Dawn screamed and lifted her arms in defense. Abbie slammed against her, knocking her into the counter. The gun flew out of her hand and landed on the floor. Abbie scrambled for it and managed to get to her feet and turn the gun on Dawn.

Dawn struggled to get up but slipped on the coffee and grounds that now covered the floor where she lay. Red splotches appeared on her face, neck, and arms where the coffee had burned her skin.

Abbie stepped back, still reeling. Her breath came in snatches. "Stay where you are."

"Help me." Dawn sobbed as she stretched out her arm. "It hurts."

"Don't move. I'll call for help." With the gun still aimed at dawn, Abbie picked up the phone. To the operator, she said, "I'm at the B&B in Cold Creek. I need the police here right away. It's urgent."

Abbie kept the gun trained on Dawn and used her free hand to steady herself. "Where is Emma?"

Dawn shook her head. "I don't know."

"You're lying." Abbie's hand shook as she waved the gun at the woman. "You took her."

"If I tell you, will you let me go?"

The words shook Abbie to the core. She held the gun firm. she would have promised Dawn anything at that point.

"Please." Dawn gasped; her face twisted in agony. "If you turn me over to the police, I'll deny everything. Let me go now, and I'll tell you where she is."

Abbie lowered the gun. "Tell me."

"She's in…" Dawn shifted onto her hands and knees. groaning in pain. She stood, took two steps toward Abbie, and collapsed.

Abbie jumped back. "No… no. Where is she?" Her screams went unanswered.

Chapter Thirty-eight

Jake had been with Jeff when he got the garbled message over his radio. "It's Abbie," Jeff shouted back at him. "She needs help." The two men raced toward the B&B. Fear coursed through Jake's veins as he conjured up all kinds of scenarios. Had she found Emma? Had Abbie been hurt?

Throwing open the door, he stopped at the threshold. Dawn lay on the floor at Abbie's side. The gun he'd bought or one like it lay on the floor and Abbie had a hold of Dawn's lapels, shaking her and screaming at her to wake up.

Jeff scooped up the weapon. What happened? Did you shoot her?"

Jake pulled Abbie off Dawn, and she immediately began beating on his chest. "Dawn did it. She took Emma. She took my baby and she killed Barbara."

"Shh." Jake pulled her close and stroked her back. "Calm down, Abbie. It'll be okay. Just tell us what happened."

It didn't take long to sort things out, but even then, Jake had trouble processing Abbie's story. Dawn came to and began writhing in pain. The ambulance arrived and the medics were able to give her something to sedate her. Between the agonizing screams, Dawn accused Abbie of ruining her life.

Abbie sat beside Jake now, silent and withdrawn. She wrapped her arms around herself and stared at the door. The medics had strapped Dawn to the stretcher after covering her burns with cool wet towels. "She knows where Emma is. She said she would tell me if I let her go. now it's too late."

"No, it's not." Jake put his arm around her. "We'll find Emma."

* * * * *

We'll find her. Jake's words settled into Abbie's mind. She turned to look into his eyes. Those blue, blue eyes. In them she saw hope, and she felt her resolve strengthen. He was right. They would find Emma. Now that they knew who had taken her, they had a better chance. Abbie couldn't give up. She would never give up.

Before leaving, Jeff promised to work on Dawn to get her to confess.

"Dawn started to tell me where she'd hidden her. She said Emma was in…something."

Jake nodded. "We should search the B&B again. There's a good chance Emma is here or at least close by. We need to think about where Dawn might have hidden her."

The search team, buoyed by the fact that Emma had likely been hidden close by, began to go through the town again, beginning with the bed and breakfast. But Emma wasn't at the B&B.

Within the hour, police had arrested both Dawn and Keith. Dawn confessed to killing Barbara and trying to kill Abbie. The money from the bank robberies had been buried in various places around the Victorian. The suitcase Keith had put in his pickup was one of them. They had taken the money out of the suitcase and stored it in the pantry, where the police found it. Keith refused to tell them where he'd buried the rest of the

278

money, saying he might be willing to make a deal with the district attorney.

He claimed to have no idea that Dawn had killed Barbara or taken Emma.

Abbie voiced her concerns about Cassie, and Jeff arranged to have Peggy pick her up after school.

By the following day they'd covered the area around Cold Creek two more times and expanded the search to include the woods and hunters' blinds around Bear lake.

Abbie felt certain that Dawn had been the one to cut Emma's hair and abduct her, but Dawn was now denying it, saying she'd only said that to get away. Abbie didn't know what to believe.

Dawn had changed her tune about the bank robberies as well. Now she insisted that Keith had taken her hostage and forced her to join him.

Keith told the authorities that Dawn had been the one to instigate the robberies and that there had been a dozen of them overall. Abbie didn't care about any of those things. she just wanted Emma back.

Emma had been gone for three days, and searchers were talking about giving up. Abbie dragged herself to her bedroom after Jake insisted that she get some sleep. How could she sleep when Emma was out there somewhere?

She felt certain Dawn had taken Emma and she felt just as certain that Dawn would have taken care of her.

The tears came again, along with her constant prayer to keep Emma safe.

Abbie was about to drift off when the thought came to her. She needed to talk to Dawn personally. Maybe she had read the woman wrong all along. Before this, Abbie hadn't seen her as a killer. But she had seen the woman interact with her daughter— with Callie. She was a mother. Abbie quickly dressed, and after calling Jeff, received permission to visit Dawn.

"She's still at the hospital," he told her, and said he would meet her there.

Seeing Dawn, her face, hands, and chest covered in bandages, filled Abbie with empathy. She had disfigured the woman—perhaps for life.

She was going to kill you.

"What do you want?" Dawn glared at Abbie when she came in.

"I know you took Emma. I also know that you don't want Emma to get hurt."

"You don't know anything."

"I know you love your daughter. I know that you killed Barbara and tried to kill me to protect your family. I know you did what you felt you had to do to keep from losing them and the life you've built for yourself."

Dawn turned to face the wall.

"Dawn, you're a mother. Please. Tell me where Emma is. She'll die if she doesn't have food and water, and you're the only one who knows where she is."

"You should have gone away. I tried to warn you."

"I know that now. But Dawn, if I hadn't bought Cold Creek, someone else would have. Do you really think you could have kept everyone out?"

"When we realized that Barbara knew who we were, Keith wanted to pick up and move. Just like that. I wanted to stay. We had friends here, and Cassie was doing so well in school. I had to do something." Dawn turned back toward Abbie. "What's going to happen to Cassie?"

"She's with Peggy right now. I suppose she'll be placed in foster care and maybe adopted out."

Dawn closed her eyes as tears slipped down her cheek.

"Please, Dawn. Think about how you would feel if someone took Cassie. You'd know how desperate I am." Abbie swallowed hard. Did Dawn's silence mean she was reaching her, or that Dawn had closed her out?

"We're not that different, you and I," Abbie said. "After my husband died, my mother-in-law decided I wasn't fit to take care of Emma. She went to the authorities and was granted custody."

Abbie went on to tell Dawn about the kidnapping and how she had run from the law for two years. "I decided it was time to stop running."

Abbie hesitated. "You and Keith committed some serious crimes. I have a feeling that if you cooperate fully, things will go better for you."

"We'll both be facing life in prison."

Abbie thought so, but aloud she said, "Maybe not. There might be a possibility for parole."

"I'll tell you where Emma is, but you have to promise me something."

"What? I can't undo what's been done."

"Take care of Cassie for me."

Abbie covered her mouth, tears clouding her eyes. "Of course."

"Promise. No lies. I don't want Cassie to suffer because of what Keith and I did."

"I promise." Abbie would have promised her the moon to get her to talk. Would she, in the end, take Cassie in, raise her as her own?

"I took good care of Emma," Dawn dabbed at her eyes when Abbie handed her a tissue. "I made sure she had food and water. I even read to her a couple of times."

"Where is she?"

"There's a root cellar about a hundred yards from the B&B where there used to be a house, but it burned down. Isabelle will know which one I mean."

"Thank you." Abbie gripped the bedrail and glanced over to where Jeff was standing on the other side of the curtain. He nodded at her and hurried out of the room, calling for help on his radio as he went.

"Cassie." Dawn grabbed at Abbie's sleeve. "Promise."

"I will do everything I possibly can for Cassie."

"Bring her to see me."

"I will if I'm allowed."

Abbie ran after Jeff and rode with him in the patrol car. He had already phoned Isabelle to learn the exact location of the property Dawn had described. The trip lasted fifteen minutes at the most; to Abbie it seemed like hours.

Jake had been informed as well and was there when she and Jeff arrived. Jeff ordered her and Jake to stay put while he and an officer opened the panel covering the root cellar. The cellar was lit by a bare bulb hanging from the ceiling.

Abbie broke away from Jake. Listening, waiting. Then she heard it. A faint cry she would have recognized anywhere.

"Emma." She tore down the steps, nearly falling into Jeff.

"Mommy."

Jeff relinquished his hold on the child as she fell into her mother's arms. Someone wrapped them in a blanket.

"Mommy don't cry. I knew you would come." Abbie, too choked up to speak, just held on. Glancing around she noticed that Dawn had left cereal, peanut butter and jelly sandwiches, and water for Emma.

There had been a cot and blankets and a child's potty chair. The experience had to have been traumatic for Emma, but she seemed to rally quickly once she and Abbie were reunited. Still, Abbie insisted they take her to the hospital to make certain she was all right.

* * * * *

A week later, life seemed to be leveling out for Abbie and Emma. Her little trouper was getting ready to share her room with her soon-to-be big sister, Cassie. Dawn and Keith had signed their parental rights over to Abbie and given her permanent custody of their daughter.

As promised, Abbie had taken Cassie to visit her mom. Dawn explained everything. Abbie teared up just thinking about it. Cassie, of course, had been devastated, and Abbie doubted she fully understood what was happening.

A trial date had been set, but Dawn and Keith were looking at life sentences. Justice would be served.

Though the police had learned more and shared their findings with Abbie, she still couldn't reconcile what had driven Dawn to take such drastic steps to protect her family.

She'd killed Barbara because her old friend had recognized them and was going to turn Keith over to the police. She'd shot Barbara and dumped her body in the lake, then pushed the car over the cliff and planted the newspaper article in Travis's kitchen to cast suspicion on him.

It was Keith who had stolen Floyd's old pickup and run Brent off the road. When Abbie saw it after the fact, she realized it had not been the one parked near her home. In the end, they concluded that the pickup parked there had nothing to do with the case.

Dawn had also ransacked Barbara's apartment looking for any evidence the woman might have had there. She'd found Barbara's journals and burned them. Dawn had grown desperate in her attempts to keep Cold Creek the same as it was when they'd moved there. In the end, she'd failed.

In a way, Abbie understood that desperation. She'd broken the law in order to keep Emma. It didn't seem possible, but she and Leah had worked out their differences.

Murray had made the trip to Oceanside, and he and Leah stayed with the Grants for a week. Leah's demeanor changed completely from when Abbie had lived with them. Leah not only enjoyed her visit with Lyle and Carlene, she made a visit to Cold Creek to see what this artists' retreat was all about.

"Maybe you'll need someone to run the bed and breakfast," Leah ventured on the eve of their departure.

Abbie turned to meet her gaze and realized she was serious. "Do you mean it? You'd actually consider living in Cold Creek?"

"Well, it looks like Daniel plans to stay, and you'll be busy with your town."

Murray cleared his throat. "We've been talking about retiring, Abbie. If you think you might like us hanging around, we'd be pleased to consider it."

"We'd be right there to take care of Emma," Leah said.

Abbie flung her arms first around Leah, then Murray. "I can't think of anything I'd like more."

"Now hold on just a minute." Carlene jumped into the fray. "You can't have Emma all the time. I want her at least once a week."

Murray and Lyle looked at each other and laughed. Abbie had never seen them happier.

At eleven, Abbie sat alone in the living room. The grandparents had retired for the evening after having negotiated who would have Emma and when.

She smiled as she replayed their banter in her mind. It was Leah who'd reminded them that they might want to let Abbie have her on occasion.

Leah had surprised her with something else as well. She'd asked Murray to bring Abbie's art supplies when he came. They were still in the living room where Murray and Daniel had set them earlier. Maybe Leah hadn't disliked her artistry so much after all.

Hearing footfalls on the porch steps, she felt her heart pick up its pace. It slowed back down when she realized it was Skye and Daniel. They settled into the porch swing.

Both Skye and Daniel had been smiling more lately, and Abbie suspected that she might be receiving a wedding invitation before the year was up. Skye was beginning to look healthy and happy for the first time in years. she still needed to gain weight, and the bruises needed more time to heal, but that would come in time.

Feeling left out, Abbie tipped her head back on the sofa cushion. She hadn't seen much of Jake since they had found Emma. He'd stopped coming over for their morning walks. She'd invited him to come for dinner several times, but he always seemed to have work to catch up on.

Abbie suspected he'd changed his mind about loving her. Maybe that was just as well. She had plenty to do without being in a relationship. Still, Abbie missed their talks and walks and more than that, his kisses. She missed looking into those blue eyes.

She thought back to the first time she'd seen him. How romantic that night had been. What were the chances he would find her the way he had?

Divine intervention, her mother had called it. Abbie agreed. She could tell herself it didn't matter, but it did. If she had any sense at all, she'd go to his house, knock on his door, and ask him if he'd forgotten about their walk. Maybe she would.

She heard the door open and close. Probably Skye coming in. When her sister didn't say anything, Abbie turned to look. There in the entry stood her blue-eyed handsome stranger.

"Hi." She shifted to get a better look.

"Did you forget about our walk?"

She laughed. "No, but I thought had."

He stepped toward her at the same moment she stood. Holding out his arms he said, "Could I have this dance?"

She bit her bottom lip to keep it from quivering and moved into his arms. "There's no music."

"It's in here." He pressed her hand to his heart.

She melted against him. "Where have you been?"

"Blaming myself."

"For what?"

"For nearly getting you killed. Putting Emma in danger. None of this would have happened if I hadn't gone to Grand Forks to get you."

She leaned back. "Silly man. If you hadn't come for me, I'd still be looking over my shoulder and living in fear. Mom and Dad were right. It was time to stop running. They were right about Cold Creek as well. And they were right about you."

Laying her head on his shoulder, she added, "I do blame you for one thing though."

He pressed his lips against her forehead. "What's that?"

"For making me fall in love with you." She tipped her head
back and raised up just enough to kiss him.

About the Author

Award-winning author and speaker, Patricia H. Rushford, has written over sixty books, including several mystery series: The Helen Bradley Mysteries, The Angel Delaney Mysteries, and The McAllister Files, which she wrote with a police detective. She's also written the popular Jennie McGrady Mysteries and the Max & Me Mysteries for kids. And Now the Artisan Mysteries. Her mystery novel, Silent Witness, was nominated for an Edgar Award by Mystery Writers of America and won the silver angel for excellence in Media. Her romantic suspense novel, Morningsong, won the golden Quill award for Inspirational Romance.

Patricia's most recent works include: Strangers in the Night, Watercolor Dreams, Deadly Deception and The Quiltmaker's Daughter, romantic suspense novels. Most of her mysteries are set in the beautiful Pacific Northwest where she lives with her husband. She enjoys sharing the sights, sounds and culinary delights of the northwest with her readers. The Oregon and Washington coasts provide the settings for many of her novels.

Patricia, who worked for 18 years as an RN, holds a master's degree in counseling. In addition, she conducts writers' workshops for adults and children and has been the Director of the Oregon Christian Writer's Summer Conference and co-director of Writer's Weekend at the Beach. Patricia has appeared on numerous radio and television talk shows across the United States and Canada.

Books by Patricia H. Rushford

FICTION

The Artisan Mysteries (Romantic Suspense)
Deadly Deception
The Quiltmaker's Daughter
Watercolor Dreams
Strangers in the Night
Sins of the Mother

The Angel Delaney Mysteries
Deadly Aim
Dying to Kill
As Good as Dead

The Helen Bradley Mysteries
Now I Lay Me Down to Sleep
Red Sky in Mourning
A Haunting Refrain
When Shadows Fall
Death on Arrival

The McAlister Files
Secrets, Lies and Alibis
Deadfall
Terminal 9
She Who Watches

Novels for Guidepost Books
Strangers in Their Midst (Mystery and the Minister's Wife series)
Chasing the Wind, Measure of Faith, and *With Open Arms* (Stories from Hope Haven)

Mysteries for Kids

The Jennie McGrady Mysteries
The Max & Me Mysteries

Non-fiction:

It Shouldn't Hurt to Be a Kid
What Kids Need Most in a Mom
The Humpty Dumpty Syndrome:
Hope and Healing for Broken People

The Artisan Mysteries

I write books, mostly mysteries, but I am an artist at heart. I write, paint, quilt, knit and crochet. Writing is a medium I use to create characters and plots, painting scenes with words and bringing them to life on the canvas of pages. A few years ago, I developed the idea of writing a mystery series featuring artists who work in various fields, such as oil painting, watercolors, clay, quilting to name a few.

Deadly Deception

Artist, Carolyn Hudson, finds herself in a compromising position when she awakens in a hotel room in a pool of blood. The dead man lying next to her is acclaimed politician, Adam Burke, who had, only a week earlier, commissioned her to paint his portrait. She has no idea how she got there. She only knows that she was drugged and soon learns she is the killer's next victim. Carolyn must go into hiding and accept police protection. Still, nothing can prevent her from investigating on her own and clearing her name, even if it kills her.

The Quiltmaker's Daughter

In *The Quiltmaker's Daughter,* Alaina Neilson, a sometimes artist, fulltime miserable excuse for a human being, is taking a Caribbean Cruise with her best friend to recover from yet another failed marriage. Her life is a mess and it's about to get worse. Her estranged mother, a master quilter, suffers a stroke. Though reluctant, Alaina knows she should go home, but isn't sure she can. Her mother had abandoned her years ago, and Alaina feels nothing but resentment for her.

Still, Alaina can't fight the urgent need to see her mother before she dies. Once home she is not only faced with her mother's debilitating illness, but with a suspicious stranger who has eased his way into her mother's life, the theft of some of her mother's highly valued quilts, and murder.

Watercolor Dreams

Lindsay's decision to leave the family's lucrative business to become an artist nearly kills her father and opens a Pandora's box of family secrets. Deception, lies and murder follow Lindsay as she struggles to pursue her dreams. Mark Owens, Lindsay's crush from high school, has come home to take over the business and wants Lindsay to stay. Can Mark and Lindsay uncover the truth before the killer takes another life.

Connect with Patricia

On Amazon:
http://www.amazon.com/Patricia-H.-Rushford/e/B000AR89Y2/ref=ntt_athr_dp_pel_pop_1
On her Website: http://www.patriciarushfordbooks.com
On Facebook: https://www.facebook.com/patricia.h.rushford
On her Blog: http://www.patriciarushford.blogspot.com/
On Pinterest: http://pinterest.com/patrushford/
Also, on Twitter and Goodreads